TWO BOTTOMS IN THE NINTH

TWO BOTTOMS IN THE NINTH

ZAVO

alyson books
NEW YORK

MANUFACTURED IN THE UNITED STATES OF AMERICA

Published by
ALYSON BOOKS
245 WEST 17TH STREET
NEW YORK, NEW YORK 10011

Distribution in the United Kingdom by
TURNAROUND PUBLISHER SERVICES LTD.
UNIT 3, OLYMPIA TRADING ESTATE
COBURG ROAD, WOOD GREEN
LONDON N22 6TZ ENGLAND

ISBN-13 978-1-60751-048-2

Cover design by Victor Mingovits

CHAPTER ONE

Having finished my business with postmaster Soames, I exited the post office and paused on its wooden steps to breathe in the fragrant spring air. As it always did at this time of year, my mind turned to baseball. Spring training for the Devils would begin next week, and once again I faced the prospect of spending the season on a local, independent team instead of realizing my dream of playing in the minor league, and eventually working my way to the majors. My thoughts were interrupted by the bustling of a small crowd in front of Hansen's Grocers. The focus of the hubbub seemed to be a large white flier pasted in the front window. I walked over to see what it was all about, and my heart leapt in joy from the instant I read the headline:

JOIN THE FLORIDA STALLIONS!
ENTER THE BUSH LEAGUE TRYOUTS

EVERY YOUNG MAN'S DREAM TO BECOME A BASEBALL PLAYER CAN BE REALIZED. START IN THE BUSH LEAGUE AND WORK YOUR WAY TO THE MAJORS! TRAVEL AND SEE THE EASTERN UNITED STATES. GREAT PAY! MEALS AND LODGING PROVIDED. JOIN US TONIGHT AT 6 P.M. SHARP IN THE MILLER FALLS GRANGE HALL.

JONATHAN HUGHES AND RICHARD STANLEY,
OWNERS AND MANAGERS OF THE STALLIONS

Well, the commotion was understandable. Life in Miller Falls, Georgia, was about as exciting as watching grass grow, so much so that sometimes we joked about that being the sec-ond-favorite local sport after baseball. Those of us who played on the numerous local independent teams did it for more than just love of the game. Any young player worth his salt knew it was near impossible to make it straight to the major leagues without possessing phenomenal talent, but as an independent league player you just might get noticed by a talent scout from the minors if they happened to be passing through the area. So it was certain there would be a large crowd of hopefuls at the grange tonight.

After committing the placard's message to memory, I turned homeward with a downright jaunty step in my stride. As I strolled, kicking stones that littered the dirt road before me, my heart and mind fought over the chance that my dream to become a major league baseball player could someday really come true.

I ambled on with thoughts of the flier filling my head, leav-ing the road about a mile from my house to head across a large cornfield. I walked between the rows of foot-high cornstalks so as not to hurt the tender young plants. I was purposefully skirt-ing my house to avoid my parents, and to scratch an itch that was growing inside my denim overalls. I came out on the other side of the field, parallel to a good-sized lake, descended a small hummock, and began walking along the lakeshore. I began whistling a tune, which was soon echoed from the vicinity of a massive, gnarled oak tree. Its large branches snaked out sev-eral feet over the placid lake. As I approached the tree I could see someone sitting against it on the other side, a strong back seemingly fused to the massive trunk. As I stepped around the tree I looked down into Nelson's smiling face. He rose grace-fully from a checkered blanket and gave me a ferocious hug and deep kiss before holding me at arm's length.

"Hello, Andrew. I didn't think you were going to make it today."

"Sorry, Nelson, I guess I lost track of time."

He was wearing denim shorts and nothing else. He stood well over 6 inches taller than me, and I was only a bit shy of 6 feet. His blond hair shone brightly in the late March sun, curling over the tips of his ears, with several stray wisps falling onto his broad forehead. His pale green eyes sparkled, full of mischief, separated evenly by a long and slender nose. His mouth was large and wide, outlined by two full lips, and my dick twitched at the knowledge of what they were capable of. His jaw was firm and had a decided squareness to it that was indicative of his steadfast Southern heritage. His cheeks and the area above his upper lip were covered in light-blond stubble; the stubble continued down his throat and transformed into full-length darker hairs as it hit his chest and stomach, which were both muscular, but subtly so. My eyes roamed from his medium-sized light-brown nipples to where I knew the hair on his stomach continued full-force below the waistband of his shorts. Accentuated against his sun-browned skin was a vivid strip of white—the band of his underwear. Pausing to admire the slight masculine flare at his hips, my gaze continued down to his crotch, noting the massive lump I knew so well before taking in his muscular, hairy legs. The visual drink ended at his oversized feet, which were topped with wisps of blond hair.

Nelson placed his hands on my waist and kissed me again, then playfully pulled me to him. His ripe masculine smell was overpowering, and I immediately felt his rising stiffness pushing against me. He let go of my waist and placed his hands on each side of my head, pulling it closer till our lips touched. His mouth parted and his tongue reached out to mine; I could taste and smell the peppermint gum he must have recently chewed. I slowly unbuttoned his shorts and reached inside, encountering the forest of hair at the root of his thick cock. I wrapped my hand around the warm piece of flesh and felt it grow within my grip. Nelson moaned softly and pressed insistently against me.

With my other hand I dug deeper, encountering his enormous nut sac and gently prodding it with the tip of a finger.

"Let me get these shorts out of your way."

I removed my hands and Nelson pulled down his shorts and briefs, stepping out of them and standing in front of me in all his naked glory. He quickly turned around, offering his ass to me, then bent over and grabbed his ankles. His ass cheeks were covered in familiar blond hair. I got on my knees and parted the twin globes of flesh, exposing his crack lined with thick tufts of hair and his brown spot. I blew softly against it, and he moaned his appreciation. I wet my finger and pressed it against the hole, then spit against the opening. I inserted my finger and went deep, while Nelson spit in his hand, grabbed his prick and began stroking it. After several lunges I replaced my finger with my tongue, licking up and down Nelson's hairy crack and then circling around his shit hole before hitting the target dead center. I stuck the tip of my tongue in as far as it would go, then lapped his sweet spot like a thirsty dog at a bowl of water. Nelson was now moaning continuously, his hand moving faster and faster on his dick. Suddenly he stood up and turned around, his meaty cock held firmly in his right hand. He gave it one more stroke and I saw the fat head flare, signaling his impending release.

"I'm gonna shoot!" he cried.

A large gob of his white fluid shot from the head of his dick, caromed off my cheek, and landed on my earlobe. More and more of his spunk followed, covering my face. When he was spent I took the large knob into my mouth and sucked it clean. After I released it, Nelson knelt in front of me and licked his cream from my face. He gave me a sticky kiss on the lips, stood up, and ran and dove into the lake. I went to the edge of the lake and lay on my back in the luxurious grass with my legs spread in invitation. Although it had been an unseasonably warm early spring, I knew the water was still chilly from the recent winter.

Nelson swam only two laps before heading back to shore and spotting me supine. He smiled mischievously as he stepped out of the water and knelt between my outspread legs. I was fully hard in anticipation. Cold droplets of water fell onto me, causing my entire body to break out in gooseflesh. He swirled his tongue over my cock head, then trailed it up and down the thick shaft of my stiffer. On his next upward lick he took the fat knob into his mouth and slowly sank down the length of my prick. When his face was nestled in my thick black crotch hair, I began to pump my hips, driving my cock into Nelson's mouth as he placed his hands on my thighs for balance. He allowed me to do all the work as he kept his mouth in a perfect O of suction around my pistoning dick. All too soon I felt the familiar stirrings of my explosion rising from deep within me. I drove into Nelson's mouth a final time and held my member there as my cum began flowing nonstop. He swallowed everything I had to offer, then licked my pole clean. He crawled on top of me, his lips seeking mine. I could still taste my juice on his tongue.

He kissed me several times, then stood up, ran to the edge of the lake, and dove in again. I quickly joined him and after a few laps we swam back to shore, climbed the grassy bank, and sat on the blanket beside the large oak tree. We stretched out on it side by side, holding each other till the water's chill subsided. The spring sun felt wonderful on my skin. Nelson ran his fingers lightly through the black hair on my chest, then flipped around so that we were laying with our crotches to each other's faces: Nelson's favorite position. His cock was fully hard—as was mine—and straining toward me as if it had a mind of its (CK) own. I glanced down to see him engulf the head of my dick and suck on it softly. The angle of my view allowed me to see my stiffer slide down his throat as he slowly swallowed it. He stopped when he reached the thick root, simply holding it in his mouth and letting me feel its warmth and overwhelming wetness, then sliding back up to the head. He let it pop from his mouth, then

looked at me as if to say, "Get busy down there," before engulfing me once more. I looked at his fat prick scant inches from
my face, its one eye staring at me and exuding its early fluid. I
lapped this up with my tongue, causing Nelson to jump slightly.
I ran my tongue in lazy circles over the fat crown, jabbed my
tongue in the slit a few more times, then took the silky knob
into my mouth. I sucked it greedily before swallowing Nelson's
cock till my nose was buried in his bristly crotch hair.

Nelson began moaning softly and pumping his hips as
I bobbed up and down on his prick. After several minutes I
paused and simply let him thrust into my mouth, his balls slapping against the bridge of my nose. I released his stiffer and
licked his ball sac, then pulled him toward me and worked my
tongue down to his hole. I trailed it along the crack of his ass,
teasing him but never quite hitting his brown spot. After several
more swaths I began making lazy circles around his opening,
drawing ever closer to it. When my tongue finally flicked across
it, Nelson bucked his hips and renewed his efforts on my own
dick. As I continued to lick his asshole, I grabbed his member
in my left hand and began jerking it with short, quick strokes.
As Nelson began thrusting his cock harder, I jerked him faster.

"Here it comes, Andrew!"

I took his stiffer back into my mouth right as the first gob
of his spunk shot forth, hitting the back of my throat. It was
quickly followed by a succession of thick spurts. I swallowed it
all at the same time my own explosion began. Nelson wrapped
his lips around the head of my dick and swallowed as quickly
as he could. When I was spent, he released my cock, flipped
around so that we were eye to eye once more, and licked his
juice from my lips. He kissed me again and rolled onto his back.
Very shortly, soft snores were escaping from between his lips.
It wasn't long before I followed suit. When I woke, Nelson was
still snoring softly beside me. I rolled onto my side to face him.
His chest rose and fell with his even breathing. I followed the

contours of his powerful chest and stomach with my eyes and from there down to his crotch, where his flaccid cock lay as if asleep, half its previous size and innocence incarnate.

As I watched the shadows from the setting sun slowly inch across Nelson's torso, I thought of the flier I had seen and the implications it could have for me, Nelson, and my family. I knew when Nelson woke I would need to tell him I was trying out for the Stallions. And I also knew that he would be happy for me, because he knew of and supported my dream to be a professional baseball player, and because he knew how desperately I wanted to get out of this town, even considering the implications that would have on our friendship.

As these thoughts raced through my mind, Nelson opened his eyes and rolled over to face me. He smiled his bright smile and I smiled back. We never stopped to wonder about or analyze our relationship. We weren't in love with each other, but we enjoyed each other's company and had great sex together. I had been hot and heavy with my boyfriend Parker for almost a year, which Nelson had encouraged and been fine with until things started to turn sour. Even then, he had tried to like Parker right up till almost the very end. And what an ordeal that had been. Nelson was a real friend.

He rose up on one elbow and stared into my eyes. "Do you have something you need to tell me?"

He knew me so well that he had sensed something was about to change between us. I cleared my throat, my nervousness plainly visible.

"When I was coming here to meet you today, I saw a flier announcing that the owners of a baseball team from Florida, the Stallions, would be in town this evening recruiting for this year's team. You know my dream is to become a major league player some day, and that starting small in one of the local bush leagues is how many of today's great players began their careers. It could be my ticket out of this godforsaken town."

Nelson looked at me without speaking, then his smile appeared again.

"Andrew, we've always been the best of friends, with the little extra spice of these moments we spend together. But we both know we will not build a life together. I'm very happy about this chance for you. I know baseball is your heart and soul, and I know you will be a damn fine addition to the Stallions."

"Thank you, Nelson. Will you go with me tonight? You know how my folks feel about my dream of playing baseball. They've never supported it, and I can't tell them about tonight or ask them to attend."

"I'd be glad to."

He kissed me a final time on the lips, and then we stood up and got dressed. We walked back up the hill and through the cornfield to the main road. Here we parted company, agreeing to meet at the same spot at a quarter past five in the evening. I ran all the way home, my mounting excitement almost too much to contain as I reached the house. I hurried through my chores, ignoring my father's suspicious looks, and raced through supper as if I were going to receive a prize for finishing first. It was only when I went to leave the house wearing clothes barely a notch below my Sunday finest that my mother could no longer hold her tongue. She was at the sink doing the dishes, and I silently blessed her for not questioning me in front of my father.

"What's got you so excited, son? You were eager to do your chores, you ate my meatloaf—your favorite meal—so fast I doubt you even tasted it, and now here you are leaving for parts unknown all dressed up."

"I'm meeting some of my friends tonight to discuss organizing a chess club for after school."

She had that look on her face parents get when they don't believe a word you've said, but she didn't press the issue.

"OK, well, don't be out too late."

I raced out the door before she probed any further, my step light, my whole body filled with excitement.

. . .

Nelson and I walked into town in silence, each absorbed in our own thoughts. Even though we arrived at the grange hall half an hour early, there was already a sizable crowd gathered on its flagstone steps. But it appeared that the doors were to remain locked till 6 o'clock.

The ancient building, which had been here as long as I could remember, was the site of all the Saturday night dances as well as innumerable social events that, even in recollection, made me want to yawn. As Nelson and I waited at the foot of the steps, I was disconcerted to note that most of my teammates from the Devils were accompanied by fathers, mothers, brothers, or aunts and uncles—a bold show of familial support from kin, unlike my parents, who were dead set against their son leaving the farm. Why couldn't my folks understand that it wasn't enough for me to be a farmer and eke out a meager living in this hopeless town? In their minds it was a good enough place for them to raise a family, and they couldn't see how I could want more, so much more than Miller Falls had to offer. At 6 p.m. sharp the grange doors opened and the crowd flowed in, quickly filling the wooden benches that lined the interior.

At the end of the rows of benches was a dais fashioned of sheets of plywood laid over numerous sawhorses; it looked precarious at best. A handsome older man, dressed in a snappy suit and tie, approached an oversized microphone and whistled to draw the milling crowd's attention. Silence fell, the only noise being the rustling of the townsfolk as they adjusted themselves on the hard, wooden benches.

"Good evening, ladies and gentlemen." The man's booming voice echoed through the building.

"My name is Jonathan Hughes, and I am one of the owners of the Florida Stallions. We are a Bush League team headquartered in Boca Raton, Florida. I want to thank you for joining Mr. Richard Stanley, another part owner, and me at tonight's meeting."

At the mention of Mr. Stanley's name, Mr. Hughes waved his arm to his right, indicating a man I had not seen before. He was sitting in a low chair, and my view of him had been blocked by several taller Devils team members sitting in front of me. I stood up to get a better look. I estimated Mr. Stanley to be in his early thirties. His well-fitted suit clung tenaciously to the muscles of his body. He had been clean-shaven sometime this morning, but the black stubble of his beard and mustache was already springing back to life. His hair was also jet black, clipped short, and slicked back with a heavy pomade. His eyes were a steely blue, almost gray, and separated equally by the bridge of a finely chiseled nose. They were alive and full of interest as he scanned the faces of the eager young men in the crowd. As his gaze neared and then hit upon me, I purposefully met and held it. He stared back unflinchingly, and a raw sexual spark seemed to jump over the heads of the people sitting in front of me and envelop my entire body. I ran the tip of my tongue over my lips several times, then smiled and stuck my middle finger in my mouth. I sucked on it eagerly, my eyes never leaving his, then slowly withdrew it. The invitation was not lost on the handsome man, and he nodded imperceptibly and smiled a small smile before turning his attention back to Mr. Hughes.

"Our third partner, Mr. Jordan Connors, who also happens to be the team's coach, could not be here due to a bad flu. We called this meeting tonight as part of our yearly recruitment practice. We are looking for five players to fill the spaces in our roster left by those who moved on to the major leagues at the end of this past season or, for various reasons, decided not to continue playing for the Stallions. Thus far, we have chosen two of the five replacements in our travels. We're hoping this is our last stop; we got a late start this spring due to reasons I won't bore you with, and we need to return to our headquarters the day after tomorrow to begin spring training in earnest. Tryouts will be held tomorrow morning beginning at 9 a.m. sharp at the Devils' field. If you think you have what it takes to be a Stallion, please sign up with Mr. Stanley or me at the table in front of the podium."

When Mr. Hughes had finished speaking, several young men got up from the benches and converged on the signup table, forming a small, excited knot. Mr. Hughes stepped down from the podium and joined Mr. Stanley at the table to greet each of the signers. As I headed there myself, with Nelson trailing me, a small gathering of people parted in the aisle and I suddenly found myself face to face with Parker.

CHAPTER TWO

It was obvious Parker had just signed up for tomorrow's tryouts. I could have kicked myself for being so foolish as not to realize he would be here. We shared the same dream of pitching in the major leagues, which had become a major bone of contention between us during our relationship. Parker didn't appear at all surprised to see me, and actually stopped as if he wanted to speak to me. I was almost frozen in place as I stared at him. He looked as if not one day had passed since we had last seen each other. And I was ashamed to admit that I felt the old sexual attraction rise unbidden to the surface. He seemed to sense something in me, because he smiled expectantly. But that smile vanished when he saw Nelson. Nelson saw him almost at the same time, and they each took stances as if they were ancient foes. Even though my body had betrayed me, I was determined not to speak to him, and Nelson apparently helped Parker change his mind about approaching me, because he turned and headed in the opposite direction. Nelson pushed past me and started to go after him, but I caught his arm. His chest was heaving slowly from his agitation.

"Don't bother, Nelson. He's not worth it."

"He ain't, Andrew, but he still has one coming to him from me. He treated you horribly, and needs to atone for that."

"It's over and done with. It's best to just let it go and move on."

We watched the cocky young man as he strode through the crowd, then turned and took our place in line. As we waited, I saw Mr. Hughes get up from the table and begin talking to a rather good-sized, older gentleman in a pinstriped suit. The man was flanked by three younger men. It was hard to miss the family resemblance, so I assumed they were his sons. Then it was my turn and I found myself facing Mr. Stanley. He smiled at me and handed me a clipboard.

"Please fill out this form."

He deliberately brushed my hand with his as I took the clipboard from him. As our hands touched, a small thrill of excitement raced up my arm and coursed through my body. I could tell that Mr. Stanley had felt something as well, for he gave me a knowing smile. As I filled out the form, Mr. Hughes returned to the table. I glanced over to see if the four gentlemen he had been talking to were still around, but the crowd had swallowed them up. When I finished the form, I handed it back to Mr. Stanley; again he deliberately brushed my hand. He reviewed the form to make sure everything had been filled out, then extended his hand.

"I look forward to seeing you tomorrow, Andrew."

As we shook hands he held mine longer than etiquette dictated, and I could tell by the look in his eye and the pressure he was exerting on my hand that he had taken a fancy to me.

"Yes, Mr. Stanley, till tomorrow."

I left the grange hall with Nelson close on my heels. I kept an eye out for Parker, half-expecting—or maybe hoping—that he would be waiting for me. But he was nowhere to be found. As Nelson and I walked home, I stopped for a moment and turned to him.

"What did you think of Mr. Stanley?"

"He was kind of nice-looking for an old guy. I mean, if that's what you're into. Why, did he hit on you?" He laughed and punched me in the arm.

"Let's just say he showed his interest. And he's only around ten years older than us, Nelson. We'll see what happens tomorrow at the tryouts. Do you have time tomorrow morning to come with me?

"Oh, I wouldn't miss this for the world. How could I pass up a chance to see Parker again?"

He laughed at his own sarcasm, which made me a little uneasy about his intentions. But I didn't call him on it, and we walked in silence till we came to the fork in the road where Nelson would turn off to his house. He gave me a quick hug.

"Goodnight, Andrew. I'll see you tomorrow morning at 8:30 sharp."

"Goodnight."

. . .

When I got home my parents were in the living room, listening to the radio; Mom was sewing and Dad was reading the paper. They both acknowledged my greeting, but neither asked for details of my evening. I bid them both goodnight and raced up the stairs to my room, where I quickly got ready for bed. However, sleep proved impossible, so I lay awake for several hours, reading the latest pulp magazines from the five-and-dime. I don't know how late it was when I drifted off, but when I woke I still had a magazine clutched in my right hand. When I looked out my window, the gray of dawn greeted me. I dressed hurriedly and raced downstairs and out to the barn to start my chores. Dad was already there and had started the milking.

"Morning, Dad."

He acknowledged me with a nod of his head. After feeding all the animals, mucking out the stalls, and collecting the eggs, I helped my dad with the milking. When we were finished, we went inside for breakfast.

"Good morning, Andrew," Mom said in her cheery morning voice. She gave my father a peck on the cheek in greeting. "Have a seat, men, your breakfast is ready."

"Thanks, Mom."

Mom had cooked a feast for us that consisted of ham, bacon, pancakes, scrambled eggs, potatoes, and red-eye gravy. I sat in my chair with a thud and a second later a large plate of food was placed in front of me. I waited while Mom served Dad and herself and grace was said, and then dove in hungrily. When I had finished eating, I ran upstairs to my room, grabbed my glove and bat, and raced back down to the kitchen. My mom was doing the dishes, but my dad was nowhere in sight. I kissed her on the cheek and was almost out the door when she asked me to hold on a minute. I turned to face her.

"I take it you're off to a baseball game, Andrew?"

"Yes, Ma."

"I forgot to mention last night that I saw a flier in Mr. Hansen's store window announcing a baseball meeting at the grange, and then tryouts this morning. Do you know anything about either one?"

I came to a halt, knowing I had been caught. In these cases, it was always best to tell the truth, which I now blurted out. When I had finished, instead of giving me an angry or disapproving look, she smiled brightly at me, then kissed me on the cheek.

"Andrew, your father and I have come to realize that your life isn't going to unfold here in Miller Falls. And while we are not thrilled about this idea of you being a baseball player, we will do what we can to support you. Good luck today."

Hiding my amazement, and not wanting to press my luck, I grinned and ran out the door and through the yard to the main road. It was true what they said: Mothers always know.

I slowed my pace to a walk as I neared Nelson's turnoff. He was waiting for me right on time.

"Morning, Andrew. Are you ready to start the next big chapter in your life?"

"Let's wait till the tryouts are over before we make any predictions, Nelson," I said, but I was secretly pleased by his enthusiasm. When we arrived at the baseball field, there were close to a dozen hopefuls already there, including several of my Devils teammates. Among them was Kent Meyers, our stellar first baseman. I greeted them but did not see Parker. Relief as well as regret flooded through me. Both Mr. Stanley and Mr. Hughes were already there as well. A small bus, painted silver with a rearing black stallion on its side and hood, was parked to my right. Seemingly against my will, my thoughts strayed back to Parker. What had happened this morning to prevent him from showing up? Better yet, why did I care? It had been a year since we had called it quits. Was I still in love with the guy? Nelson startled me off my train of thought as he wished me luck and went and sat on the wooden bench behind the backstop.

"Good morning, Andrew," Mr. Stanley greeted me. Mr. Hughes echoed his greeting.

"Good morning."

I was pleased that Mr. Stanley had remembered my name. He had forgone last night's suit for a blue T-shirt with a rearing black stallion on it. The shirt hugged his torso nicely. His arms were muscular and covered in a thick black fur. His outfit was completed by an old pair of baseball pants that left nothing to the imagination, and a ratty pair of sneakers. Mr. Hughes wore the same suit he had on last night, so it was evident he wouldn't be physically participating in the tryouts. Mr. Stanley glanced at his watch and blew a whistle that was hanging on a cord around his neck.

"Let's gather round, men. It's 9 a.m. and we need to get the tryouts started. There is a big group here today, and it's going to take most of the day to see you all in action. Promptness and reliability are two of the many traits we look for in our new recruits. And, unfortunately, as I told you last night, there are only three positions left to fill."

As he finished speaking, I heard a vehicle approaching and turned to see a pickup truck heading toward the playing field. As it drew closer I recognized Parker behind the steering wheel. What a fool I had been. Of course he would be here today, come hell or high water. He was a great ballplayer, and his ambition would not allow him to pass this opportunity by. The truck came to a stop and Parker saw me as he exited the truck and ran to us.

"I'm sorry I'm late, Mr. Stanley. I got held up with chores."

"That's OK, you're actually right on time. But we will accept no others after you."

He turned to address the group that had gathered in front of him.

"As Mr. Hughes mentioned in last night's meeting, we will be heading back to Florida tomorrow morning. Those of you who make the team are welcome to travel with us on our bus or provide your own transportation. Any questions?"

Parker immediately raised his hand.

"What will the pay be for our first year?"

I groaned inwardly but was not surprised. It was all about money to Parker, and it probably always would be. I was glad we were no longer together.

Mr. Hughes fielded this question for Mr. Stanley.

"There's no need to discuss salary till the tryouts are over and we have made our choices."

I could see Parker was disappointed by his answer, and inwardly I was glad. He stared at me for a moment, then turned his head the other way. As we walked toward the baseball field, Mr. Hughes joined Nelson on the bench. He had a clipboard, a tablet of paper, and what looked like a stopwatch. For the next several hours each young man took turns batting, fielding balls, and running the bases. Those trying out as pitchers took turns showing what our arms were capable of. As the sun reached its zenith, Mr. Stanley called a break so we could eat lunch. Unbeknownst to us, he and Mr. Hughes had brought a large ice chest filled with sandwiches, hard-boiled eggs, and bottles of soda.

When we had finished eating we were right back at it, and it was late afternoon before Mr. Stanley finally called it quits. I was tired, sweaty, and covered from head to toe in dirt. But I felt I had presented myself well.

"You men have a seat on the bench while I confer with Mr. Hughes."

We had all seen Mr. Hughes busily scribbling notes throughout the tryouts. We took seats on the bench while he and Mr. Stanley went into the bus to talk. They were inside for a good half hour, and some of the men were starting to get anxious. We were all relieved when the two men exited the bus and approached us. Mr. Stanley held up his hand for attention, and our conversations stopped immediately.

"I want to thank everyone for taking the time to participate in today's tryouts. It was a pleasure to meet all of you, and whether you are chosen today or not, we wish you the best. We have chosen three recruits from the tryouts this morning. It was not an easy decision, because we saw a lot of talent here today. However, as we indicated, there are only three spots left on the roster, and those spots go to the following: Andrew Duggan, Parker Williams, and Kent Myers. Will the three new recruits please stay behind for a moment? My best wishes to the rest of you."

My heart was pounding with joy. As the rest of the young men left the playing field, the three of us excitedly lined up in front of Mr. Hughes and Mr. Stanley. I made sure Kent was between Parker and me. Mr. Stanley cleared his throat.

"Again, gentlemen, congratulations on being recruited for the Florida Stallions. Mr. Hughes and I are staying at the hotel in town. We are going to return to our room to finalize the contracts. Please join us at six o'clock tonight to review and sign them. Afterward we'll celebrate our new partnership with dinner on us. If there are no questions, we'll see you soon."

Beyond my elation about being chosen, I was not pleased to hear that Parker had also made the cut, but I couldn't pretend I was surprised. His athleticism was surpassed only by his sexual prowess. As Mr. Hughes and Mr. Stanley reached their bus, I saw Parker intercept them. The three men spoke briefly, then Parker headed slowly for his truck, and the two managers boarded the bus and drove away with Mr. Hughes behind the wheel. I congratulated Kent, and walked over to receive a huge hug from Nelson. As I did so I saw Parker reach his truck and pause to stare at me. As I returned his gaze, my mind drifted back to almost a year ago today. He had been my first love, and our breakup was as fresh in my mind as though it had happened yesterday.

CHAPTER THREE

Parker Williams lived in Newport, a town about 20 miles from Miller Falls. We had first met two years ago when his team, the Talons, had faced mine, the Devils, in the final game of the Independent League season. As pitchers for our respective teams, I was a rightie and Parker was a natural left-hander. He had a wicked fastball and a curve that decimated my teammates. In one at-bat I managed to turn an infield grounder that bounced just outside the reach of the third baseman into a double. As I stood on the bag and adjusted my jock, Parker turned and looked at me, seemingly in grudging respect that I got a hit off him.

I could not help but admire his physique. He stood several inches over 6 feet, and his uniform hugged his body, accentuating every curve and muscle. His arms were thick and covered in reddish-brown fur, and the hair on his head was the color of newly minted pennies. His eyebrows matched the hair on his arms and stood guard over blue eyes pale as the summer sky. His nose was long and curved slightly at the bridge as though it had once been broken and had not mended correctly. His cheeks and throat were covered with reddish-brown stubble. His mouth was small but sported thick lips that glistened with the balm that protected them from the sun's harsh rays. As my gaze moved down his chest and stomach, I was transfixed by the bulge at his crotch. Although often this type of display was merely induced by wearing a protective cup, what I spied was more than even that device could handle. He had eyed me longer than politeness warranted, and I adjusted my jock again to see what reaction it provoked. He smiled, revealing two rows of perfect white teeth, then lowered his free hand to hip level and subtly gestured to his crotch. I nodded my head slightly, feeling a flush of excitement course through me, and he smiled and turned around to face the next batter.

Due largely to Parker's pitching prowess and my distraction, we lost 8–0. As I was walking to my dad's truck after the game, I ran into Parker in the grassy parking area.

"Nice hit. My name's Parker. Parker Williams. As you can probably guess, I'm from Newport."

"Pleased to meet you, Parker. I'm Andrew Duggan, from Miller Falls."

We shook hands with instant rapport, sparking an intense sexual connection. He was even more handsome close up, and his handshake was strong, with fingers that were thick and quite long. Reddish-brown hair also graced the backs of his hands.

"Well, Andrew, do you have any pressing business, or would you like to unwind and kill off a bottle of whiskey? I know a spot where we won't be disturbed."

"Nope, I've got no reason to hurry home; I'd love to hang out with you. Let me go tell my dad."

Finding myself desperately wanting to spend time with this man, I literally ran to where my dad had parked to tell him I would be home later and that I didn't need a ride. Glancing at me skeptically, he started the truck and drove away. I watched till he was out of sight before rejoining Parker, following him to the end of a row of cars and into a fairly new pickup truck. Once we were inside he placed his hand on my thigh and gave it a good squeeze, then leaned over and kissed me full on the mouth.

"Nice," he said, then started the truck. As he drove along numerous dirt roads, he talked nonstop about baseball, the current Independent League teams, and life in Newport in general—all the while feeling me up quite earnestly. Finally, after turning onto yet another dusty road, he immediately pulled off into a copse of trees, parking beneath the canopy of several large maples. Parker leaned over and kissed me again, this time sliding his tongue inside my mouth. I could feel his spit mixing with mine as he pinched my nipples through my uniform. He finally removed his tongue and exited the truck. I followed suit. He rummaged behind the seat before shutting the door and walking around to the tailgate. When I met him there I saw that he had a blanket tucked under his left arm and a bottle in his right hand. Parker pulled down the tailgate and spread the blanket on it. He patted it and smiled.

"Have a seat, handsome."

I slid onto the blanket and spread my legs, and when he stepped between them I locked my knees against his hips. He placed his hands on my shoulders and kissed me again, deeply and passionately. My body was already responding to him; my cock was hard and throbbing in my pants. He grabbed the bottle of whisky and took a long pull from it before passing it to me. I followed his example, letting the liquid burn down my gullet.

"This is from a batch of my daddy's grade-A corn whiskey."

I murmured my appreciation, unable to speak because of the burning in my mouth.

We shared the bottle of whiskey in between kisses, all the while exploring each other's bodies with our hands. Before long the liquor had taken effect, and I was as horny as a three-peckered billy goat. Parker reached into his pocket and pulled out a silver tin the size of a gas cap. It was a container of the grease baseball players use to keep their mitts supple, something all players have a readily available supply of. He pushed me flat on my back and began unbuttoning my pants. He then reached down, undid the laces of my cleats, pulled them off, and placed them on the tailgate next to me.

He pulled my pants and briefs down my legs and over my feet, leaving my socks on. The early spring air caused gooseflesh to rise on my arms and legs. He folded both garments and placed them next to my cleats before picking up the tin. He took the top of his baseball uniform off, quickly followed by his undershirt. His chest was thick and brawny, his nipples large and dark brown. His navel was small and deep. Both his chest and stomach were covered in the same reddish-brown hair as his arms. As he gazed into my eyes he undid his belt and the buttons on his pants. He slid them, along with his underwear, down to his ankles. His cock was long and thick and fully hard, and stuck straight out from his crotch. A thick forest of hair grew above the thick root.

He popped the lid off the tin and scooped up a generous glob of the clear gel with his fingers. I raised my legs in the air, exposing my hole, and he covered it with the grease and gently inserted a finger inside me. He worked it in and out a few times before withdrawing it. After spreading the remainder of the grease on his dick, Parker grabbed me underneath my knees, pushed my legs back and stepped between them. He placed the head of his cock against my slick hole and pushed gently.

After the usual initial resistance, the knob of his massive member popped through and penetrated me, slowly but surely parting the walls of my asshole. When he was completely inside me, he stood still, letting me feel the full measure of his prick. He then withdrew just as slowly as he'd entered, till only the tip remained in me, then pushed back in. Once he hit bottom the second time he began thrusting in and out in long, deep, unhurried strokes. With each one the head of his cock hit the pleasure muscle deep within me, eliciting a continuous series of grunts and moans.

I lost track of time; the only sounds were the occasional bird, a cow lowing in a distant field, Parker's thighs slapping against the back of mine, and our chorus of groans. Then I could feel my own explosion coming quickly, but I was to be outpaced by Parker.

"I'm gonna blow, Andrew!"

He sank into me a final time and I felt the flood of his release. Surprisingly, this triggered my own juice to come bubbling out of me, and it quickly crisscrossed the black hairs of my stomach. Parker seemed quite proud that I had shot my load simply from the effect of his probing cock. He scooped it from my belly and ate it, then sprawled atop me till his dick softened. When he pulled out of me it was with a soft, squishy sound. Grabbing the blanket from underneath my ass, Parker climbed into the bed of the pickup truck and spread the blanket full length.

"Come and join me."

I crawled beside him and we lay on our sides, Parker cradling me in his arms. The first stars were beginning to appear in the night sky and the evening was beginning to turn colder. Parker held me tighter, the warmth of his body seeping into my own. I had closed my eyes and was listening to the sounds of the early night when I felt the head of Parker's cock slide invitingly between my ass cheeks.

"Do you want to go again, Andrew?"

In reply I wrapped my left arm around his neck and pulled him to me. He kissed me on the back of the neck while pressing his fat crown against my opening once more. No grease was necessary since I was still slick from our first encounter. The head popped through easily, and he slid all the way in, spreading the walls of my asshole wide.

"Your ass feels real nice, Andrew."

He lifted my leg to give him better access, and began sliding in and out of me with long, quick, deep lunges. The second time was to be no slow affair—it was for Parker's benefit and his alone—but the thought of pleasing him thrilled me beyond reason, and I think I fell in love with Parker Williams that very night. After he exploded inside me for the second time, we lay in the bed of the truck for what seemed like hours, covered up with the blanket, watching the stars and finishing the bottle of whisky. And before we left our sanctuary, he had me one more time. I would learn over the next year how great his stamina was, often enabling him to come three or four times over several hours of lovemaking.

When he finally drove me home, the eastern sky was beginning to lighten. He kissed me goodnight and asked if we could get together the next night after practice. I readily agreed, and that was the beginning of my first relationship. And what a tumultuous year it turned out to be, one that I would definitely end up regretting.

Because Parker was my first boyfriend—not to mention the fact that he was exciting, handsome, and an ardent lover—I overlooked many faults I sensed early on. It became increasingly clear that he came with a lot of baggage. When the next season started, a rivalry sprang up almost immediately between the two of us over each other's pitching prowess. He kept track of our individual wins and was always quick to point out that he had more. And when he lost a game, which was rare, he was irate and inconsolable. What was worse, the whiskey we drank that first night together was nothing compared to the amounts Parker soon began to consume, and he was a bad-tempered drunk. It was at these times that, strangely enough, he was the most amorous, so our sexual romps took on a meanness and unnecessary roughness that I began to despise and avoid. But things really turned sour the day I told him about Nelson. Looking back on it now, I realize I deliberately told him of Nelson to precipitate the end of our relationship, knowing Parker couldn't understand.

On several occasions Parker and I invited other men to join us in our sexual escapades, and each time, Parker was the one to bring in the stranger. Sensing a familiarity between Parker and these men, I was pretty sure that they were either old lovers of his or recent solo conquests; it was clear that Parker saw this as his role in our relationship, and I thought, "So be it." But at the

same time, when Parker was drinking he became insanely jealous of any man who even looked at me outside of these planned
sessions with strangers. It led to numerous fights. During one
such altercation at a bar a few miles out of town, I threw the
mention of Nelson in Parker's face, and he almost went ber-
serk. He took a drunken swing that I easily avoided, and the
momentum propelled him to the ground. I had left him that
night, walking home to find Nelson on the front porch waiting
for me. He always knew what could make me feel better; taking
my hand, he led me into the barn and up the ladder to the hayloft. But as soon as he had emptied his seed inside me, I heard
Parker's voice. He was hollering for me and pounding on the
door of my parents' house. Nelson and I quickly got dressed. I
was headed to the ladder when Nelson grabbed my arm.

"Don't go down there, Andrew. Let your dad take care of
this."

Just then I heard my father's voice say something angry but
incomprehensible, followed by the sound of the front door
being slammed. An eerie quiet ensued, but it was soon shattered as Parker came storming into the barn, where Nelson
and I stood in the loft above him in plain sight. After quickly
surveying the ground floor of the barn, Parker's gaze turned
upward, and the look of malicious triumph on his face when he
saw us sent a chill down my spine.

"Andrew! Come down here. I want to talk to you!"

"He ain't coming down, Parker, and it's best you leave before
you get hurt."

"You must be Nelson," Parker sneered. "Come down so I can
have a word with you as well."

"Stay here, Andrew," Nelson said, and before I could stop
him he quickly descended the ladder.

Parker gave him a moment to light on the ground before
attacking him with two swinging fists. But his drunkenness

was still making it easy to avoid his blows; Nelson quickly side-stepped his flailing fists and rained several blows on his head and face. Knocked to the ground, Parker lay sprawled, with blood running from his nose. He managed to regain his feet, but the fight seemed to have been knocked out of him. He did not make any more moves toward Nelson. Instead, he glared up at me.

"We're through, Duggan, you stupid loser," he slurred.

"I couldn't have said it better myself, Parker. Now get your drunken ass the hell out of my barn."

"Gladly. And you've got one coming from me, Nelson!"

"Anytime, Parker!"

Parker made no reply. He stomped out of the barn and out of my life.

· · ·

My thoughts snapped back to the present as Nelson's embrace eased. He must have sensed Parker's and my staring contest; upon being released, I turned to see Parker standing by his truck as if trying to convince himself to come over and talk to me. When Nelson purposefully stepped in front of me Parker seemed to get the message, and got in his truck and left. As he drove away, Nelson whirled on me, his anger plain to see on his face.

"What the hell was that about? Do you still have feelings for that jerk? Have you lost your mind?"

My own anger quickly flared up. "Mind your own business, Nelson!"

Without waiting for him to respond, I turned and walked away. I fumed all the way home, angry because of what Nelson had seen, angrier because he had been right, and angriest at myself for being a fool and for yelling at Nelson. My mom was in the kitchen when I got home and she was quite pleased that I had made the team. She also asked that I let her break the news to my father, which I was more than happy to do.

I told her about dinner in town, during which I was to sign my contract. She hugged me and told me she was very proud of me. I went upstairs and changed into my Sunday best, washed my face, brushed my teeth, and combed my hair. When I came back downstairs to leave, my mom fussed over me and told me to have fun.

The hotel Mr. Stanley had referenced was the only one in town, the Claremont. I had never been inside, but knew that the dining room was on the ground floor, as well as the kitchen and the owner's quarters. The second floor consisted of a half-dozen rooms, each with its own bathroom. It was owned and run by an elderly German couple. I had heard they served good food, and with tonight being the start of my new future, I was ready to enjoy all they had to offer.

As I approached the hotel, I saw the Stallions' bus parked in front. When I pulled open the large oak front door of the building, I was immediately greeted by the smells of pot roast, homemade bread, and apple pie. The dining room was to my left, set apart by a low wall, which enabled me to see there were no customers as of yet. I glanced at the wide, dark oak staircase right as Mr. Stanley came down it.

He extended his hand as he reached me and I clasped it firmly, his own grip matching mine. That exhilarating sensation passed through me and once more I could tell Mr. Stanley felt it too. He glanced around the restaurant, then placed his hand on my crotch and rubbed vigorously. My cock responded and began swelling to its full length. As it did he squeezed its fat head. I moaned softly and pressed against his hand. He grabbed my right hand and placed it on his crotch, where his own dick was just as hard. And it was a big one.

"Nice," he murmured, then withdrew his hand as a tired-looking woman with her hair in a bun came bustling out of the kitchen.

"Feel free to seat yourselves, gentlemen. I'll be right with you."

We entered the dining room and sat at a table facing the door. Within minutes an older gentleman brought us water. Mr. Stanley ordered two beers and when the old man returned with them, Mr. Stanley held his up in a toast.

"Congratulations again, Andrew, and welcome to the Stallions."

I clinked his bottle and took a long pull from my own. It was ice cold and delicious.

"Mr. Hughes is finishing up the remaining contracts, but should be down momentarily. Parker Williams will not be joining us because he had to help his father with the spring planting. He came to the hotel after the tryouts and reviewed and signed his contract. So it will just be you and Kent Myers joining us for dinner. Parker also has some obligations that will prevent him from riding our bus to Boca Raton, so he will be driving to Florida the day after tomorrow."

I felt instant relief when I realized that Parker would not be on the bus with me. That was a ride I had not been looking forward to. As I took another long pull on my beer, Kent entered the restaurant, followed by Mr. Hughes, who was carrying a worn valise. Mr. Stanley flagged down the old man and ordered a beer for each of them.

"Greetings, everyone. Sorry for the delay," said Mr. Hughes as he pulled a set of papers from the valise. "Here are the contracts. Please read and, if you agree to the terms, sign at the bottom on the dotted line. There are no mysteries here: By signing you each affirm your intention to play for the Florida Stallions for one year's time. You will be paid monthly, and room and board will be paid for. Contracts may be terminated at any time for poor performance or unwanted conduct. If you wish someone else to review for or after you, you will have until tomorrow morning to return the signed copies to me."

I quickly read the terms of the contract, signed my name at the bottom, and handed the contract back to Mr. Hughes. In my mind there was no need for anyone else to review. Kent signed shortly after me, and when Mr. Hughes had both contracts he slid them back inside the valise.

"Okay, men," Mr. Hughes exclaimed, "now that business matters have been taken care of, let's enjoy our dinner so we can adjourn to our room upstairs and celebrate our new partnership. The pot roast is highly recommended here."

After our order had been taken, I asked Mr. Hughes where the other two recruits were this evening.

"They both have family in this area they haven't seen in some time, and they opted to spend tonight with them. They will meet us here tomorrow morning."

After a dinner that included pot roast, mashed potatoes, homemade bread, and a slice of apple pie, washed down with several more beers, I was feeling full and slightly intoxicated. Mr. Stanley paid the bill and the four of us climbed the wide wooden stairs to the second floor. He unlocked the first door on the left and we followed him inside.

The room was spacious, with only one large bed. Two heavy walnut nightstands stood on each side, each with a small lamp atop it. To the right of the bed was a large armoire, also walnut. Two large windows overlooked the main street, with an oversized armchair with matching ottoman in between them. A moderate-sized bathroom completed the room. It contained a claw-foot bathtub and a small toilet and sink. I saw a wooden ice chest in the bathtub. Mr. Stanley went immediately to it and came back into the room with a bottle of champagne. He poured glasses for everyone and handed them to us.

"To the future success of the Stallions!"

We raised our glasses, clinked them together, yelled "cheers" in unison, and took a deep drink. Mr. Stanley loosened and removed his tie, and sat down in the chair. I sat on the ottoman, and Mr. Hughes and Kent sat side by side on the bed. As the night progressed and the ice chest produced many more bottles of beer, the discussion centered on, of course, the upcoming baseball season and the glories of past seasons.

The room began to get warm due to the effects of the alcohol and our proximity to one another, so Mr. Stanley opened the window. Cold, fresh air wafted into the room. Soon Mr. Stanley had removed his shoes and socks, and then his shirt. This left him sitting in the worn armchair in just his undershirt and pants. The undershirt nicely outlined the muscles of his chest and stomach; large tufts of black hair clumped in his armpits, and a forest of it peeked out from the revealed half-moon of his chest. The front of the undershirt was stained with his sweat, which I could smell. I couldn't tear my eyes from him, and as I continued to stare he began rubbing his right nipple with his bottle of beer. When he withdrew it the nub of his tit poked up underneath the cotton material. He did the same to the left one, his eyes never leaving mine.

"Do you like what you see, Andrew?"

"Yes, very much."

"Then take your shirt off and join me."

In response I stood up, pulled my shirt over my head and dropped it on the floor, followed closely by my T-shirt. Mr. Stanley studied my chest and stomach with undisguised interest, confirmed by his next statement.

"What luck that I chose the hairy one. And you're in great shape as well."

He patted his thighs and I went to him and straddled his lap. He ran his hands over my chest and stomach, curling my jet-black hair between his fingers, then pulling on my tits till their nubs were as hard as pebbles. Then he leaned in and took the right one into his mouth. I moaned softly and placed my hand on the back of his head, both in support and encouragement. Releasing it, he gave the left one the same treatment, then let it fall from his mouth and kissed me, his tongue sliding between my lips and finding my own. Our tongues wrapped around each other as if in some weird dance until he withdrew his and licked his way down the front of me till he reached my belt. He undid the buckle, pulled it through the loops, and tossed it on the floor with the rest of my clothing. He unbuttoned my pants and wormed his hand underneath my briefs, spearing the thick shaft of my cock.

"Take your pants off."

The whispered command prompted me to my feet. I quickly pulled my pants and briefs down to my ankles and stepped out of them. My dick sprang free and slapped against my belly.

"Very nice. Leave your socks on."

He rose from the chair and pulled his undershirt off. His thick chest was blanketed with black hair, the dark-brown nipples barely visible. The hair covered his stomach as well, growing twice as fuzzy in his navel. Without further ado, Mr. Stanley continued undressing till he stood naked before me in all his hirsute glory. His member was fully hard and long and thick, and stuck straight out from his body like a pole. His balls were enormous, hanging low in their sac of flesh. He struck several bodybuilder poses, jokingly, then settled back into the chair once more. I stepped over to him till my legs were pressed against the chair, my prick directly in line with his face; he didn't need to be told what to do. He leaned forward and swirled his tongue over the head of my cock. He ran his tongue through the tiny piss slit, lapping up my early cum and forcing a shudder through my body. He sucked the fat knob, then leaned back in his chair and patted its thick arms.

"Climb up here."

I did as ordered, completely oblivious now as to anyone else in the room. I balanced on my knees on the chair's arms as Mr. Stanley gripped my ass cheeks and in one swift movement swallowed my entire stiffer. I looked down to see his nose buried in my crotch hair. He stayed on my cock, breathing loudly through his nose, then slid up to the crown once more, gagging slightly with saliva hanging from his chin. He sucked the fat head once more before swallowing my prick again and sawing up and down on it. I again placed my hand on the back of his head and began pumping my hips to match his bobbing head. As he sucked my stiffer he began probing beneath my ball sac with his finger. When he hit my shit hole he began pushing at the tiny opening. When it resisted his efforts, he slid the same finger in his mouth alongside my dick to wet it, then took up his quest once more. This time the hole yielded, and after his finger slid through the puckered ring, he penetrated as deeply as the angle would allow.

He began timing the thrusts of his finger with his sawing on my cock. I felt the pressure building within me as my release boiled to the surface. He sensed it was coming and on his next upward saw he simply held the fat knob in his mouth as I unloaded my seed. He didn't miss one bit of the massive flow, and when the last drop had fallen he licked first the head clean and then his lips. I bent down and kissed him, then eased off the arms and into his lap, aligning his stiffer with the crack of my ass. It was an incredible feeling. I squirmed against it, eliciting a series of soft moans from him. I leaned into him and he kissed me long and hard. As we parted I heard several loud groans coming from behind us. Mr. Stanley nodded his head in the direction of the bed and I turned to discover that Mr. Hughes and Kent had not been idle while Mr. Stanley had been savoring my prick.

Mr. Hughes was lying naked on his back on the bed, his head toward the pillow, his large feet facing us. Kent was naked and inverted above him, balanced on his knees and elbows. Mr. Hughes was gripping him at the waist while Kent's dick slid in and out of his mouth. At the same time, Kent was sucking on Mr. Hughes's huge member for all he was worth. With his right hand he was stroking the bottom half of the large cock, and with his other he was fondling Mr. Hughes's enormous sac of balls. As we continued to watch the pair, Mr. Hughes began thrashing on the bed and thrusting his prick in a frenzy into Kent's mouth. Suddenly, Kent released the thick piece of meat from his mouth and began pumping it furiously. Within seconds a large wide gob of cum erupted from the flared head, landing on Kent's right cheek. More of the white fluid shot forth, resembling a mini-volcano. When Mr. Hughes was spent, Kent wiped the stuff from his right cheek with a finger, sucked it clean, then proceeded to lap up the remaining splotches that had landed on the older man. When he was finished Kent stayed in position above Mr. Hughes, who began sucking Kent's cock with a new vigor. It was quickly apparent by the look on Kent's face that his own explosion was imminent. Sure enough, he began moaning loudly and pumping his hips faster. He suddenly paused and we could see Mr. Hughes's throat muscles working as he swallowed Kent's seed. When Kent was done he swung around and lay next to Mr. Hughes, an arm slung across the older man's hairy chest. They both looked over at us expectantly. Kent was the first to break the silence.

"It's your turn again."

I turned to Mr. Stanley and he smiled at me.

"Let's give the crowd what they want. There's a tin of glove grease in my pants pocket."

I slid off his lap, fished the container from his pants pocket, and took my place once more. I popped the tin open, scooped out a generous amount and coated Mr. Stanley's prick. I then rose up a bit and wiped the excess on my hole. I started to turn around when he asked me to face him. I swung around and planted my knees on his hairy thighs. I grabbed Mr. Stanley's thick cock and aimed it for my sweet spot. When the fat head passed between my ass cheeks and hit my brown hole, he held me in place till the knob popped through the taut opening and I slid down onto his prick till he was completely inside me. Mr. Stanley let out a loud groan and began grinding his hips. He leaned into me and began biting and sucking on my tits again. As he worked the now-rigid nubs I rose up on his stiffer till just the large crown was still inside before slowly lowering myself once more.

I placed my hands on Mr. Stanley's shoulders and began riding him, forcing his pole deep into me each time. His eyes were glazed with his lust as he began pumping his hips, increasing his thrusts into me. He grabbed my stiffer in his right hand and began stroking it in time with his lunges in and out of my asshole. I leaned forward to kiss him, my tongue sliding into his mouth. He sucked on it eagerly. Sweat was running down his chest and stomach, dampening the hairs of both and pooling in his crotch. The strong smells from our coupling filled the room. When he began thrusting even harder into me, I knew his eruption was quickly approaching. And with his hand on my cock and his enormous prick up my ass, I knew I wouldn't be far behind him.

"Here it comes," he yelled so loud I thought for sure the entire hotel heard it. I felt his spooge flooding my asshole. When he was done shooting, Mr. Stanley renewed his efforts on my own stiffer, while at the same time leaning in and sucking and biting my nipples once more. I cried out as my eruption overtook me and my jism began spilling onto his chest, crisscrossing the black hairs. When I was spent Mr. Stanley kissed me a final time, then rubbed my spunk further into his chest hairs, making a sticky mess. I rose up off his softening cock and felt some of his fluid leak out of my hole.

"I need to piss," I said as I headed naked across the room.

When I came out of the bathroom, I took a good swallow from the beer I had grabbed from the ice chest. I sat in the armchair while Kent got up from the bed and began dressing.

"I have to get home before my parents start getting worried. I'll meet you all tomorrow in front of the hotel."

He leaned down and gave Mr. Hughes a kiss, then did the same to me and Mr. Stanley.

When he had gone, Mr. Stanley joined Mr. Hughes on the bed.

"Do you have to go now too, Andrew, or can you stay a bit longer? We'll make it worth your while." As Mr. Stanley finished speaking he grabbed Mr. Hughes's cock and began slowly stroking it.

"I can stay a little while longer."

As if in response, Mr. Stanley increased his strokes on Mr. Hughes's stiffer and the large piece of meat filled to its full proportions. The older man turned on his side while the younger one did the same, only headed in the opposite direction. Each one had his left leg in the air, forming a V. Mr. Hughes stuck out his tongue and licked the head of Mr. Stanley's member, then engulfed the fat knob and began slowly sawing on it. Mr. Stanley did the same to Mr. Hughes's prick. Each sucked the other's stiffer in slow, relaxed, up-and-down movements, their soft moans mixing with the sounds of their sucking. I grabbed the tin of grease, slicked up my stiffer, and began pumping myself as I stood at the foot of the bed and watched the two managers slowly and lovingly suck each other off. I kept my strokes to a slow pace as well, hoping that we could all release at the same time.

While continuing to savor Mr. Hughes's cock, Mr. Stanley began running his finger along the older man's hairy ass crack. After several runs along the fuzzy slit, he slid his finger between the two hairy cheeks, searching for the treasure hidden between. It was obvious when he found the tiny opening and gained access, for Mr. Hughes's moaning increased tenfold. Mr. Stanley began sliding his finger in and out while at the same time he stopped sawing on the older man's prick and simply held it in his mouth. I think he sensed Mr. Hughes was getting close to shooting and, indeed, Mr. Hughes began pumping his hips faster before releasing Mr. Stanley's cock altogether and growling as his release began. Mr. Stanley swallowed it all, then gave Mr. Hughes his seed in return. When both men were spent they uncoiled themselves and sat on the end of the bed, watching me as I brought relief to myself. When the first drop exploded from the head of my dick it arced in the air and landed on my stomach. More droplets followed. When I was done I crawled on the bed and settled in between the two managers. They wrapped their arms around me and I quickly nodded off.

When I woke up I was still wedged between Mr. Stanley and Mr. Hughes, a hairy chest against both my front and back. I was still quite drunk. The lamp on the nightstand allowed me to see the clock, and I was shocked to discover it was a little past midnight. I had been asleep for a few hours. My parents were going to be worried to death and also probably very angry. As I was dressing there was a loud knock on the door. Without a clue as to who it could it be at this hour, I shook both men awake; we dressed hurriedly as the knocking became more insistent and then turned to pounding. When Mr. Stanley was fully dressed, he motioned Mr. Hughes to go in the bathroom. Mr. Stanley opened the door partway so I could not see who was outside. I heard hushed voices that were quickly raised, and suddenly Mr. Stanley was sent reeling backward. The door opened all the way and in stepped a livid man. He looked at me for a moment, then turned his stony glare on Mr. Stanley, who was rising from the floor.

"Who the hell are you and what do you think you're doing barging into my room at this hour?"

Before the man had a chance to reply, I stepped between the two of them. "It's OK, Mr. Stanley. This is my father."

CHAPTER FOUR

"Go get in the truck, Andrew," was all he said, and the look on his face was one I had never seen before. He ignored Mr. Stanley completely as he turned and left the room. I followed him out the door and down the stairs, stumbling a little due to the lingering effects of the beer. I'm sure I smelled like a bucket of cum as well. My father stopped and, without a word, put his arm underneath my shoulder and guided me out of the hotel to his truck. Surprisingly, he was not rough in his treatment of me as he put me in the passenger's side and got behind the wheel. As we drove away he turned to me, a look of concern on his face.

"We won't speak of this to your mother. Nelson told me where to find you. I know the reputation ballplayers have. When I was your age my best friend made it to the majors. Anyway, your mother was in bed and asleep when I left the house. I'll tell her you were with Nelson and lost track of time. You're a man, Andrew, and if you're going to drink like one, you need to do it responsibly. Or not do it at all."

"Yes, sir," was my feeble response.

"So, can I assume you have made the team?"

I turned to him and was surprised to see a smile on his face.

"I know this will come as a shock to you, Andrew, but your mother and I had a long talk after you left tonight. She told me of the meeting at the grange and the tryouts this morning. If this is what you want for your life, we won't stand in your way."

Overcome with emotion, all I could muster was, "Thanks, Dad."

We drove the rest of the way home in silence. When we arrived at the house the only light on was the one in the kitchen. I fumbled my way upstairs and fell spread-eagled on my bed. When I woke in the morning I felt like I had been kicked in the head by a mule. My body wanted to lie in bed all day, but my mind interjected, telling me I had chores to do before I left for Boca Raton. Boca Raton? As that thought surfaced, I leapt out of bed, dressed, and went downstairs. My mother was not in the kitchen, so I hurried to the barn so I would miss her. I went through my litany of chores in a complete fog, not notic-ing the small smiles that often appeared on my father's face as he watched me. I hadn't seen or heard from Nelson since our fight yesterday, and I wondered if he had been eager to tell my Dad where I was. But it looked like I wouldn't have time to track him down this morning before I had to meet Mr. Hughes and Mr. Stanley at the hotel. As I helped my father finish the milking, I heard the barn door bang shut. When I turned to see who had entered, Nelson was standing just inside it. He had a sheepish grin on his face. My dad stared at him for a moment, then walked past him on his way out the door.

"Good morning, Mr. Duggan."

"Morning, Nelson."

When my dad was gone, Nelson stood facing me in silence.

"I'm sorry about yesterday," he suddenly blurted out. "And I'm sorry about telling your dad where you were."

"Don't worry about it, Nelson. And just so you know, I signed the contract last night, and am now officially a member of the Florida Stallions. I leave this morning at 9 for Boca Raton."

"That's wonderful news, Andrew. I'm so proud of you." He came and gave me a big hug, then slid his hand down to my crotch and began massaging my cock. "Do we have time to go up to the loft before you leave?"

"I think we can squeeze in a quickie."

We climbed the ladder to the loft, and I pulled a blanket from a trunk we stored there for such occasions. I spread it on the hay, and then we both shed our clothes and lay down. We did not speak as we fell into an embrace, our mouths meeting in a kiss. His familiar scent filled my nostrils as he pushed me onto my back. I raised my legs and Nelson spread my ass cheeks. His tongue found my shit hole and he licked the sensitive spot before spitting on it several times. He then spit into his hand, spread it on his stiffer, and entered me swiftly. He plunged deep, his crotch hair tickling my ass cheeks, then withdrew and entered me powerfully once again. This was no slow-motion act but a hard and fast ride. He bent over me and kissed me on the mouth. I thrust my hips in time with his lunges, nibbling on his nipples and the lobes of his ears. Our small cries and the sound of flesh hitting flesh were the only noises in our little alcove.

Nelson increased his tempo, and I knew he was close to coming. He gave a long guttural grunt and shoved his cock home one final time. As his jism filled me he spit into his hand again, grabbed my pole, and began stroking it furiously. I bucked my hips as his speed increased, and within minutes my own juice was crisscrossing my stomach. Nelson bent forward and licked my belly clean, then pulled out of me. When we were dressed we climbed down from the loft. We hugged and kissed goodbye, and we both promised to write as often as we could. Nelson also promised a visit as soon as he could get away. When we came out of the barn my parents were waiting for me on the front porch, my battered suitcases beside them.

"See ya, Mr. and Mrs. Duggan," Nelson threw back over his shoulder.

My dad nodded to Nelson in response, while my mom smiled and waved. I went onto the porch and hugged my mother goodbye. There were tears in her eyes.

"I will miss you, Andrew. Please be careful and write to us every week."

I hugged her again, then released her, planted a kiss on her cheek, grabbed my suitcases, and walked to the truck, followed by my dad. After placing the suitcases in the back, I climbed in the passenger side, and we both waved goodbye to my mom. We drove to town in silence and pulled up in front of the hotel. There were no long goodbyes; as I retrieved my suitcases my father got out of the truck, came around to my side, and shook my hand.

"Good luck, son. I wish you the best and know you will make your mother and me proud."

As I watched his battered old pickup head down the main street, I felt a small twinge of anxiety. Was I making a mistake in leaving the only life I had ever known to pursue a dream that might not pan out? What if I was not as good a player as I thought? What if I didn't even last a full season on the Stallions? I quickly pushed these thoughts from my mind as I saw Mr. Stanley and Mr. Hughes emerge from the hotel, trailed by two handsome young men. Several scenes from the hotel room last night flashed through my mind. I felt my cock stirring beneath my briefs at the memories of Mr. Stanley shooting his seed.

I joined the group just as Kent was being dropped off by a rather severe-looking older man and woman. We greeted one another and stood beside each other next to the bus.

"Good morning, Kent and Andrew. This is our new short-stop, Tobias 'Dizzy' Gibson, and our new catcher, Trevor Mason."

"Please, everyone calls me Dizzy."

"Nice to meet you," said Trevor.

First Tobias and then Trevor shook my and Kent's hands. Each grip was firm and strong, the hands hard from many hours of labor. Tobias was a few inches shorter than me, but power-fully built. He had light blond hair that was closely cropped. His eyes were a greenish brown, and he was clean-shaven. He was wearing a sparkling clean white T-shirt, jeans, and leather work boots. The lump at his crotch was sizable. Trevor matched Tobias in height and musculature. His hair was light brown and slicked back. His cheeks and chin were covered in dark-brown stubble. He was wearing a navy-blue T-shirt that fit him like a second skin, blue jeans that were worn and tight, and a ratty pair of sneakers. His cock and nut sac were both clearly outlined beneath his pants, and both were impressive.

As we turned to board the bus, there must have been an expression of dismay about its condition on one of the other players' faces, because Mr. Hughes hurriedly explained that they would be buying a new bus a few weeks into the season. Until then, he assured us, this had gotten them all the way here from Florida and would most assuredly get them back. Mr. Hughes took the seat behind the wheel and started the engine, which sounded as if it were on its last legs. The interior of the bus was just as shabby, with many of the seats torn and ragged. Two seats behind the driver were missing, and the area was occupied by two suitcases with room for more. I was the first on; I stored my suitcases and took the last seat on the right. Kent sat to my left, while Dizzy s took the seat in front of me, and Trevor took the seat in front of Kent. Mr. Stanley sat down next to me as the bus pulled away from the hotel.

I stared out the window as familiar landmarks were replaced by ones I had never seen. I had lived in Miller Falls my entire life, and had never been very far from its outskirts. This was going to be a great adventure, and I was very excited at the prospect. However, I was quickly discovering that adventurers, young and old alike, often tire from physical exertion; I was still worn out from last night's activity as well as my tryst with Nelson this morning. Soon I was having trouble concentrating on what the people around me were saying, and suddenly my head snapped forward and woke me jarringly awake. Mr. Stanley placed his arm around my shoulders and leaned into me.

"Go ahead and get some sleep, Andrew," he whispered in my ear. "It's a day-and-a-half drive to our headquarters in Boca Raton. We'll drive as far as we can today till it gets dark, and then get a motel for the night."

"Okay, Mr. Stanley," I murmured, my head already lolling on my shoulder. I didn't hear the last bit of what he said as I drifted off to sleep. I thought at first it was the motion of the bus that awakened me, but as I opened my eyes and my surroundings came into focus I realized several things simultaneously: my pants and underwear were down around my ankles, and Mr. Stanley was stroking my rock-hard cock.

"Hello, sleepyhead."

"Hello, yourself."

I looked to see what the rest of the recruits were doing; most of them appeared to be asleep, including Kent. Mr. Stanley smiled at me, then reached over and unbuttoned my shirt and helped me out of it.

"Lift your arms."

I did so, and he took my T-shirt off over my head. He ran his hand through the thick black hair on my chest and stomach, then wet his index finger and stuck the tip deeply into my navel, causing me to lurch forward on the seat and laugh. Simultaneously, Mr. Stanley took my left nipple into his mouth and began sucking on it, quickly wringing small whimpers of delight from me. As he continued working the tender nub with his teeth and lips, I placed my hand on the back of his head to direct his efforts. After a bit he switched to the right and gave it the same treatment. The smell of his aftershave combined with his strong masculine scent and a touch of sweat filled my nostrils.

He suddenly eased off my nipple and, releasing my prick, undid his belt. He then fished one of the familiar tins of grease from his pants pocket before unbuttoning them and sliding them and his briefs down to his ankles. Mr. Stanley expertly popped the lid off the tin with one hand, scooped some out, and coated his cock with it. He leaned into me again and whispered in my ear, "Stand up." When I did he slid underneath me and spread my ass cheeks. I rested my elbows on the seatback in front of me; I saw Dizzy still asleep, his head resting against the window. I gasped when I felt Mr. Stanley's wet tongue in the crack of my ass. He proceeded to lick all along my crack, then circled the tender opening and probed gently. After several swipes with his tongue, he greased up my chute, stuck a fat finger inside me and wiggled it around several times. Mr. Stanley then withdrew the large digit, grabbed me at the waist, and slowly pulled me down toward his pole. The large knob slid between my ass cheeks and popped through my opening, and I sank down on his huge cock till the fat head poked the secret muscle buried deep inside me. Mr. Stanley moaned softly and hugged me tightly, then began planting kisses on my back.

I sat still for several seconds, letting my asshole adjust to this massive intruder, then rocked back and forth a few times. Mr. Stanley moved from my back to my ears and began nibbling on the lobes. He then began thrusting his hips, smacking the pleasure muscle again and again.

"Let me drive," I whispered.

I rose up slowly on Mr. Stanley's stiffer till only the large crown remained inside me, then sank back down. I quickly picked up the pace, rising and falling on his dick faster and faster, almost in a rocking rhythm; his moans grew in number and intensity. The noises from our coupling evidently awakened Kent and Dizzy, because suddenly they were both on their knees on Dizzy's seat facing us, their eyes alight with desire. Dizzy was shirtless; the top half of his torso was hairless and thickly muscled. His nipples were light brown. He rested his elbows on the top of the seat and watched as Kent leaned over the back of the seat and kissed me deeply, his tongue darting into my mouth and exploring it fully. After several more kisses he came around to our seat and squeezed in on his knees between our seat and the back of his. It was a tight fit. He began licking my dick, starting at the thick base and running his tongue up the shaft, over the fat head, and back down the other side, only to begin all over again. Clear fluid was seeping from the slit in the crown, and on his next pass Kent made sure he got every precious drop.

As I continued to ride, Mr. Stanley and Kent kept thirstily sucking my cock. Mr. Hughes suddenly pulled off the main road onto a dirt road, then immediately left this road and parked underneath a copse of maple trees. I watched as Mr. Hughes came from behind the steering wheel, walked up the center aisle, and slid into Dizzy's seat behind him. I heard Mr. Hughes undo his belt and—still fully clothed, from the waist up at least, which was all I could see—enter Dizzy from behind. Though I couldn't see the penetration, it was evident from the pleasurable expression on Dizzy's face and the soft whimpers escaping from his half-open mouth. The next sounds I heard were Mr. Hughes's thighs slapping against Dizzy's ass cheeks as he hammered him from behind.

I had forgotten about Trevor, but suddenly he was standing next to Kent completely naked, his cock swollen and bobbing invitingly. His arms and legs were heavily muscled and covered in thick, dark-brown hair. His chest and stomach were similarly covered. Puffy, pinkish nipples capped the swells of his well-muscled tits, and the flare at his hips was quite pronounced, along with the V above his crotch. While still riding Mr. Stanley, and with Kent still sucking my cock, I turned sideways, and took the head of Trevor's dick into my mouth. I sucked on it softly, swirling my tongue over the blood-engorged knob, then slowly engulfed his prick till my nose was buried in his crotch hair.

He placed his hands on the back of my head and began slowing pumping his stiffer into my mouth. On each lunge my nose was buried in his thatch of hair and I inhaled deeply of his male odor. Saliva was soon dribbling from the corners of my mouth, dampening his thatch. I sawed back up on his cock and let the large head plop from my mouth. I pressed his pole flat against his stomach and ran my tongue up and down the thick shaft, teasing the veins and pulling at a few errant hairs at the base.

While I went to town on Trevor's dick, Mr. Stanley was still plowing steadily into me, Kent was contentedly slobbering on my pole, and Dizzy's eyes were closed in pure ecstasy as Mr. Hughes continued to fill his backside with his substantial member. I could feel my explosion building, and when Mr. Stanley reached from behind me and began pulling on my tits, that sent me over the edge. Without releasing Trevor's cock and without warning, I began spewing my seed into Kent's mouth. He didn't miss a beat, swallowing the first drop and everything else I gave him. At the same time, I felt the first glob of Trevor's cum hit the back of my throat. I swallowed it eagerly, and it was followed quickly by a barrage of more spooge. As I struggled to take the entire load, Mr. Stanley bit down gently on my left earlobe and began filling me with his juice.

When Trevor was spent, I licked his prick a final time. Then he stepped into the next seat and began dressing. Kent got up from the floor of the bus, kissed me on the mouth, and slipped into the aisle and back to his seat. As I eased off Mr. Stanley's still-hard dick, Mr. Hughes began yowling behind Dizzy as if he were a cat in heat. He cried out long and loud, then slumped onto Dizzy's back, and began planting kisses there. Dizzy turned toward him as far as his position would allow, and received a sloppy kiss on the mouth, after which Mr. Hughes withdrew from the young shortstop, adjusted his clothing, and stepped into the aisle.

"Okay, fellas, the siesta's over," Mr. Hughes said, his smile expressing his true thoughts on the short repast. "The sooner we get back on the road, the sooner we hit Boca Raton. We'll drive till the late evening, then stop at a motel for the night."

He returned to his seat behind the wheel, started the bus, and pulled back onto the main road, and we resumed our journey as if nothing had happened. It was a few hours after sunset when we pulled into the parking lot of a very rundown motel. We parked in front of the office, so designated by the broken neon sign that actually read OFF, and Mr. Stanley went to see about rooms for the night. After several minutes he returned, announcing that the motel had only two vacant rooms, so we would need to share. He and Mr. Hughes would share one room, and the four recruits would share another. As we exited the bus, each of us grabbing what luggage we needed for an overnight stay, Mr. Stanley handed me the key.

"Mr. Hughes and I are in Room 1, right next to the office. The rest of you are in Room 12, at the end of the row. There's a little diner behind the motel. Let's meet there for dinner as soon as you guys have washed up."

When we reached Room 12, I unlocked and opened the door and searched for a light. I was not impressed with what it revealed. The room was very small, with dark paneled walls, two double beds, and a nightstand between. A small round table stood beneath the only window, flanked by two chairs. A door to my right led to a tiny bathroom crammed full to accommodate the sink, toilet, and shower stall.

We dropped our suitcases on the beds and left the room in search of the diner, which we found behind a small grocer's. The diner was tiny as well, with two customers at the counter and a waitress who looked as tired as I felt. After we slogged through a meal of greasy meatloaf, mashed potatoes, and peas, the waitress brought us our bill. Back at the motel, we bid Mr. Hughes and Mr. Stanley goodnight as they entered their room, and then we filed into ours.

"Okay, guys," Kent said, "who's heading out for the beer?"

"Are you sure this is a good idea with both managers so close?" Trevor piped up. "I'm sure they have strict rules around drinking."

Kent and I looked at each other and both burst out laughing. "I'll go get the beer," I chuckled. "I don't think it will be a problem this one time."

I ran to the grocer's, which was just shutting down for the evening, and bought a case of beer. As I returned to the room I noticed a man coming the other way, carrying two valises stuffed to the brim and wearing a fedora lopsided on his head; he stopped at Room 11. He seemed distressed and didn't notice my presence. He set the valises down, fished a key out of his pants pocket, and fumbled it into the lock.

"Evening, Sir."

He started when I spoke, then collected himself and turned to me. As he did so, his profile was highlighted by one of the motel parking lot lights. He was disheveled and in need of a bath and a shave, but quite handsome and older than I had at first thought. His shabby suit clung to his stocky frame. There was a gold band on his finger.

"Good evening to you as well, young man. What brings you to this motel on this fine evening?"

I heard the insincerity in his voice, and in the few seconds it took me to reply I didn't miss the fact that his gaze traveled the length of my body twice, each time pausing meaningfully at my crotch.

"I'm traveling with the Stallions, a baseball team from Florida. I just joined yesterday, and we are busing back to headquarters in Boca Raton. I'm sharing this room with three other recruits, and our managers are down in the room by the office." My look and tone became a bit more suggestive. "I just bought some beer if you'd like to join us for one. Or two."

"That would be real nice. It's been a very long day." He held out his hand. "My name is Henry. Henry Jones." His handshake was firm.

"I'm Andrew Duggan."

"Hold on while I put these valises in my room."

After Henry had deposited them inside his room, he followed me into mine. Kent was sitting on one of the beds, reading one of the latest pulp magazines. I could hear water running in the bathroom.

"Kent, this is Henry. He has the room next to ours and I invited him over for a beer."

Kent rose from the bed and clasped hands with the man.

"It's nice to meet you, Henry."

I opened three beers with my jackknife and handed one to each of them. I took a long pull from mine as Henry and I sat down at the table and Kent resumed his position on the bed. The three of us quickly struck up a conversation. Henry was a farmer from Idaho who had fallen on hard times when his land went bust. He had moved his wife and children in with his in-laws and hit the road as a Bible salesman. While not religious himself, he knew a few people who had been able to make a living at it. The valises he had left in his room were stuffed with Bibles. As he finished speaking, Dizzy emerged from the bath-room naked and drying himself with a towel. Trevor emerged a moment later in the same state. It was obvious they had been in the shower together.

As I introduced them to Henry, he could not take his eyes off Dizzy. Noticing this, Dizzy stepped forward to shake hands with him, moving close enough that Henry could have grabbed his dick if he wanted to. As Henry shook hands, he never once took his eyes from Dizzy's fat prick.

"Would you like to put it in your mouth?" Dizzy asked softly, dropping the towel.

Henry seemed to be momentarily paralyzed by the question, but the yearning in his eyes was hard to miss. As we waited expectantly, he found his voice.

"I have never done this before," he stammered as he reached up and grabbed Dizzy's cock.

He squeezed and pulled the fat member and watched wide-eyed as it grew in his hand. When it was fully hard Henry began stroking it softly, then cupped the young shortstop's heavy ball sac before taking the fat knob into his mouth and sinking halfway down the thick shaft. He held it in his mouth for several seconds, then slowly released it. He gazed up at Dizzy, appearing awestruck with what he had just done.

"Your cock smells incredible. And it tastes like nothing I've ever known before."

Without further ado he swallowed Dizzy's stiffer once more, almost getting to the root before choking slightly. He placed his hands on the young man's thighs, paused a moment, then engulfed the rest. He began sliding up and down on the huge prick, sucking noisily and making a humming noise like he was enjoying a fine meal.

If it really was Henry's first time handling a cock, he was a fast learner. Dizzy placed his hand on the older man's shoulders and began pumping his hips slowly. The rest of us sat mesmerized by the sight of the novice cocksucker servicing Dizzy, whose eyes were closed and head thrown back; he was moaning through his slightly open mouth. With his free hand he was pinching and twisting his own nipples. Sweat glistened on his chest and stomach. His groans increased, as did the pumping of his hips, plunging his prick in and out of Henry's mouth.

"I'm coming," Dizzy suddenly cried.

Though he claimed this was his first time, as a man Henry should have known what was about to happen. Dizzy's spooge came at him so fast and heavy he had no alternative but to swallow it, and as fast as he could. His eyes were open wide, either in delight or surprise. When Dizzy was spent he wiped the head of his cock across Henry's lips then stepped back from the seated man. Henry looked up at Dizzy with an almost worshipful expression on his face.

"I didn't realize so much could come out of one of these." He licked his lips, then took a pull from his beer. When he set it down, he wiped his sleeve across his mouth. "I'd like to suck all your dicks, if that's OK."

A chorus of eager "yeses" sounded in the room, and Trevor asked to be next.

"Let's do it on the bed, Henry. It's more fun when you can lick the guy's balls."

The Bible salesman fairly leapt out of the chair, and as Trevor lay naked on his back on the nearest bed, Henry crawled eagerly between his legs. Dizzy took the chair Henry had just vacated, and the three of us watched him go to town on Trevor's tool. As the hours ticked away, we drank beer and watched Henry suck cock as if today was judgment day. And he put on quite a show, sucking, licking, bobbing, and slurping. He couldn't seem to get enough, stopping only once to go to the bathroom. I swear he had guzzled enough jism to fill one of the beer bottles.

After dumping my third load down the older man's throat, I went to the bathroom to piss. When I returned Henry was on his hands and knees on the bed, naked, wiggling his ample hairy ass toward Trevor, who was kneeling behind him. Trevor was licking Henry's shit hole for all he was worth, and Henry was making all kinds of animalistic noises. Trevor suddenly withdrew his tongue and grabbed a tin of grease that was lying on the bedspread. He popped the lid, slathered his pole, then slid two fingers inside Henry, working them in and out quickly. The salesman squealed like a stuck pig as the fingers worked his hole. When he was all slicked up, Trevor placed the head of his cock against Henry's hole and pushed insistently. When it popped through Henry screamed, "For the love of God!" loud enough that I was sure the motel manager would come running to investigate. He continued to moan, writhe, and quote what sounded like scripture as he took Trevor's full length.

Trevor held his dick deep inside Henry, making him feel its full girth, then withdrew quickly and began skewering Henry's ass. At this point the salesman lost all control; he began meeting each thrust of Trevor's with a backward one of his own, all the while continuing to make enough noise to wake the dead, including imploring Trevor to "pound his corn chute." Fearful that the exclamations would wake someone, Kent stuffed a dirty sweat sock in the man's mouth.

Thus began the next round of Henry's sex schooling. We finished off the beer as we took turns drilling his ass. And as with his cock-sucking initiation, Henry could not get enough dick inside him. The small of his back and his ass cheeks were covered in spunk. After my second turn the beer finally overcame me, and I lay down on the unoccupied bed. As I drifted off to sleep I saw Dizzy mounting Henry for a third time. The next sound I heard was a thunderous pounding on the motel door, followed by a stentorian voice.

"It's the Oak Grove sheriff. Open this door now or I'll break it down!"

CHAPTER FIVE

Kent was sleeping in the bed next to me but woke quickly at the pounding. I could hear the water running in the shower and see Trevor and Dizzy in the bed next to us. They were struggling to rise and make sense of the incessant noise. We had all fallen asleep with the lights on.

I jumped out of bed. "Everyone get dressed, quickly. I'll go see what the sheriff wants."

When I was fully clothed I went to the door, undid the chain, and opened it. An enormous man was standing in the doorway, completely blocking the view to the outside. I could safely say he was the largest man I had ever seen. He looked as if he was going to bust out of his tan uniform at any moment. A large gold star was pinned to the right pocket flap of his shirt. His arms and legs were twice the size of mine, the former covered in thick brown fur. Despite the undisguised anger on his face, I could not help but stare at the large mound at his crotch. When he spoke his voice was deep, sending chills racing up and down my back.

"I'm Sheriff Johnston." His eyes scanned the room. "I'm looking for a man named Henry Jones. His wife called my office this morning and reported him missing. He checked into this motel last night and was supposed to call her, but she has not heard from him. Have you seen him?"

The sheriff had not missed my staring at his crotch, and he stepped closer to me as if to give me a better look. As he did so his scent assailed me—a mixture of sweat, cologne, and pure man—and I placed a hand on the door frame to steady myself. The sexual energy emanating from him was palpable. I finally found my voice.

"Pleased to meet you, Sheriff Johnston. I'm Andrew Duggan and these are Kent Myers, Trevor Mason, and Tobias Gibson. We're members of the Florida Stallions baseball team."

He looked me up and down as if measuring the truth of my words. "Do you know a Henry Jones?"

Before I could answer him, Henry emerged from the bathroom, naked and drying his hair, the towel blocking his sight.

"Guys, I can suck each of you off once more before I have to leave. Who wants to go first?"

Before any of us had a chance to warn the horny Bible salesman, the sheriff spoke up.

"I'll go first."

Henry lowered his towel and saw the sheriff. A look of puzzlement appeared on his face.

"Are you by any chance Henry Jones?"

"Yes."

"Your wife's real worried about you. When you didn't call her last night, she managed to track down my number."

"Sorry, Sheriff. I was invited here last night for a few beers and I guess I lost track of time."

The sheriff laughed.

"I can see how that could happen, Mr. Jones. You should give her a call to let her know you're OK. Right after you suck my dick, that is."

The mountain of a man closed the door behind him, took off his holster, and laid it on the table. Leaving his hat on, he undid his belt, unbuttoned his pants, and slid them, along with his briefs, down to his knees. What the five of us saw seemed simply unbelievable. Even soft, his thick dick hung halfway to his knees.

Henry was awestruck. The sheriff taunted him. "It ain't quite long enough to suck from there, Mr. Jones. And I don't have all day."

Henry swallowed visibly, went to the giant, and knelt before him. He grabbed the monster cock and pulled it gently to him. It was as thick as his wrist, and I wondered fleetingly if, when it filled with blood, the sheriff would feel lightheaded. I soon had my answer as the piece of flesh assumed proportions to match the rest of the man. I had only seen a cock this size once before, and it had not been on a human. Undaunted, Henry took the large knob, which was the size of a small apple, into his mouth. He sucked it energetically, then swallowed as much of the thick shaft as he could. When he reached the halfway point it was clear that he had reached his limit; his jaws looked as if they were going to snap and his eyes were beginning to protrude from their sockets. Without a word of complaint, the salesman wrapped both his hands around the portion of the sheriff's stiffer he couldn't fit into his mouth and stroked it furiously as he bobbed on the huge piece of flesh. The sheriff slowly unbuttoned his shirt and took it off, followed by his T-shirt. He revealed a barrel chest and a thick stomach, both covered in the same fur as his arms. His beefy tits were capped by thick, dark-brown nipples the size of half-dollars.

Without waiting for an invitation, I went to his right side and took that teat into my mouth. I worked it with my teeth and tongue, bringing it to a hardened state. At the same time, Trevor moved to the sheriff's left side and began working that nipple. The hirsute man moaned his appreciation, then raised his arms above his head. At once Trevor and I each turned and stuck our faces in the armpit offered to us. The hair in mine was thick and tufted, resembling a tiny forest creature. I ran my tongue through the brown clump; it was damp, and smelled and tasted of sweat and a deodorant similar to the cologne that had overwhelmed me earlier. These odors spurred on my efforts, and I began bathing his huge underarm with my tongue. Trevor did the same with his pit, while the giant between us whistled softly through his lips. When I had further dampened the hairy pit, I moved back to the swollen nipple facing me; Trevor did the same, almost in synchronization. The sheriff lowered his arms and placed his hands on Henry's shoulders. He began pumping his hips faster, his enormous bag of balls slapping against Henry's chin.

"Let me blow on your face," the sheriff said huskily.

Henry didn't need to be asked twice, and immediately released the man's cock. The sheriff grabbed his stiffer and gave it a few quick strokes. He literally roared as the first large gob of his fluid erupted, hitting Henry's right cheek. More and more of the thick white stuff shot forth, coating the Bible salesman's face. The last one hit him right on the tip of the nose and hung off it. When the hairy giant was done shooting, he wiped his mess from Henry's face and fed it to the kneeling man, who ate every drop. When Henry was done, he stood up and began dressing; the sheriff did so as well.

"Thanks, gentlemen. And Mr. Jones, don't forget about your wife."

He tipped his hat to us and left the room, quietly closing the door behind him. Henry stood by the table, a pleased expression on his tired face.

"Thanks again, guys, for the best night of my life. I will never forget any of you. And good luck with the team this season."

He hugged each of us goodbye, then left our room without looking back.

"Okay, guys, let's go meet Mr. Stanley and Mr. Hughes before they show up here and we have to start explaining."

When we got outside I wasn't in the least surprised to find Henry in the parking lot talking to the sheriff. They both waved to us as we headed down the sidewalk.

Once we had collected Mr. Hughes and Mr. Stanley, our tired group assembled at the motel diner for breakfast. We all ate heartily of the less-than-desirable food, famished from our night of breaking Henry in. When we had finished eating, we gathered our luggage and boarded the bus once more. As we pulled out of the parking lot Mr. Stanley announced that we should make it to the Stallions' headquarters toward late afternoon. This was greeted with a loud cheer from the recruits.

The trip proved to be uneventful for the remainder of the morning. Everyone kept pretty much to themselves, napping, reading, or staring out the window absorbed in their own thoughts. We stopped at a gas station a little past noon to fuel up. Mr. Stanley bought us each a sandwich and a cold drink from the station grocer's, and we ate them as we hit the road once more. As I watched the endless miles of open field rush past us, my thoughts swirled around my parents, Nelson, and unbidden, Parker. I had to face the fact that Parker was going to be in my future, at least for a year. There was simply no way I could avoid him. And because we were both pitchers, the ties that bound us would be that much tighter. I forced this train of thought from my mind, shut my eyes, and willed myself to sleep.

"Boca Raton, next stop!"

Mr. Stanley's announcement brought me quickly out of my sleep. Excitement swept through the bus. In less than ten minutes I spotted a large white sign that welcomed us to Boca Raton. I gave a huge cheer that was echoed by the rest of the recruits. As we drove through town I drank in the local sights. It was much bigger than Miller Falls, of course, and had an air of prosperity that Miller Falls lacked.

The town was neatly laid out in a square, and lined on each side by brick buildings of various sizes, shapes, heights, and hues. The inside of the square was one long, rolling park, at the center of which was an enormous statue of a military figure on horseback. Several small ponds flanked the statue, along with numerous benches, many of them filled with happy-looking locals. As we neared the end of town, I saw amid bushes a large flag raised next to a howitzer: a monument to the recently ended war.

After leaving town, we stayed on the main road for a short distance before turning right onto a dusty side road. After we had traveled a few miles, in the distance emerged a large rectangular building set back several hundred feet from the road. As we drew closer, a baseball field came into view as well, in addition to a large, three-story house. We turned in the driveway. The bus stopped in front of the house, and Mr. Stanley proclaimed that we were home. The recruits emerged from the bus chattering like magpies, trying to take in everything at once. We waited anxiously while Mr. Hughes drove the bus around back to park it in a large red barn.

The house's exterior had just seen a fresh coat of paint. A flagstone path led up to a large front porch that ran the length of the house and wrapped around both sides. Several cushioned chairs dotted the porch, along with a small octagonal table. Upon closer inspection one could see, though, that the house was in need of some repair. Several of the clapboards were spilt and needed replacing, there were cracks in what we could see of the foundation, and the porch stairs looked like they'd collapse if any serious weight were put on them. However, it was apparent that in its day this had been a stately farmhouse. To its right stood the barn, which Mr. Hughes was returning from, with an enclosure next to it that appeared empty. Numerous outbuildings were situated behind it, most of them surely housing farm machinery.

"We'll take a quick tour of the grounds before heading to the main offices."

With that, Mr. Stanley and Mr. Hughes led us off to explore our new surroundings. Behind the boarding house stood an outdoor shower made of four wooden walls at least 6 feet high. An opening the size of a closet door granted access. There were six showerheads, three each on the walls parallel to the house, and each had its own pump for water. The shower floor was the grass of the back lawn.

Leaving the showers, we passed a shaded, wooded, park-like area abutting a good-sized pond. At the edge of the pond were two ancient elm trees, each with a tire swing hanging from one of its many branches. A dock extended into the pond, and in the pond's center was a wooden platform. We looped around the pond and headed behind the office to the baseball field. The rest of the team was practicing, but I didn't see any coach or similar figurehead, so it was clearly more of a casual workout. The field was freshly mown, although the grass was a sickly brown, almost the color of late-summer grass. The foul lines were in need of fresh paint, and the home-run fence was dilapidated. Wooden bleachers flanked both sides of the backstop. In the distance we saw a man pushing a large lawnmower.

"That's it for the grounds," Mr. Stanley shouted to be heard above the sound of the approaching mower. As the machine drew closer, Mr. Stanley waved the man over. When he was only a few feet from us the man turned the mower off and walked over to meet us. He was middle-aged and stood several inches above 6 feet. He was wearing a baseball cap with a rearing black stallion emblazoned on it. The hair protruding from the cap was light brown speckled with gray. He was unshaven, and his full beard and mustache were also filled with gray. Thick, caterpillar-like eyebrows rested over piercing light-blue eyes.

His dirty gray T-shirt was ripped at the collar, revealing a patch of suntanned skin covered in thick brown hair. The shirt also accentuated his muscular chest and hugged his slight paunch. His arms were large and powerful, and covered in the same brown fleece that continued onto the backs of his hands and from there to his knuckles. He was wearing thin, light-gray workout pants that had the appearance of a second skin. The swell of his crotch was enormous, and seemed to barely be contained by his pants; the head of his cock was clearly outlined.

His outfit was completed by a pair of ratty sneakers that were stained green from the grass he was cutting.

"Fellas, this is Jordan Connors, our coach, but we simply call him Coach."

The older man stepped forward and shook hands with each of us. When it was my turn I could feel his overwhelming manly strength. He eyed me steadily before releasing my hand.

"Greetings to each of you, and welcome to the headquarters of the Florida Stallions. I look forward to seeing each of you bright and early tomorrow morning for our first practice."

When he finished speaking he returned to the lawnmower, started it once more, and resumed his methodical mowing.

"The last piece to see is the locker room and the offices," Mr. Stanley said, excitement evident in his voice.

Seen up close, the large building was also in need of repair. Some of the metal sheets were pulling away from the sides, and much of the metal was rusted. We faced a double set of large metal doors, one of which Mr. Hughes had trouble opening. As we filed inside behind the managers, we found ourselves in a short corridor formed of cement walls. The corridor took a right turn after 50 feet, then a quick left turn, and we entered a large rectangular room lined with metal lockers.

As our eyes adjusted from the brightness of the sun outside, I was immediately overwhelmed by the combined smells of piss, sweat, spunk, and the overriding scent of male. We walked past the lockers and continued down the hall, passing a shelf to our right that held folded towels. On our left, three sets of double windows, four feet apart, showed a vast, green lawn. Where the windows stopped, the offices began, identified by lettering on their glass doors as Mr. Stanley's, Mr. Hughes's, and Coach's. The showers were located across from them, with at least a dozen showerheads. At the end of the hallway was a second set of double doors that Mr. Stanley explained granted access to the ball field. To the right of the doors was an examining room (Coach doubled as a doctor, Mr. Stanley explained) and an exercise room. Next to that was a small laundry room.

As we turned to backtrack our route, Mr. Hughes excused himself to go speak to the team. Mr. Stanley said he would take us to the main house and get us settled in. We followed him single file back to the house and up the front steps. When he opened the outer screen door he discovered that the main door to the house was locked. His frustration was evident as he knocked loudly on the door and we waited for a response. When nothing happened after a few minutes, he knocked a second time, even more loudly than before. Suddenly the door opened and an old woman stood staring at us through a large pair of spectacles.

"May I help you?" she asked in a dry, leathery voice that sounded as if it hadn't been used in years.

"It's me, Mrs. Jenkins, Mr. Stanley, general manager of the Stallions. We're back from our recruiting trip and have brought home five new hopefuls for you to watch over."

Recognition dawned in the old woman's eyes. "Why, indeed it is Mr. Stanley. My apologies, young man, these old eyes aren't what they used to be. Please, come right in."

The interior of the house was cool, dim, and immaculate. To our right I could see a large kitchen, with a gleaming white tile floor, shiny countertops, and a wooden table that looked as if it would seat a small army. To our immediate left was an enormous living room, with a radio the size of a Model T, and well-worn, oversized, comfortable-looking furniture. The walls were formed of dark wood, most likely walnut, and the floor was of the same wood, only in a lighter shade. A hallway ran parallel to the living room, which we later learned led directly to Mrs. Jenkins's personal quarters. In front of us loomed a wide, dark staircase that ascended to the right, its end out of sight. The scent of furniture polish hung thick and heavy in the air.

"Gentlemen, this is Mrs. Jenkins. Mrs. Jenkins, please welcome Andrew Duggan, Kent Myers, Trevor Mason, and Tobias Gibson. Parker Williams will be here later today."

She acknowledged each of us with a slight nod of her head.

"Boys, I'm going to leave you in her capable hands while I go tend to business. Once you are unpacked, please meet me down at the locker room so I can introduce you to the rest of the team."

He planted a kiss on the old woman's cheek and left the house. She eyed us up and down as if she had an aversion to men our age and would rather be rid of us altogether than welcome us into her home.

"Your rooms are on the third floor, boys. The veteran team members are occupying the second floor. Please follow me."

The old woman started up the stairs at a pace that seemed destined to get us there by nightfall. We dutifully fell in line behind her and did our best to hide our laughter as her knees creaked and cracked as much as the stairs did. At the second-floor landing she paused to show us a bathroom. It held a small sink, a claw-foot tub, and a toilet. She explained that we were welcome to use the outside showers if we didn't want to wait our turn with the tub.

"Those showers get cold water only, but many of the boys use them to cool off after practice or a game. You are also free to use the showers in the locker room, of course. Questions?"

When no one had any questions, we began the climb to the third floor, which mirrored the second. Mrs. Jenkins assigned Dizzy the first room we came to, which she noted was also occupied by a current player. She paired Kent and I off in the next room and then explained that the last would be Trevor's to share with Parker Williams. Parker. I had not thought of him in a while. That was good. But he would be arriving today and living in the room next door to me. I reminded myself not to dwell on that, but rather focus on becoming an integral part of the Stallions.

"Now, boys," Mrs. Jenkins began, "breakfast is at 7 a.m. sharp, every day, no exceptions. Lunch will be brought to the playing field at noon, and dinner is promptly at 6. If you are late for breakfast or dinner, you will not eat. Lights out is at 9 p.m., with no exceptions. Anyone breaking this curfew will have to make other rooming arrangements. Again, any questions?"

The old woman proved she could be very intimidating, for no one had the nerve to ask her anything.

"Good. I will see you at dinner this evening."

As she made her way back down the stairs, Kent and I went into our room. It was furnished with two single beds, two dressers with three drawers each, a small table and chair that stood in front of the window, and a smaller table between the beds with a small lamp on it. Kent and I quickly unpacked our few possessions, gathered the rest of the recruits, and headed back down to the offices. As we reached the front porch, I spotted a familiar truck coming down the dirt road toward the house. It was Parker. He stopped in front of the house and climbed out of the truck. Of course, he spotted me immediately. To my dismay, the group halted at the bottom of the steps and waited while Parker grabbed his bags from the back of the truck. When he had, he shared a warm general greeting.

"Hello. I'm Parker Williams."

Trevor took the lead, stepping forward to introduce everyone. Parker shook hands with all of us, and even though he made no outward sign of familiarity when he reached me, his eyes held a hint of anger, remorse, and something else not readily definable. For now I was determined keep our relationship to ourselves. Trevor went on to explain that we had taken a tour of the grounds, had been assigned rooms in the house, had unpacked, and were now heading back to the locker room to meet the rest of the team. He offered to show Parker his room and asked the rest of us to wait for them. Upon their return, we headed back down to the locker room.

Once inside, we found Mr. Stanley in his office. As he rose from his chair to greet Parker, the doors that led to the field flew open and the rest of the team came pouring in. They were laughing, jostling, and full of youthful exuberance, their cleats clacking on the tile floor as they headed for their lockers. Mr. Hughes was trailing them. We followed behind Mr. Stanley, who quieted the milling men to make introductions.

"Boys, I'd like you to meet the rest of the team. This is Joshua Steinberg, our third baseman and the most senior member of the team; Ethan Murdock, our second baseman; Nicholas Morton, left field; Mark Hoffman, center field; and Heath Durham, right field. Boys, these are our new recruits: Parker Williams, left-handed pitcher; Andrew Duggan, right-handed pitcher; Trevor Mason, catcher; Kent Myers, first baseman; and Tobias "Dizzy" Gibson, shortstop. Please welcome them to Florida and the team."

As each of them shook hands with and warmly welcomed us, I quickly but thoroughly checked them out. They were a mixed lot of heights, builds, hair colors, and ages. Once introductions had been made, the men began undressing in front of us unselfconsciously. Mr. Stanley was going over the training and game schedule with us new team members, but I quickly lost track of his words as sweaty jerseys were pulled over strong backs and taut, sculpted stomachs. I saw chests covered in fur of all colors: black, dark brown, and light brown, as well as chests as bare as a baby's bottom, with big dark brown or pinkish nipples. I saw hairy, well-muscled arms. Pants were shrugged down hairy, massive thighs, revealing a bevy of tantalizing jockstraps that were sweat-stained and stuffed full to almost bursting. As the jockstraps were tugged free, cocks of all shapes and sizes flopped out, dangling over ball sacs of all dimensions. I saw hairy asses and hairless asses.

The naked players all streamed past in a line toward the showers, towels slung over shoulders or held in ham-like hands. I couldn't hear a word Mr. Stanley was saying; to my ears there was only the sound of water striking tile, and then a cloud of stream slowly wafting from the showers, engulfing the room and bringing with it an intoxicating scent. After several minutes the men began filing back from the showers, many of them sporting half erections and one full erection that made my mouth water. I watched as armpits, chests, arms, and legs were vigorously dried, followed by damp hairy crotches.

As the men quickly dressed and left, Mr. Stanley finally wrapped up his sermon.

"That's it for today, recruits. Mr. Hughes and I are leaving for the day, but we'll be back tomorrow bright and early to start training. Have a good evening. And be kind to Mrs. Jenkins. Oh, and before we go, we have one last person for you to meet."

He went down the hall to Coach's office, returning in a few moments with a young man trailing him. He was very handsome, and he bore a slight resemblance to Coach.

"This is Michael Christiansen. He has been the official gopher and bat boy of the team since he turned eighteen in February. He is also responsible for greeting the new recruits and maintaining team morale. He is also Coach's nephew. We leave you in his capable hands."

With that he and Mr. Hughes left. The young man stepped forward and shook each of our hands.

"Pleased to meet you all, and welcome to the Stallions. As Mr. Stanley commented, one of my duties is to maintain team morale. I've found that the best way I can do this is by sucking cock. I love to suck it, I'm damn good at it, and I can't get enough. I'm available any time of day. During practice and games I can be found in the dugout. Or if need be, I can take care of you in here. Now, who wants to go first?"

I immediately raised my hand.

"Andrew, is it? Okay. The rest of you are welcome to watch or wait in one of the offices. It's your choice, but I've found most prefer to stay."

When he finished speaking, Michael stepped to me and undid my belt buckle and then the buttons on my pants. He pushed my pants and my drawers down to my ankles and knelt on the tile at my feet. My stiffer was staring him in the face, growing quickly. He trailed his tongue up and down the thick shaft, then took the large crown into his mouth. It was wet and warm, and he sucked gently on my knob before sinking down my shaft till he had engulfed my tool completely. He sawed back up to the head and wrapped his right hand around the shaft close to the root. With his left hand he cupped my ball sac, and began kneading it while he bobbed on the top half of my dick and jerked the bottom half.

The rest of the recruits watched with avid interest, and I could see large swells at all crotches. Michael was as good as he had said, and I soon picked up his rhythm and began pumping my hips to match his hand and mouth. All too quickly I felt the overwhelming buildup and then I was over the edge, emptying my load deep down his throat. He swallowed every fat drop before slowly releasing my cock. He licked it clean, then smiled up at me.

"Welcome to the team. Who's next?"

I stepped aside and Parker immediately took my place. His hands were at his sides as Michael followed the same routine. When Parker's cock sprang free I couldn't tear my eyes from it, so long and fat, with such a nicely shaped head. And it looked even bigger than when we were together. A rush of images flashed through my mind of that monster prick plunging into my mouth or ass, or spewing its juice onto my face or down my gullet.

I heard a soft moan and tore my eyes away from Parker's dick, only to find Parker staring intently at me. Seeing that he had my attention, he pulled his shirt up a bit to reveal his muscular, hairy stomach. He then took his T-shirt completely off, displaying the abundance of red hair on his chest as well. I couldn't count the number of times I had run my hands through that hair and shot my jism onto it, only to immediately lick it off. Parker reached up and began tweaking both his nipples. I felt my breathing increase and the room get several degrees hotter. Before long Parker was moaning loudly and thrusting his hips faster. His chest glistened with sweat, and several rivulets ran down his chest and stomach and into his crotch hair.

"I'm gonna coat your tonsils, bat boy."

Michael never missed a beat as Parker emptied into him. Having been on the receiving end of that flood more times than I could count, I knew Michael had his work cut out for him. When Parker was spent he pulled up his pants and drawers, put his T-shirt back on, and, to my surprise, stood next to me, so close he was almost touching me. As we watched Michael service the rest of the recruits, our hands touched and a wave of sensation swept up my arm and down through my torso. I fought the overwhelming urge to take Parker into my arms. Seemingly against my will, I turned to him, only to find him staring directly at me. The lust in his eyes was so strong I raised my arms to him. He stepped closer to me and kissed me full on the lips. Sparks went off inside me. His tongue was inside my mouth and he was sucking on my tongue. He placed his hand on my crotch and squeezed my cock several times. I suddenly pushed his hand away.

"Please don't, Parker. I'm not ready for this."

"Sure, Andrew. Sorry, I didn't mean to push you. But since that night I saw you in the grange hall I've thought of you constantly. I can wait, if that's what it takes."

We watched Michael in silence. When Dizzy had dumped his seed, Michael rose from his knees.

"Again, welcome to the Florida Stallions. I hope you enjoyed our little session, and don't forget there's plenty more where that came from. Now, we need to get to dinner or we won't eat tonight."

I looked at the clock on the wall and was surprised to see it was ten minutes till 6. We left the locker room and raced to the house. When we entered we found Mrs. Jenkins and a young girl placing dishes on a sideboard in the kitchen. Whether by design or accident, Parker somehow managed to seat himself directly across from me. I was all thumbs as I passed dishes to my right or left, once almost dropping a large bowl of mashed potatoes. He was handsome and charming as ever, and his strong personality quickly delighted the rest of the team.

After dinner Joshua suggested a quick dip in the pond before lights out. Remembering the cold swim Nelson and I had taken back home just days ago, I passed, but most of the team eagerly followed Joshua out the front door, Parker included. I went back to my room, read several pages of one of the latest pulp magazines I had brought, and wrote a quick letter to Nelson. I filled him in on my trip to Boca Raton, my overall impressions of the Stallions' headquarters, and my encounter with Parker. I sealed the letter in an envelope provided by my mother, evoking enough guilt to bring me to write a letter to my parents as well. When both letters were done I set them on the small table; I would walk into town tomorrow morning before practice and mail them.

I was just getting ready for bed when Kent sneaked into the room. It was well past lights out. I could detect the scent of sex on him, and I also immediately recognized the cologne that Parker wore. I groaned inwardly. Kent lay on the bed and stared up at the ceiling, not saying a word. A sudden premonition hit me.

"You're taking a risk coming in after lights out on your first night, Kent. Did you have a good evening?"

He turned to look at me, a large, knowing smile spreading slowly across his face.

"I sure did. The quick dip in the pond quickly turned into a skinny dip and free for all. I was kissing that new pitcher, Parker, when he suggested we go back to his room. He sure knows how to use that big dick of his. So, I was actually in the house well before lights out. You know, he looks familiar for some reason."

I tensed. Although Kent had been a teammate on the Devils, I had kept my relationship with Parker a secret from everyone except Nelson. Surely my secret was safe and Kent just recognized Parker from when he faced his pitching in our games against the Talons. I kept my mouth shut and quickly crawled beneath the covers as Kent got ready for bed. After I turned the lamp out I lay awake a long time, thinking and remembering.

I had not thought about Parker in a sexual way for over a year. But seeing him in action today and being next to him after he had had sex with Michael had set my mind reeling. How did I feel about him? I remembered his anger and jealousy of Nelson—and any other man, for that matter. But he seemed fine this afternoon. Was it because we were no longer together? Was there a chance of us getting back together? And why was I thinking these thoughts now? Was it because we were thrust together again, or because I missed home and Nelson? And now I had to be prepared for Parker to be bedding the rest of the team. Of course, as horny as he always was, I guess I should have expected it. I was overcome with the feeling that the months ahead were going to be difficult, not only physically but emotionally as well.

At breakfast the next morning I found myself again seated near Parker. He was nothing but courteous as he passed me a dish or asked if I wanted seconds. It reminded me of how solicitous he had been when we first met. When I had finished eating I walked to the post office as planned, bought stamps, mailed my letters, and then headed back to the playing field for practice. The smell of freshly mown grass hung heavy in the air, as did dust from the infield, whipped up by a rather strong breeze. I heard the sound of an automobile and turned to find a beat-up pickup heading toward the field. As it drew closer, I saw that it was Coach. He brought the truck to a stop, climbed out, and came over to me.

"Good morning, Andrew. Since you're the first one to arrive, can you give me a hand getting the equipment out of the locker room?"

"Sure, Coach."

By the time we had carried bags of bats, balls, and gloves to the field, the rest of the team had arrived.

"Good morning, gentlemen. For those of you who are new, you can find old practice uniforms in the locker room. The old-timers can show you where they are. We save our good uniforms for real games."

After everyone had suited up, we spent the morning batting, fielding, running the bases, and doing endless calisthenics. I was hot, dirty, and tired as hell, but thrilled to be here. Precisely at noon, Mr. Hughes and Mr. Stanley arrived with lunch from Mrs. Jenkins, which consisted of thick ham sandwiches, home-made pickles, deviled eggs, homemade brownies, and cold soda. We ate every scrap, then dove into the afternoon's training. Both managers took a seat on the bench, and we started with more exercises. Then Parker and I took turns pitching for what seemed like hours. When Coach finally called it quits for the day, it was late afternoon.

"Good workout, men. Now hit the showers, and we'll see you back here bright and early tomorrow."

We filed into the locker room and quickly stripped out of our sweaty, dirty uniforms. I had just turned to head to the showers when Joshua stood on the bench in front of his locker and clapped his hands for attention.

"Before we head to the showers, there is a certain ceremony we must perform for the new recruits that always takes place after our first practice. It is intended to both officially welcome you as new members and solidify your allegiance to the team. Your ability to make it through this initiation by following the next series of orders will ensure your place on the roster for the rest of the season. Anyone who does not make it through will be summarily dismissed and sent home. Do I make myself clear? Are there any questions?"

He paused to let his words sink in. My own mind was racing as I tried to imagine what the orders and the test would be. And how could he have the authority to fire us from the team? No one said a word, and the room seemed heavy with anticipation.

"Okay, then, if there are no questions, new recruits please line up single file and naked in front of the lockers, facing me. The initiation has officially begun!"

CHAPTER SIX

We quickly did as he ordered. He walked down the line of new players, making eye contact with each of us but not saying a word. When he reached the end, he turned and came back down the line. All the while I couldn't take my eyes off his hairy chest or his fat cock that flopped from side to side as he walked. He was a nice specimen of manhood.

"Now," he shouted, startling everyone, "have a seat on the bench behind you and place your hands behind your backs."

We sat down immediately; I was fifth in line. Parker was to my left. Of course. Dizzy was first. Satisfied that we were following directions, Joshua, followed closely by Nicholas, went to Dizzy. While Joshua pulled Dizzy forward by the shoulders, Nicholas reached behind him and swiftly tied his hands together with a jockstrap. The two men then worked their way down the line till all of us were similarly trussed. And judging by the smells wafting from the jockstrap that bound me, they were not using fresh ones. The rest of the team then formed a line to the left of Dizzy. Joshua stepped in front of the shortstop, his cock sticking straight out in front of him. It was not overly long, but it was quite big in circumference. Dizzy dutifully opened his mouth to accept the massive member when, to all our surprise, Joshua turned around and stuck his hairy ass in Dizzy's face. He spread his cheeks and stepped back till his ass was literally touching the man's face.

Dizzy did not hesitate before licking Joshua's hairy ass cheeks with his tongue. After another drawn-out swipe, Dizzy's tongue disappeared into the crack. Joshua moaned loudly as Dizzy's tongue found his most secret spot, then he reached behind him, placed a hand on Dizzy's head, and held it firmly in place. The young man needed no further urging, and he went to work on Joshua's hole.

"Lick it, rookie," Joshua whispered.

"Time!"

I hadn't noticed that Ethan, the second baseman, was keeping time on a stop watch. Joshua pulled away from Dizzy, swung around, bent down, and kissed him deeply on the lips, then moved to Trevor, the catcher. Once again he turned around and bent over, offering his sweet hairy ass to Trevor, who was very willing to satisfy the older player's needs. At the same time, Ethan handed the stopwatch to Nicholas and took up position in front of Dizzy. The whole movement was well choreographed, and it was quite clear that this initiation had been performed numerous times in the past. Time was called again, and Joshua moved down the line. As I watched the action headed my way, I could see that each of the recruits was sporting an enormous erection, myself included. My early juice was flowing in my piss slit. But with my hands tied by the jockstrap, I couldn't give myself any relief.

Suddenly, Joshua was standing in front of me, his dick hard and throbbing, only inches from my mouth. I desperately wanted to take the thick piece of meat deep down my throat, but his warning about obeying the rules held me in check. I looked up into his eyes; they were filled with lust, and I was sure he knew what I was thinking. He stood there a moment longer, then turned and thrust his ass in my face. It was covered in quite a thick layer of black hair. He spread his ass cheeks, exposing his brown hole. His ass channel was covered in the same thick hair. I ran my tongue lightly through the hairs on his cheeks, then along the crack of his ass. I licked around his opening, teasing him, and he wiggled his ass in my face to encourage my direction. I withdrew my tongue, then darted it back in, hitting his asshole dead on and eliciting a long moan of pleasure from him. I continued to lick the hole, forcing the tip of my tongue deep into his inner moistness. I could taste the spit of the previous recruits as well as the gaminess of his hole. My arousal was quickly building and I thought I was going to shoot my load when suddenly Joshua left me and Ethan took his place.

For an undetermined time my world became asses, both hairy and smooth, and assholes, some big, some small. When Joshua was bent over in front of me for the second time I began to wonder if this was the extent of the initiation. I would soon have my answer. When the last team member had been down the line twice, Joshua stood in front of Dizzy once more. An expectant hush fell over the locker room as everyone waited for what was to happen next.

"Good work, men," he announced heartily. "But that's just part one of today's performance. Suck it," he yelled at Dizzy without warning.

Everyone jumped, but the shortstop quickly regained his composure. He ran his tongue over the fat crown of Joshua's dick, then stuck the tip of his tongue into the piss slit. Joshua shuddered as Dizzy worked the tiny opening before slowly sinking down the length of his cock. He didn't stop till his nose was buried deep in Joshua's thatch of black crotch hair. He immediately sawed back to the fat knob, then began bobbing up and down on the thick shaft. When time was called, Joshua pulled his dick forcibly out of the man's mouth with a loud plopping sound. Dizzy lunged forward in an attempt to recapture the thick prick. Joshua looked down at him, his chest heaving and covered in sweat. He seemed reluctant to leave the shortstop.

"Move now, Joshua, or you will be disqualified," Ethan bellowed, and the third baseman reluctantly moved to the next recruit. When he was standing in front of me, I sucked the large crown noisily, then engulfed his entire cock. Rather than bob up and down on it as had those before me, I simply held it in my mouth, sucking on it softly. Joshua ran his fingers through my hair before placing his hand gently on my head. When time was called I found myself staring at Ethan's gigantic prick. As with assholes in the first two rounds, my world became made up simply of cocks. Cocks of all sizes and thicknesses; the majority were the ones with the skin cut away, permanently exposing the heads. These were fashionable with the arrival of the new century. But there was also one with the skin still attached. And one was so long I could not even swallow all of it. When I was sucking Joshua's cock for the second time, I was sure part two of the initiation was wrapping up. Sure enough, when he left me he clapped his hands for our attention.

"Again, nice work all around. I know the rest of the team will agree with me that this is one of the best batches of recruits the Stallions have seen in a long, long time. There are loads and loads of talent here. And you'll all be happy to know that the fun and games will continue. We are going to untie your hands to allow you to take a few minutes to stand and stretch before we proceed."

As the jockstrap was removed, I stood up and stretched my arms above my head. Before I knew what I was doing, I found myself glancing at Parker. His prick was at full attention, and I was transfixed by it. I tore my gaze from the phallic reminder, only for Parker to catch my eye and hold it as he reached down and grabbed his dick.

"Keep your hands off your stiffers, gentlemen," Joshua barked. "The break is over. Please move to the towel shelf and stand facing it in the same order."

Parker glanced at me again before moving to stand in front of the shelf with the rest of us. After our hands were trussed behind our backs once more by the jockstraps, we stood in quiet expectation. Joshua had disappeared into Coach's office and when he returned a few minutes later he was carrying a cloth sack. He set the sack down on the shelf next to Dizzy and pulled a long object from within. Joshua quickly explained what he held was a souvenir baseball bat. These had been newly introduced to the team last season. They measured approximately 12 inches in length, and the fans, especially the kids, loved them. Along with hats and T-shirts, they were a great source of extra revenue for teams. He also produced one of the tins of grease.

"Gentlemen, when one of your teammates is not around to help you let off some steam, this will become your new best friend. Dizzy, bend over the shelf and spread your legs."

Joshua went to Dizzy and began rolling the bat across his ass cheeks, then he switched to sliding it along the crack of his ass. Dizzy squirmed underneath the ministrations of the bat, and humped his ass back to meet it. After a little more teasing, Joshua opened the glove grease, dipped his fingers in the clear substance, and coated the bat with it. He used what was remaining on his fingers to lather the shortstop's asshole. Without having to be instructed, Dizzy spread his ass cheeks as best he could with his tied hands, and Joshua placed the business end of the bat between them and pressed determinedly. The young man moaned loudly as we watched the better part of the bat slowly disappear up his asshole. When he could take no more, Joshua let the bat rest. Dizzy was moaning continually now. Joshua slowly withdrew the small instrument, then pushed it back in. He then began long, deep, slow thrusts in and out as Dizzy writhed beneath him.

When time was called Joshua moved to the next man, and Ethan stepped behind Dizzy, bat in hand. When it was Parker's turn he took the bat eagerly, and began thrusting his ass back at Joshua. Then I felt the bat pressed against my cornhole. The bat was several inches longer than the biggest dick I had ever taken, which happened to be Parker's. When the end of it banged into the secret muscle buried deep within me, I cried out and ground my stiffer onto the shelf as my fluid plopped onto its surface. Joshua rested the bat a moment before beginning the in-and-out plunges. I pushed back against the instrument each time, moaning softly all the while.

After all the teammates had used me once, there was not a second go-round for this portion of the initiation. Again, after congratulating us on our efforts, Joshua assured us we weren't done yet.

"Okay, lads, next comes the most critical part of the initiation. It will determine who your team mentor is for the season. All of you need to remain in your positions while we rotate through you once more. This time we'll be using real cocks instead of artificial ones. Whoever makes one of us shoot his load, that man will be your mentor."

Without further ado he greased up his prick, stepped behind Dizzy, and entered him with one swift lunge. He plowed in and out of him, slapping his ass with each thrust till time was called, then withdrew and moved down the line as Ethan took his place behind Dizzy. As Parker and I waited for our turn, he suddenly turned to me and whispered conspiratorially.

"I bet you ten bucks I can make one of them shoot before you do."

I bit my tongue to keep from laughing out loud. This was so typical of Parker. But then I figured what the hell; it seemed pretty harmless under the circumstances.

"You're on, Parker."

As Joshua entered Parker and began hammering his ass, Parker heaved back against him, matching each thrust. The sound of flesh slapping against flesh echoed within the room. Parker gave it a valiant effort but, try as he might, it was not to be for him this round; time was called and Joshua swiftly entered me. He sank deep in one swift motion, then began rabbit-like thrusts in and out of me. As Parker had, I met each thrust of his with a back one of my own, and used the well-trained muscles in my ass to clench his cock on each plunge. However, he had more stamina than I had given him credit for, and made it to the next round. He withdrew from me and moved back to the head of the line.

Before long, Joshua was inside Parker for the second time. Try as he might, my ex-lover could not make the man come. When Joshua moved to me and Ethan was inside Parker, I became more determined than ever to milk him dry before Parker could do the same to Ethan. I clenched and unclenched the muscles in my ass, determined to win our ridiculous bet. Just as time was called and Joshua withdrew he cried out, and I felt his warm slop spraying onto my back. I heard Parker angrily whisper, "Damn."

Because Joshua had blown his load on my back, he was now my mentor and I stepped out of the line. Within minutes the rest of the team were also reaching individual climaxes, signaling who they would be mentoring. Parker had landed Ethan. Joshua clapped his hands once more for our attention.

"Okay, men. That's it for the initiation. And I'm pleased to say you all passed with flying colors and will be valued members of the Stallions for the next year. Now follow us to the showers where, as the final rite, you will wash down your mentor."

The five of us walked single file to the showers behind the rest of the team.

"Stand here while we turn on the showers."

We stood just inside the shower room while each of the players stood under a showerhead and turned on their individual sprays. On a small table just inside the shower room were numerous bars of soap and a stack of washcloths.

"Okay, recruits, grab a bar of soap and a washcloth from the stack on the floor, go to your mentor, and make sure he is shiny clean after a hard workout and initiation."

I grabbed a bar of soap and a washcloth and went to Joshua. He smiled at me mischievously as the water ran down the front of his body. He was a fine specimen, standing well over 6 feet, 6 inches tall. His chest was massive and covered in black hair, the nipples large, full, and brown. His stomach was rippled with muscles and also furred; the flare at his hips accentuated his masculinity. His arms and legs were covered in the same thick, black hair, matching the thatch of hair growing above his fat cock, which was already hard and pointing straight at me. I scrubbed the bar of soap across the washcloth.

"Close your eyes."

He did as I'd ordered, and I scrubbed his face, then moved down to his neck.

"Okay, rinse."

When he had rinsed I scrubbed the washcloth once more with the soap, then began washing his enormous chest. He sighed contently as I worked the rough cloth over his nipples, bringing them to hard points. He stared at me and nodded his head slightly. I took the left teat into my mouth and sucked on it gently, then the right. I alternated between the two, using my teeth and my tongue to elicit a series of moans from this giant of a man.

"Finish my shower before I shoot too soon," he moaned softly.

I left his tits alone and began washing his stomach. Then he turned around to let me scrub his muscular back. From there I washed his ass, making sure to scrub his hole vigorously. When I was finished he faced me once more, his dick still as hard as a tree trunk. I lathered more soap into the washcloth and began washing his legs and his feet. When I had finished I paused for a moment to look at the action around me. All of the recruits were either on their knees, swallowing pricks, or being gripped at the hips and pounded into steadily from behind. The sexual stamina of these ballplayers was truly amazing.

I instructed Joshua to rinse off and asked what position I should assume for the final part of my extensive initiation.

"Turn around and face the wall," Joshua whispered hoarsely.

I moved beside him and placed my hands flat on the tile wall. He lubed my hole with soap and quickly entered me. Grabbing me by the hips, he began deep in-and-out lunges. After a dozen or so thrusts, their power increased and I felt his warm fluid flooding my insides. He withdrew, rinsed off, and left the shower. I followed him to his locker and dried him from head to toe, then watched him dress. The others did the same around me.

When only the recruits were left in the locker room, we showered ourselves. Michael, who had been dismissed before the initiation began, returned to collect our uniforms and our jockstraps—including those that had bound our hands during the rite—and disappeared down the hallway in the direction of the laundry room. After dressing, we returned to the boarding house and hung out in our rooms till it was time for dinner. After dinner I went straight to bed and fell fast asleep, worn out by the exhilaratingly strenuous day.

· · ·

The next four weeks were spent in training, and in a world of routines. We were awakened each morning by Mrs. Jenkins, who wholeheartedly believed in starting each day with a massive breakfast. The combinations varied from day to day, but the food consisted largely of eggs, biscuits, oatmeal, bacon, ham, sausage, pancakes, grits, and corn cakes. Plus glass after glass of milk fresh from the dairy a few miles down the road. It was stick-to-your-ribs food, according to Mrs. Jenkins, intended to give us lots of energy for that day's practice. After breakfast it was off to shower, and typically we chose the outside showers because a nice cold shower in the morning would really wake us up. Plus, we were trying to keep costs down by only using the hot water in the locker room after practice.

After a necessarily quick shower, it was back inside to dress. Also to reduce expenses, we continued to practice in the old uniforms supplied by Coach. Practice began with a dozen laps around the field, quickly followed by push-ups, sit-ups, jumping jacks, and a myriad of other exercises I had never heard of. Then we performed endless batting, running, and fielding drills. After several grueling hours, it was time for lunch, which was always brought to us by Mr. Stanley and Mr. Hughes.

After lunch the real work began. We divided into two teams and played a series of practice games for the next several hours. Coach drove us hard, and we gave our all for him. Each of us came to realize how much was riding on this season; it was going to make or break the Stallions. Eventually, Coach would call it quits for the day. We then all filed into the locker room and engaged in some form of sexual activity. More often than not, Coach joined in or at least watched. After satisfying our lust, we would shower and head back to the boarding house for dinner. The evenings were spent playing cards or checkers, reading, listening to radio programs, or writing letters. By the time lights out was called, everyone was eager for bed.

The number of practices before our big first game was dwindling fast. One evening I was in the locker room, taking a long shower after a particularly exhausting practice. The rest of the team was gone, having hurried to eat dinner and head into town to see a motion picture. I knew my lateness would force me to forgo eating, but I felt I more greatly needed to rejuvenate my aching muscles. I stood under the shower spray, letting the scalding water wash the dirt and stiffness from me. After another ten minutes, as the water began to get cold, I reluctantly turned it off, grabbed my towel, and slung it over my shoulder.

As I emerged from the shower I heard voices raised in anger and saw Coach standing in front of the lockers talking to a group of well-dressed men. As I approached, the oldest of the four suddenly grabbed Coach by the neck of his shirt and pushed him back against the lockers. There was already a welt forming on Coach's cheek, and a small trail of blood ran from the right corner of his mouth. As they heard me approach all eyes turned to me simultaneously; a dead silence fell over the locker room. Suddenly self-conscious, I wrapped the towel around my waist. The older gentleman released Coach, who immediately wiped the blood from the corner of his mouth.

"Who the hell are you?" the man roared.

My tongue seemed to have disappeared, for no words would form in my mouth. This man's commanding and menacing presence seemed to have robbed me of the power of speech.

"Giovanni," Coach stammered, fighting to control a slight trembling in his voice, "this is Andrew Duggan, one of two new star pitchers. He's from Georgia, and joined us several weeks ago. With him on our team, plus the rest of the recruits we picked up for this season, I foresee great things happening for the Stallions."

The man named Giovanni studied me intently. I felt as if I were under a microscope.

Coach continued, seeming to gather strength at the sound of his own voice.

"Andrew, this is Giovanni Sabatini and his sons, Antonio, Lorenzo, and Nino. Mr. Sabatini is an avid follower of Bush League baseball, and is quite enamored with the Stallions."

I studied the four men as I tried to quell my rising panic. This was not a good scene by any means, and the air was thick with menace. I guessed Antonio and Lorenzo to be in their late twenties, maybe early thirties, but Nino looked closer to my age. Giovanni was completely gray, and to have sons as old as Antonio and Lorenzo, he had to be in his late forties or early fifties. Whatever his exact age, he was still handsome, even with the beginnings of a paunch. The three sons varied slightly from their dad in height and weight, but all of them had his dashing good looks. They were all of average height and a little on the stocky side, but none could be called fat. All were dressed in the latest fashionable suits, hats, and shoes, in varying shades of dark blue and black.

During my examination of them, the four men were also looking me over in a weirdly predatory way that left me vaguely uneasy. It didn't escape my notice that Nino eyed me longer than the rest, his gaze traveling from head to toe and lingering the longest at the lump my crotch made beneath the towel. When he finally raised his head our eyes locked, and though no smile split his face, his eyes immediately displayed an interest in me that was too potent to miss.

"Welcome, Andrew, to Florida," Giovanni said.

He extended his hand and I grasped it in mine. His handshake was crushingly strong, as were those of Antonio and Lorenzo. When I shook hands with Nino, he gave my hand an extra hard squeeze and ran his finger lightly across my palm; the meaning was not lost on me.

"Mr. Connors," Giovanni addressed Coach, "let's go into your office and finish our discussion in private. I find that money matters usually are best discussed this way. Andrew, it was nice to meet you."

He draped his arm across Coach's shoulder and turned to Nino. He was now all camaraderie and kindness.

"Nino, you stay here and keep an eye on things. Including this one." Giovanni indicated me with a nod of his head and a smile on his face.

"Sure, Pop," the young man replied.

With that, the four of them walked down the hall and disappeared into Coach's office, leaving Nino and me alone. I studied the young man standing in front of me. He was strikingly handsome, with pale blue eyes beneath thick black eyebrows. His nose was slim and tapered to thin, flaring nostrils. His lips were full, and I felt the overpowering urge to taste them—that, or slide my dick between them. He was clean-shaven, but the dark outline of his beard and mustache were plain to see.

"So, you're the new pitcher for the Stallions."

His question snapped me back to attention; I was surprised by the deepness of his voice. "One of two, yes."

"That means you're good at handling balls."

I almost laughed at his absurd come-on. Maybe those lines worked for the types he was used to courting, but they had no effect on me. Or did they? I found my mouth replying before my brain realized it had formed an answer.

"Yup. The bigger the better. The same goes for the size of the bats I prefer."

Nino stared at me intently, then his face broke into a large grin and he laughed out loud.

"Okay, let's agree right now to kill this corny dialogue."

I laughed as well. "Agreed."

Nino sat down on the bench and tugged his pants up a little, causing the material to stretch across the lump at his crotch, thus outlining the head of his cock as well as his ball sac; both were sizable. The display was obvious, and I didn't disappoint him; I stared openly at his crotch to let him know his interest was reciprocated, then went to my locker next to him, and opened the door.

"Let's see what you're hiding," Nino whispered.

He reached up and loosened the towel at my waist, causing it to fall to the floor. He grabbed my semi-hard cock and tugged on it gently. He then held it in his hand as it swelled to its full length and girth. Without further ado he spit into his hand and began stroking my cock, all the while kneading my balls with his free hand. This was no slow dance, but a fast limbo to get me off. I moaned and thrashed under his ministrations till the first splash of my seed shot forth and landed on his expensive pants. His soft, urgent whispers implored me to shoot my load and I readily complied, filling his hand with my jism. When I was spent he licked his hand clean, then stood up and kissed me on the mouth. We were interrupted by the voices of the returning men. As they approached I quickly dressed, buttoning the final button on my pants just as they came abreast of Nino and me. Coach was not with them, and the three Sabatini men didn't look very happy either. Giovanni snarled, "Let's go" to Nino, and the four men left the locker room. When I was sure they were gone, I went to find Coach. He was sitting in his office, at his desk, staring out the window. I startled him when I entered.

"Sorry, Coach. Am I interrupting something?"

"No, Andrew. I'm just doing some thinking about my life."

"What did the Sabatinis want with you, Coach? They seem like real bad sorts, and it sounds like money is involved."

He didn't respond for a moment, and I could tell he was either scared or angry, or both. I had been raised on a farm in rural Georgia, but I read the paper and listened to the news on the radio. I knew rumors were swirling around the Sabatinis, the speculation being that they were racketeers. And supposedly the feds were investigating them. Was Coach running on the wrong side of the law? I quickly pushed the thought from my mind.

"They are bad sorts, Andrew. And they want a piece of everyone else's good luck."

He seemed to want to say more, but did not.

"Nino seemed to be OK, and I could easily be friends with him."

I was not ready for Coach's reaction.

"You stay away from all the Sabatinis! You hear me, Andrew? Nino may appear to be nice, but he's rotten, just like the old man and the other two sons. They will bring you nothing but trouble."

"Okay, Coach. I'll see you tomorrow."

He didn't respond as I left his office and headed for the house.

· · ·

The next day after practice I was leaving the locker room when I was surprised to find Nino standing outside. He smiled when he saw me, but I could tell he was nervous.

"Hi, Andrew," he said, almost shyly. I found this hard to believe after his performance in the locker room.

"Hi yourself, Nino," I said, my voice sounding stupid to my own ears. "What brings you back here?"

Nino stared at me and looked as if he were about to flee. I tried to reassure him. "Don't worry, there's no one else around."

I saw relief flood his face, and then he was the shy young man once more.

"I was wondering," he began haltingly, then seemed to pick up courage as the words came pouring out of him, "if you would like to join me for a beer?"

Coach's warning echoed in the back of my mind, but I found myself saying, "On a hot day like today, Nino, a cold beer sounds like a fine idea."

"Great, we can take my car."

The man couldn't hide his elation, and fairly danced instead of walked on the way to his car. It was one of the latest models, all shiny red, with big headlights and miles and miles of chrome. Nino went to my side of the car and opened the door, waving me in with a grand gesture of his right arm. I stepped in and sat down on the plush seat. Nino hopped in the driver's side and turned the key; the engine roared to life, and we were off. Nino drove expertly, shifting at exactly the right moment, and almost seemed to be a part of his car. His large, white teeth were exposed in a permanent grin. I studied his large hand on the shifter, noting the black hair that covered the back and also tufted at the knuckles. As we drove down the main street of the tiny town, Nino seemed to know exactly where he was headed, and within minutes we parked outside a tiny bar. Nino did not get my door this time, but simply waited patiently on the sidewalk for me to get out.

We went inside, which was cool and dark but rather smoky. There were a few patrons who seemed to eye us warily, then turn away. The bartender greeted Nino by name, which solidified my thinking that Nino was familiar with this town. We ordered beers and chatted nervously till they arrived. After the first few sips we both loosened up and became more talkative, and as we started on our second beer I suddenly realized I was developing an attraction to this man. He seemed to sense it as well.

"Let's get out of here, Andrew. I have a house a few blocks down the street."

We left the bar and drove down the street a bit to an enormous, three-story stone house set back from the street and fronted by a large yard. A massive black wrought-iron fence kept the curious out. Nino turned into a cobblestone driveway closed off by a large gate of the same iron. He hopped out of the car, produced the necessary key, and soon the large gate was swinging open. Nino got back in the car, drove onto the property, closed and locked the gate behind us, and stopped the car at the front of the house in front of a set of wide stone steps. No lights shone in the house. Once more Nino opened my door and gallantly waved me out of the car. He grabbed my hand, and we walked up the steps to the front door. I was overwhelmed by the house and stood staring at him.

"Actually, this isn't my house," he confessed, "but one of many houses my family owns on the East Coast. Papa and my brothers travel so much on business that they felt it best to have comfortable lodgings. I've been away at college, so this is my first official trip with papa. But I've been here many times before."

I was surprised to hear that Nino had been to college, and evidently my surprise showed on my face.

"Both papa and mama believe that a man should be educated to some extent. Since my grandparents came from the old country over half a century ago, we have tried to better ourselves. Of course, they mandate that once we finish at least two years, we must come back to work in the family business."

"And what is that?" I asked, innocently enough.

He paused a long time before replying. "Let's just say my family is in the shipping business, and that we have multiple interests across North America, predominantly along the eastern and western seaboards. Can we leave it at that?"

Could I leave it at that? I silently asked myself. Coming from life on the farm in Miller Falls, this element of danger was new to me. I was willing to wait and see what happened. I told myself that I wasn't doing anything to break the law, so whatever happened to Nino would not rope me in as well.

"We can, Nino."

We stepped into the foyer and faced a long hallway that led to a well-lighted kitchen. As Nino closed the door behind us, I stared in awe around me. I saw dark woodwork everywhere, with elaborate scrollwork. A gigantic staircase wound up to the right and disappeared into cavernous heights above us.

"Millie, Hank, it's me, Nino!"

I heard footsteps coming from the kitchen and suddenly the light was cut off by a large figure moving toward us. As it drew nearer I saw an old black woman equal to two Ninos in size. She wore a large blue dress with little white daisies all over it. As she neared us, she spread massive arms that engulfed Nino in a ferocious hug.

"Young Mister Nino, it's so good to see you again. It's been too long since your last visit."

When I was sure that she had crushed the life from Nino, he pushed her gently away.

"I missed you too, Millie. This is my friend, Andrew."

I braced myself as I received the same hug from the old woman. I literally felt the breath being squeezed from my body.

"Welcome to you too, Mister Andrew."

"Is there anything for us to eat, Millie?"

"You're in luck, Mister Nino. I have a large ham in the oven that is almost done, and roasted ears of corn, sweet potatoes, and collard greens cookin' on the stove. I also baked fresh corn bread."

"That sounds great, Millie. Andrew and I will be in the study. Will you please bring us the usual?"

"Right away."

She retreated down the hallway and disappeared once more into the kitchen.

"The study is upstairs."

I followed Nino up the enormous stairs, which continued to the third floor. But at the second floor we turned left and proceeded down a long hall, passing many doors to unknown rooms. At the end of the hall we stopped at a heavy oak door. Nino opened it and gallantly waved me into the room. He pushed a button on the wall and lights came on, revealing walls covered from floor to ceiling in bookshelves, without an empty space on any shelf. The furniture was leather, with large, heavy feet and grand, sweeping arms. The floors were of a dark wood, and covered generously with elaborately designed rugs. Even though it was early summer, the room still had a slight chill to it, most likely from the house's stone facade. An enormous fireplace a small boy could stand upright in took up almost an entire wall. A bear rug was spread before it. As I continued to survey the room, a rather short, wizened black man came into the study.

"Greetings, Hank," Nino said as he shook hands with the older man.

"It's good to see you again, young Nino."

As with Millie, I could tell there was genuine affection and respect between these two.

"Let me get a fire started for you and young Andrew."

Without further preamble, he gathered kindling and newspapers that were stacked to the right of the fireplace, and soon had a blaze going. He added several birch logs from a wooden crate, and the fire quickly came to life. He excused himself and paused while leaving the room to allow Millie to enter. She was carrying a silver tray on which were two rocks glasses, a clear bottle of dark liquid, two slim cigars, and a small box of matches. She placed the tray on the coffee table.

"Will you be needing anything else before dinner is served, Nino?"

"That's all for now, Millie. Thank you."

Millie gave him another big hug as well as a kiss on the cheek, then turned and left the room, closing the door behind her. Nino walked to the table, pulled the cork on the clear bottle, and filled both glasses. He sat down on the oversized leather sofa and patted the spot next to him.

"Come join me, Andrew."

As I settled next to Nino, he handed me one of the glasses. I took a tentative sip, and Nino could tell I was not familiar with the liquor.

"It's Scotch. It's best sipped slowly."

As I took another sip, Nino picked up one of the cigars, bit off the end, and lit it. Once smoke was curling lazily from its tip, he handed it to me and lit the second one for himself. This was my first cigar, and I coughed a little as I blew out the acrid smoke, but the cigar itself had a not unpleasant taste. As we sat and smoked and drank the Scotch, Nino asked about my hometown, my family, and how I had come to be a member of the Stallions. As I finished my life history and was just about to ask him about his family—most specifically, its connection to Coach Connors—we were interrupted by a soft but imperative knock on the study door.

"Come in," Nino responded, as he drank his last bit of Scotch. He snubbed his cigar out in the ashtray, then did the same with mine. The door opened and Millie stood silhouetted in its frame.

"Dinner is ready, Nino."

"Thanks, Millie. We'll be right down."

She closed the door and, as I began to stand, Nino leaned into me and kissed me full on the lips. He tasted of Scotch and cigars, and his cologne filled my nostrils. As I returned his kisses his tongue wound its way into my mouth, exploring the cavity fully before withdrawing.

"We'll finish this after dinner," he whispered softly.

As we left the study and descended the stairs, we were greeted by wondrous odors coming from the kitchen. We traversed the hall that led to the kitchen but bypassed it to enter an elegant dining room. Again, the walls were of a fine dark wood, as was the floor. A large crystal chandelier hung over the table, reflecting prisms of light around the room. The table, a massive affair in itself, was set with the finest china and silverware, as well as magnificent water goblets. A sideboard stood to the right of the table, laden with food. A large, succulent ham rested in a silver baking dish, stewing in its own juices. Numerous intricately carved serving bowls held sweet potatoes, collard greens, corn bread, and a large platter of corn on the cob. It was enough food to feed an army. Nino excused Millie and we served ourselves. I hadn't realized how hungry I was, but I was soon dishing a second helping of everything.

When we were done eating we excused ourselves, thanked Millie for everything, climbed the stairs, and settled once more in the study. The fire was still burning brightly, and the room was filled with its warmth and glow. On the coffee table the bottle of Scotch and the glasses had been replaced by a bottle of champagne and two long-stemmed glasses. Nino popped the cork and filled each glass, set the glasses on the floor by the bear rug, and closed and locked the door to the study.

Without saying a word, he undid his tie and pulled it from around his neck. He then unbuttoned his shirt, slowly, teasingly, and tossed it onto the couch. Thick, black hair flooded from above the collar of his undershirt. The muscles of his chest were clearly outlined, as were his nipples, which were large points beneath the material. The thin shirt also prominently displayed his strong, sculpted stomach. He had appeared stocky before, but he proved to be all muscle. He pulled off the T-shirt and began unbuttoning his pants, revealing his white underwear. The black hair on his stomach and chest continued unabated beneath his underwear, creating a stark contrast to the white of his briefs. He slid his pants down his hairy, powerful legs, took off his shoes and socks, and stepped out of his pants. I could see the outline of his cock beneath his underwear; he was already hard. He dropped his underwear and stood before me in all his naked glory. He was the embodiment of manhood; I admired him, temporarily unable to speak.

"Your turn," he said softly.

I mimicked Nino, and began performing a slow, tantalizing, silent striptease. I maintained eye contact with him at all times. When I was completely naked, he surveyed my body up and down, his desire evident in his eyes as well as his body. His dick stuck straight out from his body like a club. His balls hung low in their sac of flesh. He walked past me to the fireplace and lay down on the bear rug.

"Please, join me."

I did as I had been bidden. The feel of the fur against my skin was incredible. He handed me a champagne glass and held his up to me.

"To new relationships, Andrew."

"To new relationships."

We clinked our glasses, and I quickly drained mine. He took it and placed both glasses on the hearth.

"Roll over," he whispered.

I rolled onto my belly. Nino straddled me at the hips and began vigorously massaging my shoulders. His hands on my flesh felt wonderful after the strenuous workout on the ball field that day. After working several minutes on my shoulders, he moved to my upper back; he then scooted down to sit on my ass and began working my lower back, then flipped around and began deeply rubbing my upper legs. I was soon almost lulled to sleep by his skillful fingers. However, he got my full attention when he spread my ass cheeks and trailed his finger up the crack, passing lightly over my hole, then returning to flick the end of his finger over it. His finger was then replaced with his tongue, and he thoroughly licked my crack, pausing often to give special attention to my opening. I moaned softly and arched my ass back against him. When his finger returned to my ass it was wet. He poked at my spot, then pushed insistently against the opening till his finger slid in deep. I gasped when he began slowly sliding the large digit in and out of my chute.

I began humping my ass to match his thrusts. He suddenly withdrew his finger, grabbed me at the waist, and pulled me roughly onto my knees. He spread something on my opening, then I felt the head of his prick against it. He didn't plunge in, but teased me for a bit, rubbing the head over the opening and up and down my crack. My own dick was as hard as a rock, and my early juice was flowing. Nino reached underneath me, grabbed my stiffer, and gave it a few hard pulls. After he released it I felt the large crown pressing against my opening till the ring of muscle relaxed and the fat knob popped through.

He slid in easily, sinking to the hilt till the head was bumping against the muscle buried within my channel. He paused, slowly withdrew completely, then pushed back in and began slow, leisurely plunges. I pushed back against him each time, forcing him deep inside me, his huge cock spreading the walls of my asshole, the head of his prick dinging my pleasure muscle each time. Sweat was flowing freely from my body, in part from our exertions, but also from the fire burning only a few feet from us. I quickly lost track of time as my senses focused on the piece of flesh sliding in and out of me, and the noises connected with it: our combined groans, and the sound of flesh slapping against flesh. As Nino increased the pace of his thrusts, and his grunts increased in length and intensity, I knew he was close to coming. Suddenly, he heaved a final, massive time, and I felt his spunk flooding my asshole. When he was done, he withdrew slowly, and my shit hole returned to its former shape.

Without warning, he flipped me on my back and began licking my cock. He trailed his tongue up and down the shaft, then sucked the fat knob into his mouth, and greedily lapped up the clear fluid in the slit. After sucking earnestly on the crown, he released it and began swathing my crotch hair. When he was done, he pushed my right leg out and began licking the crack where it joined to my body. This was a first for me, and I couldn't believe the sensation; it was ticklish and a turn-on at the same time. He did the same to the left leg, then moved back to my cock, engulfed the head, and sank down to the root. He began sawing up and down vigorously while at the same time probing my asshole with a wet finger. The combination did the trick and all too soon I was spewing my stuff down his throat. He licked me clean and then stood up and stretched, the fire casting his shadow against the wall.

He refilled our glasses and then lay down beside me and pulled a section of the rug over both of us. We drank the champagne in silence. Then he lay on his back, I rested my head on his chest, he wrapped his arms around me, and I was soon fast asleep. When I woke it was still dark, but I could tell it was very early in the morning. Nino was sound asleep beside me. The fire had long since burned out. The next time I awoke was to Nino softly planting kisses on my cheek. Early morning light was coming through the tall windows.

"Good morning, Andrew."

"Good morning."

"Millie just knocked and said breakfast is ready. After we eat I'll take you back to the boarding house."

We got dressed and went downstairs to the kitchen. Millie was positioned at the stove, and Hank was just coming in from the backyard. After plowing through a breakfast of ham, eggs, pancakes, and biscuits and gravy, plus coffee, we said our good-byes to Millie and Hank. Nino kissed her on the cheek, and I received a big hug from her. We then each shook hands with Hank, left the house, and climbed into Nino's car. The engine roared to life and we drove between the gates out onto the street. We didn't speak as we drove back to the boarding house, each wrapped in his own thoughts. When Nino's hand was free from shifting he clasped it in mine. As we pulled into the driveway of the house, Coach and Mr. Stanley were just coming down the porch steps. When Coach saw Nino, his face hardened. When I got out of the car, Nino did as well. He started to speak to the two men, but Coach cut his words short.

"You're not welcome here, Nino. In fact, none of your family is."

With that he punched Nino in the mouth, knocking him to the ground.

CHAPTER SEVEN

As Coach stood over Nino, his fist raised, Mr. Stanley expertly pulled the large man's arms behind his back and held them tight. Coach strained against him but was no match for the manager's wiry strength.

"Jordan, this is not the time or place for this."

Nino got up from the ground and dusted off his clothes. A rivulet of blood trickled from the right corner of his mouth.

"I have no personal problems with you, Mr. Connors," he said. "What's between you and my father is strictly business, none of which is mine."

"You expect me to believe you don't know anything about your father's business dealings? Do you take me for a fool?" He writhed in Mr. Stanley's grip.

I could see that Nino was close to losing his cool as well. I quickly stepped between the two men.

"Coach, let's not do this now. For whatever reason, you don't like Nino, and that's between you and him. I happen to like him, and I will be spending time with him, regardless of whether you approve. Why don't you and Mr. Stanley go down to the locker room?"

"That's a great idea, Andrew," Mr. Stanley said between clenched teeth. "But I echo Coach's sentiments. Nino, you are not welcome on this property. If you need to see Andrew, do so elsewhere."

Grudgingly, Coach allowed Mr. Stanley to steer him toward the office. I turned to Nino, whose anger and hurt were plainly written on his face.

"I'm sorry, Nino. I think it's best for now to abide by their wishes. Tomorrow is our first game, and I was hoping you were going to be here to bring me luck."

He looked at me for a moment before replying.

"Andrew, I know my father's not a saint and, for that matter, neither are many in my family. While I am not like them, I am cursed by my last name. I would like to change this somehow, but for now I apologize—I can't make it to the game tomorrow. I must go out of town on business. But rest assured I will come to you at the boarding house once I return. No one is going to keep me from you. Not your coach nor my father."

Before I had a chance to ask him what he meant, he got back in his car and roared away. I watched him disappear in a cloud of dust before going inside to change and head down to the field for practice. When I arrived, Coach was in the outfield, and he avoided me the rest of the day. I knew he was only concerned about me, but I was irritated by his dislike of Nino simply based on whatever was transpiring between him and Giovanni Sabatini.

When practice was over I wanted to be alone, so I took a cold shower behind the house, then went straight to my room, skipping dinner. I read my pulp magazines till I fell asleep. I woke the next morning feeling surprisingly refreshed for all I had on my mind, especially the scene between Coach and Nino. If Nino came to see me at the boarding house, it would directly be disobeying Coach's and Mr. Stanley's wills. What would Coach do if he found out? Ban me from the team for my conduct? I pushed the thought from my mind. It was opening day and time to focus on a win.

I quickly dressed and headed downstairs for breakfast. The entire team was already seated, and the game-day excitement was almost palpable. Our first game was against the Gators, and as usual we were opening the season at home. I had waited

years for this moment to happen, and now that it was unfolding, it had an air of unreality about it. We hurried through
the massive meal, then excused ourselves and ran as a group
down to the locker room to shower and change into our real
uniforms. They were grey with black piping on the pants and
a black rearing stallion on the right breast and on our caps.
While getting ready, we were surprised to learn that the Gators
had not arrived the night before.

As we moved onto the field to warm up, we found our team's
bleachers full of fans from the town. Just then a large navy blue
bus, twice the size of ours, pulled into the boarding house's
driveway. A second, smaller bus was behind it. Both had large
alligators painted on their sides, jaws agape. Coach and Mr.
Stanley went to the bus to greet the visiting team. As they dis-
embarked we discovered that the smaller bus had brought a
contingent of fans. We soon also learned that engine trouble
had forced them to spend the previous night sleeping in the
bus by the side of the road. But they seemed ready to get down
to business now.

As their fans took up positions on the visiting team's bleachers, the Gators stormed the field to do their warm-up exercises,
and before long the game was underway. The Gators immediately proved to have a formidable offense, earning three runs
in the first inning, which greatly angered Parker, our starting
pitcher. However, we quickly answered back with two runs in
the bottom of the first. Parker cooled his anger and held the
Gators scoreless for the next two innings. And true to his word,
Michael was in the Stallions' dugout—hidden from the fans in
the bleachers and players on the field—busily sucking cock and
keeping up morale. His ministrations helped us earn two more
runs. In the fifth it became clear Parker could have used some
attention of his own from Michael, as he gave up a two-run
homer.

At the top of the sixth, Coach pulled Parker and put me in. My first official Bush League pitch produced a home run. For a moment my mind reeled with failure. I quickly recovered, however, focusing on making each pitch hit the mark and refusing to think about anything else. My fellow Stallions provided some serious run support, scoring two more runs in the bottom of the sixth and another in the seventh.

In the top of the ninth, with my Stallions still clinging to a one-run lead, there were two men on and two outs. The count on the batter I now faced was full. I could feel the sweat running down my back into the crack of my ass and soaking my jockstrap. My next pitch was low and inside, and the batter popped it high and long to center field. Mark was underneath it, and the game was over. We had won! Our fans went crazy, yelling and cheering and stamping their feet. The entire team ran toward me, and began hugging me and clapping me on the back. Seeing this, the Stallion fans poured onto the field as well. Parker hoisted me onto his shoulders and carried me around the infield. Later, after the Gators and their forlorn fans had boarded their buses and left, the Stallions and our spectators spilled into the locker room.

Mr. Stanley and Coach went to Coach's office and returned with several bottles of champagne. Corks were popped and the bottles were passed around, though we bathed each other with more of the champagne than we drank. Coach held up his hand for silence. It took several seconds for the din to subside, finally helped along by an ear-splitting whistle from Dizzy.

"Gentlemen, you've just won your first official game. A hearty congratulations from myself, Mr. Stanley, and Mr. Hughes. I predict a winning season for the Stallions!"

When he finished, a cheer rose up from the group. Finally the crowd began to thin, although the champagne still flowed. And I was certainly beginning to feel its effects. While the rest of the team began to shower and straggle back to the house, I lingered in Coach's office with him and Mr. Stanley. Mr. Hughes had already left. We continued drinking while the two men recounted wins and losses of past seasons. When the champagne was completely gone, Coach and Mr. Stanley indicated they were ready to leave, but I still hadn't showered. I said my goodbyes and left the office to undress and get myself clean.

I tipsily made my way to a showerhead, turned on the water, let it get as hot as my hand could stand, and then stepped beneath the spray. The water soothed my aching muscles. For several minutes I let the water cascade over me, then turned to reach for the bar of soap on the shelf beneath the spray. I had just started to lather my legs when a strong hand placed itself on top of mine. Startled, I swung around and found myself looking up into Parker's eyes.

He made no sound, but simply stared at me. Maybe it was the fact of seeing him all the time, or unresolved issues, or the adrenaline from our first game, but for whatever reason, I did not move his hand away. A rush of old feelings swept over me. His hand took command of the soap, moving up my leg to my crotch, where my prick was already hard and eagerly awaiting his touch. I knew if I did not do something we would soon be having sex. I pushed his hand away.

"I'm still not ready for this, Parker."

It was impossible to miss the look of disappointment on his face. And maybe a touch of anger?

"It's OK. We don't need to rush it, Andrew. Seeing you and being near you for these past several weeks has stirred old feelings in me that I thought were long since dead and buried. Do you feel anything for me at all?"

While I wanted to tell him how much I hated him, I knew it was a lie. As he had said, the familiarity we'd shared over the past few weeks had changed something. But what about Nino?

And don't forget, that inner voice said, Parker was this nice in the beginning of our relationship.

"I honestly don't know, Parker."

I turned off the water and left Parker in the shower room. I fumbled through getting dressed and ran up to the boarding house. I literally ran into Kent as he was heading out the door.

"Slow down, Andrew. What's the rush?"

Before I realized it, I was blurting out the fact that Parker and I had been in a relationship for a year. Kent placed his hand on my shoulder.

"Let's go back to the room where we can talk in private."

Once we were in our room, Kent handed me a beer from the ever-present ice chest he had under his bed. I poured out the whole story to him, and he listened without comment. When I had finished he took a long pull from his beer.

"I knew I had seen him somewhere before. Now I feel bad that I messed around with him. And I will readily admit that Parker is certainly good-looking. He has a large cock and he knows how to use it, but there's something about him that makes me uneasy. I can't quite put my finger on it, but he definitely seems overly ambitious. I would watch out for that one."

At 6 o'clock we went downstairs for dinner, returning to our room immediately afterward. I was writing a letter to Nelson and Kent was playing Solitaire when there was a knock on our door. Thinking it was Nino I jumped up and opened it, only to find it was Nicholas. He was here to play cards with Kent. About an hour later, there was a second knock on the door. Nicholas and Kent were deep into their card game, so I hopped up to answer it. When I swung it open, I found Nino standing there. He had a dozen roses in his hand, and a brilliant smile lit up his face. Without warning he pushed me into the room and kissed me on the mouth. It was only then that he saw Nicholas and Kent. His smile quickly disappeared.

"I'm sorry to interrupt. Do you want me to come back later?"

Before I could answer, both Nicholas and Kent assured him it was no problem.

"Don't worry, Nino," I added. "We're quite free-spirited around here."

With that he set the flowers on my dresser and turned back to me, kissing me once more while pushing me back onto the bed. I landed on my back and spread my legs to allow him to slide on top of me, then encircled his hips. We lay entangled, kissing, for several minutes, his weight pressing against me. I could feel his prick, hard and laid atop my own. And I knew he was only holding back because of the other players in the room. Suddenly, he came up for air and stared into my eyes.

"I heard about your win today and got here as quickly as I could. I was visiting my mother."

"But how did you hear about the game so soon?" I wondered aloud.

He paused a moment, seemingly unwilling to answer. "My father keeps a close watch on any sporting event that happens on the East Coast. But enough about him; I'm here to see you, alone or otherwise."

He hopped up from the bed, his back to Kent and Nicholas, and quickly undressed. Then he eased onto the bed once more and straddled me at the hips. He unbuttoned my shirt and helped me take it off, along with my undershirt. Leaning over, he began tonguing and biting my nipples, causing me to moan softly and writhe on the bed. After working both teats till my dick was aching, he licked a path down to my navel. He ran his tongue around the tiny opening, then darted it right in. My ass lifted off the bed and I shuddered at the sensation. Nino did this once more, then slid down till he was resting on my thighs. The shaft of my prick was clearly outlined beneath the denim of my pants. Nino pulled the cloth taut till he could see the large head as well, squeezed my stiffer several times along its length, unbuttoned my pants, and reached inside. His fingers found the head and my early fluid. He coated his fingertips with it, then drew them to his mouth and began sucking on them avidly. As he pulled my pants down my legs and tossed them in a heap at the foot of the bed, I glanced over to see Kent and Nicholas watching us with rapt attention; Nicholas's cock was sticking up and out of his underwear's piss flap, and Kent was slowly stroking it.

When Nino came back onto the bed, I opened the drawer and pulled out a tin of grease. I turned on my side with my back to him, and he lay beside me, the heat of his body against me. Suddenly I felt the head of his cock slide between my cheeks and bump up against my hole. He began humping against me insistently, but I was not going to let him go in dry. I handed him the tin, and he quickly coated my asshole with its contents. He then unceremoniously stuck a large digit inside me and poked around, then replaced it with the head of his dick. I pushed back against him as he pressed into me. The fat head popped through the ring of muscle and his pole slid all the way inside me.

My moans as he penetrated me were drowned out by the noises coming from Kent and Nicholas. They were now both naked and lying atop Kent's bedspread. Kent was on his back with Nicholas inverted above him. Nicholas's large cock was scant inches above Kent's mouth. Kent extended his neck, sucking the knob into his mouth and rolling it around against his cheek. He then opened his mouth wide and Nicholas shoved the entire piece of meat down his throat. Kent gagged slightly as the full length went in, then placed his hands on Nicholas's hips to prevent him from choking him to death with his huge prick. Kent let Nicholas's stiffer flop completely from his mouth on each upward movement, then grabbed it delicately with his lips, and resumed his sucking.

Nino did not change position, keeping me on my side so we could watch the action across from us. He lifted my leg slightly to grant him easier access, and thrust steadily into me. I grabbed the glove grease and lubed my own cock with it. I began stroking it to the rhythm Nino had established. We were both grunting like wild pigs, but Kent and Nicholas were making so much noise with their lustful cock sucking that they probably could not even hear us. The way Nino was pounding my ass I knew he was getting close, and I was quickly approaching my own explosion as well.

But Nicholas was the first to cry out, and as he stiffened over Kent I could see Kent greedily swallowing all his spooge. Nino plunged into me one final time and cried out as his spunk flooded my asshole, and I was right behind him after one more stroke, as my own jism began plopping onto the sheet, forming a tiny puddle. Almost as soon as I was spent, I saw Nicholas eagerly gulping everything Kent had to give him. Only after Nicholas had licked Kent's cock clean did he notice Nino and me watching them. He simply smiled, kissed the head of Kent's prick, flipped onto his back and slid around till his head was resting next to Kent's. He kissed Kent on the lips several times, and then they both crawled under the covers. Before long the two of them were asleep. Nino and I quickly followed suit. When I woke the next morning Nicholas and Kent were gone, but Nino was still wrapped tightly to me.

"Good morning," he said, matter-of-factly.

"Good morning."

"I need to go tend some business for my father, but I'll see you again as soon as I can." He kissed me, dressed, and quickly left the room.

· · ·

As July approached, our lives had settled into a new daily routine. We practiced Sunday through Tuesday, then played games the rest of the week. Wednesday and Thursday were reserved for home games, and Friday and Saturday we spent away. For our away games we left Friday morning and returned on Sunday. When we traveled, we most often stayed in cheap motels. However, once in a while they were not available, which forced us to sleep in an open field, wary of the brief but often violent summer thunderstorms. Away games gave my horny teammates time to seek out new male companionship in each town. It never failed that some farmer's son would find his way to our motel or camp, and before long the liquor and beer would start flowing and he'd be on his knees with a cock in his mouth or bent over taking it from behind.

Inevitably, some crushes were hard to break. Coach or Mr. Stanley spent many a morning driving lovesick farm boys, and even the occasional rich kid, home against their will. It was difficult for the managers to keep the players out of trouble. Young, horny men were drawn to the players because we were also young, horny men. Truth be told, there was not one player on the team who didn't know how to get his way out of an argument with any of the managers. A hot, eager mouth or a tight ass—hell, often all it took was a quick stroking to garner forgiveness.

Another commonality with the games was that, no matter which town we were in, one or two members of the Sabatini family always showed up. Most often it was the old man and Nino, or Nino and one of his brothers. They didn't cause any trouble or approach any of the players, but one could sense they were watching everything. And even though I wasn't the only player who had noticed them, no questions were ever asked of Coach, Mr. Stanley, or Mr. Hughes. In various team discussions it was assumed that they were bankrolling either all or part of our games, because it was obvious to everyone that the team was in dire straits financially. Whatever role they played, no one thought they were good news. But it always made me happy to know that Nino was watching me play.

The Stallions were now in third place in the Eastern Bush League. It was a late Friday morning and we were headed to Farmington, some 100 miles distant, to play the Blue Herons that afternoon. Our small bus was crowded because both Mr. Hughes and Mr. Stanley were on board, as was Michael. In fact, Michael was already working on team morale in the seat next to mine as he slurped on Dizzy's cock. The young man could never seem to get enough, and he was never one to waste a drop of juice. The day was sunny and clear, and the humidity was already climbing. And there was a chance of thunderstorms later in the afternoon. We stopped around noon for a quick lunch, then hit the road once more.

When we arrived in Farmington in the early afternoon, we were greeted by a throng of people who booed our arrival. This kind of thing happened now and then, but most often we were treated with respect and professionalism. There were only two motel rooms available, so Mr. Stanley, Mr. Hughes, and Coach took one room, and five players were assigned the second one. The rest of the team was forced to sleep in the bus. It was a miserable summer night, with a huge thunderstorm raging outside. After dinner we all congregated in the managers' room, playing cards, watching the lightning, and listening to the rain and thunder. After several games, Mr. Stanley stood up.

"It's getting close to bedtime, men. But before we turn in, can I interest anyone in a game of Sponge?"

Everyone except us five newest players raised a hand in the air.

"What is Sponge, Mr. Stanley?" Dizzy inquired on our behalf.

"Well, it's easier to show you, Dizzy. Simply follow our lead. Coach, would you like to be the sponge this evening?"

"I would be delighted, Mr. Stanley."

He stood up and stripped out of his clothes, then lay on his back on the bed. He was covered in hair from head to toe, and his large cock lay across his thigh. The rest of the team, including both managers, took off their clothes as well, so the five of us followed suit. We fell into position as the group encircled Coach in a U shape around the bed and all the old-timers began stroking their dicks, bringing them to full hardness. They performed this act in such unison it was evident they had performed it many times before. We initiates hurried to catch up with their level of stiffness.

Mr. Stanley checked around the line to be sure that everyone was ready for action, then pulled a tin of glove grease from his travel bag. He scooped some out and passed it to Mr. Hughes, who did the same and passed it on. I was last in line and when I had enough of the unguent I dropped the tin on the floor. Coach was fully hard as well and busily stroking his own stiffer. The entire ensemble followed his lead. I soon lost track of time as I divided my attention between Coach and the rest of the team. Heads were thrown back, mouths hung slack, and faces contorted in ecstasy as the semicircle of men stroked themselves as one.

We'd been at it a good ten minutes when Mr. Hughes cried out, the first to have his explosion overtake him. The first white blob shot from the head of his dick and landed on Coach's thigh. More and more of the fluid shot forth, creating white crisscross patterns on Coach's hairy stomach. As soon as Mr. Hughes was spent, Nicholas began coming, also splattering Coach with his juice. And thus it went till everyone had deposited their seed on Coach. Somehow he managed to hold out till last, then added his own thick stuff to the mixture. He was covered from head to toe in spooge. As we began to dress, he got up from the bed and went into the bathroom to shower. We said good night to Mr. Stanley and Mr. Hughes. Then those who were staying in the bus headed to it and the rest of us went into the room next door. I was asleep as soon as my head hit the pillow.

The next morning after a quick breakfast we made our way to the Blue Herons' locker room. We were fortunate to have our own section of the locker room where we could suit up; often we had to get dressed on the bus. Once we were ready, we headed to the playing field. It was immaculate, with newly cropped grass, freshly raked dirt, and newly painted lines. Large shiny bleachers flanked both team's dugouts adjacent to the backstop, and the perimeter fencing was blindingly white.

Coach had started me, planning for Parker to relieve me by mid-game, if he wasn't needed sooner. He might be; after facing just two batters in the bottom of the first I had runners on second and third, then gave up three runs to a home run that arced high over Nicholas's head and the boundary fence. Determined to stanch the bleeding, I managed to strike out the next two batters and get the next to fly out to Heath in shallow right.

In the second inning, the first three Stallions struck out or flied out, and things didn't improve much from there. We didn't score our first run till the sixth inning, and only scraped out two more on errors. By the bottom of the eighth, Parker had long since relieved me on the pitcher's mound, and the Blue Herons were beating us 8 to 3. Short of a miracle, there was little chance we could pull off a win.

In the top of the ninth, I came up to bat with one out and runners on second and third, and quickly fell behind to a 2 and 0 count. The next pitch came in at my sweet spot—low and inside—and I swung for the fence. I heard the crack as the bat connected, and as my body muscled through the arc of the swing my eyes stayed on the ball, which was sailing high into right field. I shot from the plate, headed for first. The few fans that had driven from Boca Raton were on their feet, stomping and cheering, as was the rest of the team in the dugout.

The ball dropped just short of the fence. I had been robbed of a home run, but the hit should drive in two runs at least, and possibly three if I ran my ass off. As I rounded second and headed for third I saw Nicholas cross home plate, closely followed by Joshua. I also saw Coach behind the bag at third, signaling me home. I barreled around the base and dug in toward home. The roar of both sets of fans was now deafening, so I knew the ball was quickly approaching my path. I fell into a slide at the same time the catcher sturdily positioned himself to catch and tag me with the incoming ball. As we collided, I immediately felt a white-hot pain in my ankle and saw the ball spinning crazily in the dirt.

"Safe!" the umpire cried.

I was momentarily frozen from the pain in my ankle and a dull ache deep in my right hip, on which I'd slid. The cheering of the Stallions's fans was so intense it was all I could hear. By the time the dust settled I was rocking back and forth and moaning loudly. Then Coach and Parker were both kneeling at my side.

"Are you OK, Andrew?" they asked in unison.

Was I delirious, or was that genuine concern on Parker's face?

"I think I may have sprained my ankle. And my hip is killing me."

"Parker, since you've already batted, why don't you take Andrew back to the bus and get some ice on that ankle."

Without comment Parker lifted me, protecting my ankle with one hand, and carried me to the bus. I had the sudden impulse to throw my arms around his neck like some femme fatale, but I resisted. I could see the muscles twitching in his arms as he carried me. He smelled of mitt grease and sweat. When we reached the doors of the bus he set me down on my good foot, then helped me up the steps and down the aisle to one of the back seats. I took the one on the right with my back to the bus wall and my ankle laid out flat before me.

"Sit tight, Andrew, while I go find some ice and bandages."

I watched him run to the locker room and disappear inside. He was being so solicitous. And why was I lapping it up? Was my resolve weakening? It felt so comfortable to let him take care of me, and an inner voice urged, "Don't think about it too much." There was more din from the bleachers as I watched Parker emerge running from the locker room, and in a moment he was by my side once more.

"Is the game over yet?"

"No, after your run Heath walked and Dizzy homered, so it's gone into the bottom of the ninth. Now lay back and relax. I need to take your pants off to see how badly your hip is bruised." He could sense the hesitation in me, and laughed. "Honestly, Andrew. I know every inch of your body by heart, and it ain't anything I haven't seen before. Or had in me for that matter."

His crassness forced a laugh from me as I pushed my baseball trousers down to my knees, exposing my jock. But with my throbbing ankle, that was as far as I could reach.

"You'll need to finish the job."

He tenderly pulled my trousers over my knees and off, favoring my injured foot the whole way. He paused momentarily, staring at my cock-filled jock, then expertly wrapped my ankle with a bandage and applied some ice he had wrapped in a towel to my hip. As he stood up I met his eyes; the old hunger must have been plain on my face, for without warning he leaned into me and kissed me tenderly on the lips. I found myself returning the kiss fervently, my arms wrapped around his neck.

He started to pull away. "Andrew . . ."

I placed my fingers on his lips to stop his words, while at the same time placing his hand on my jock. He needed no further encouragement.

He whispered, "Raise up a little."

When I did he slipped my jock down over my thighs, releasing my stiffer to slap against my belly. He gaped at it.

"God, I swear it has gotten bigger since I last saw it!"

He pulled my jockstrap off carefully and spread my legs gingerly, taking care to place my ankle on the floor of the bus with the towel wrapped around it, then slid in between them. He licked my ball sac, pulling tenderly at the loose skin before taking each of the large orbs into his mouth and sucking on them softly. After letting the right one fall from his mouth, he ran his tongue up my thick shaft, tracing the blue veins and twirling the tip of it around the large cock head. He then worked his way back to the root of my dick, down over my balls, and began lapping at my taint. He was headed for my asshole, but I knew I couldn't lift my injured ankle to grant him access.

"Parker, I can't lift my leg."

He understood immediately, and licked his way back to the head of my cock. He engulfed the knob and slowly sank down my shaft. I moaned softly when he hit bottom. He rested a moment before sawing back to the top, then began a slow up-and-down rhythm, all the while grasping my nut sac in his left hand. I settled back against the bus seat as Parker sucked my dick. He was as good as I remembered, and very quickly I was shooting my spooge down his throat. He swallowed everything I gave him, then licked me clean, and put my jockstrap back on. After helping me with my pants, he slid onto the seat and elevated my foot across his lap. The ice felt good against my hip. We sat in silence, each absorbed in our own thoughts around what had just happened. Soon the players began filing onto the bus. I could tell by their somber expressions that we had not beaten the Blue Herons. I quickly learned that the game ended in a loss, with the Blue Herons beating us 9 to 8.

It was a long, painful drive back to Boca Raton that evening. Parker sat with me the whole time, elevating my leg every half hour, keeping me supplied with water, and feeding me aspirin when the pain got too great. I napped occasionally. When we arrived back at the boarding house late, Parker carried me inside and up to my room. I was silently impressed by the fact that he did not even break a sweat, even while taking the stairs sideways to shelter my ankle. He laid me on the bed, positioning my sore foot carefully, and moved toward the door.

"I've arranged for Kent to stay in my room while you recover. Coach confirmed it's only a bad sprain, so it should only take a few days to heal."

"Thanks for taking care of me, Parker."

For the next few days Parker catered to my every need, and was ceaselessly solicitous. It was as if the man I had bitterly broken up with no longer existed. I had not seen Nino since before my accident—he had not been at the game—and assumed he was away on business for his father. Parker got me a pair of crutches from the general store in town so I could go watch the team practice each day. On that Wednesday I watched the Stallions defeat the White Sox 6 to 4, and we scored another win on Thursday. The team also returned triumphantly on Sunday from the away games. It was torture not to be able to play, but by the middle of the following week my sprain had healed enough that I could get around without any help from Parker or the crutches. We had just returned to my room after dinner when Mrs. Jenkins knocked on the door. Mail had been delivered for me, but I had missed it on the hall table. It consisted of two letters: one from my parents and one from Nelson. I put the letters on the table between the bed, hoping they wouldn't pique Parker's interest. But of course they did.

"Who from?"

I knew there was no use lying to him, so I told him the truth. When he heard Nelson's name he made a valiant effort to hide his disdain but couldn't quite pull it off. I remained silent, waiting for him to further broach the subject.

"I know that Nelson and I did not get along in the past."

"That's an understatement, Parker. You both hated each other, and you came to blows the night of our breakup."

He sat staring into space for a bit, trying to form a response.

"It was because I was jealous of the relationship you two had. He was always around whenever I wanted you to myself."

"Best friends have a way of doing that, Parker."

As we sat in silence, there was a second knock on the door. When I answered, "Come in," the door opened and Nino stepped into the room. His eyebrows raised when he saw Parker sitting on the bed next to me, but other than that he didn't make any untoward moves. However, the two men stared so intently at one another, it was as if they had met before. I was the first to break the awkward silence.

"Nino, this is Parker Williams. He's a pitcher for the team. Parker, this is Nino Sabatini. His father has an interest in baseball."

That last bit sounded lame even to me. The two men eyed each other warily, as though they were adversarial predators meeting on a jungle path. Finally, Nino stuck out his hand.

"Pleased to meet you, Parker."

"Likewise."

Parker turned to me.

"Andrew, I'm going to see what the rest of the team is up to."

He excused himself and left the room. Nino came and sat next to me on the bed. I told him about my injury and how I was mostly healed; he kissed me on the cheek and wrapped me in his arms. I was anxious to open the letters and when I kept glancing at the table, Nino laughed, leaned over, grabbed the letters, and handed them to me.

"Don't let me keep you from your mail," he said, smiling.

I laughed and kissed his cheek, then opened the letter from my parents first. In it they wished me well and congratulated me on the many wins the Stallions had racked up. Knowing they would never travel to see any of my games, I had been sending them articles from local papers whenever I could. The rest of the letter brought me up to speed with farm matters, happenings in Miller Falls, and the comings and goings of the extended Duggan family. They signed off with their love. Nelson's letter held big news: He was coming for a visit soon. I excitedly gushed to Nino all about my lifelong friend.

"I look forward to meeting him."

I placed the letters back on the table and Nino took me into his arms once more.

"Were you out of town again on business?"

"Yes. If I didn't know better I would think my father was deliberately trying to keep me away from you. I've never been on so many business trips."

I lay back with Nino against me. Several minutes had passed when I heard a commotion down the hall. I gave Nino a puzzled look, scrambled out of his arms and off the bed, and rushed to open the door.

Someone was shouting, "Fire, fire—the headquarters is on fire!"

CHAPTER EIGHT

Nino and I ran into the hall, down the stairs, and onto the front porch, me still slightly favoring my injured ankle. The night sky was lit with flames shooting from the building. Other members of the team, including Coach, were already there; they had run the garden hose from the house and Joshua was spraying water onto the burning headquarters. The rest of them were carrying buckets of water up from the pond, with Parker the first in line. As Nino and I approached the conflagration, an intense wall of heat pushed against us. The back half of the building that contained the showers and the offices was completely engulfed in flames, most likely a total loss.

As I stood there I heard the clanging of the fire bell. Out of the night the fire engine came careening down the road, quickly followed by a group of men from the town. The men immediately joined the bucket brigade, as did Nino and I, while the firemen began spraying the flames. When they had exhausted their supply of water they refilled at the pond. After many touch-and-go hours, during which we were joined by Mr. Stanley and Mr. Hughes, the fire was finally out. We were all covered in soot and ashes, and completely exhausted. No one spoke after the fire engine and the townspeople had left; we simply sat on the soaked grass, staring at the destruction before us. Nino's presence wasn't even challenged. Mr. Stanley finally stood up and turned to address everyone.

"Boys, you best clean up and get some sleep. Practice is cancelled tomorrow while we assess the damage."

No one spoke as we shuffled to the showers behind the house and stripped out of our clothes. Because there were so few showerheads, Nino shared mine; the freezing water did not even make an impact. When we went inside, Mrs. Jenkins fed us cold ham sandwiches, hard-boiled eggs, and peach pie. We all ate ravenously, then crawled upstairs to our rooms. I flopped on my bed and quickly fell asleep with Nino beside me. When I woke in the morning, he was gone.

After breakfast we gathered at the ruined building. We learned from Coach that the fire had destroyed almost everything: the showers; the offices of Coach, Mr. Stanley, and Mr. Hughes; the laundry room; and the exercise room. The lockers themselves were still intact and usable, due in large part to the efforts of the firemen and the volunteers from town. However, all the uniforms inside the lockers themselves had received smoke and water damage and would need to be sent to the cleaners in town. We spent that day sifting through the wreckage, trying to salvage what equipment we could. Many volunteers from town came to help us. In the end, although we had lost most of the building, we still had enough equipment, our locker room, and the indomitable spirit of the Stallions to keep us going. Mere days after the fire we were back at practice, determined to put the tragedy behind us and continue our winning streak.

· · ·

As the season drew to a close, the Stallions continued to win. I continued to see both Parker and Nino, but my main attention was focused on Nino. I knew I was playing a dangerous game, one that I probably would get caught at, but I was too enmeshed in the drama to know how to extricate myself and having too much fun to care. Plus, I was having the best sex of my life. Now Nelson would be arriving after the playoff game, which raised another issue: how to tell him I was seeing Parker again.

Because of the fire we were now forced to use the ancient outdoor showers behind the house for all our bathing. They had been built back in the farm's heyday, when the fields had been full of migrant workers picking fruit and vegetables. Mrs. Jenkins's husband had installed them to allow the workers to cool off and clean up after a hard day's work. Since the fire Mrs. Jenkins had started placing a pile of towels and bars of coarse lye soap on the back porch to keep the shower traffic out of the house.

After the last practice before the playoffs I headed to the showers with the rest of the team. I stripped off my clothes, hanging them on one of the many wooden pegs, and walked to the first showerhead. I reached up and pulled the chain to enable the flow, then began working the pump handle vigorously. It was a laborious process, often leading some of the more impatient players to bathe in the pond. As the water began to flow out of the head, I stood under it and let the coldness numb my aching muscles. I had just lathered my upper chest and arms when Kent stepped underneath the shower next to mine. He primed the pump and jumped as I had done when a cold stream of water splashed onto his head. As he began to wash his body, he eagerly informed me that Joshua had told him there was going to be a party that afternoon in a nearby field. It had been a long, stressful season, and the team was looking to unwind a little before the playoff game tomorrow, an away game. Kent spoke in hushed tones, because although Coach was often lenient with the team regarding most of its antics, including drinking and whoring, he would frown on the fact that we were doing so the night before a big game. But the players were being true to their well-earned reputation for being rowdy. And what Coach didn't know wouldn't hurt him.

When we had finished our showers, we wrapped our towels around our waists and headed to our room. On the way we ran into Parker, who also had heard about the party and offered to drive us there. After we all were dressed, we left the house. As we drove to the party location, Parker grabbed my hand and held it tight. It reminded me of the early days of our relationship, when we were still wrapped up in the joy of discovering each other. Kent pretended not to notice. We turned onto a dirt road and then took an immediate right into a grassy meadow that was ringed by large maples. These trees masked us from any casual observers.

There was a large group of men standing around a fire pit. All the players were there, as well as Michael, but there were also a half-dozen men I did not recognize, so I assumed they were locals. As we joined them music was blaring from radios in several trucks, all tuned to one of only three available country and western stations in the area. Several clear bottles were being passed around, which proved to be corn liquor. Several wooden chests contained ice-cold bottles of beer. Much of the talk revolved around the game the next day, which would decide the two teams that played the final game next week. As daylight faded and the slight chill of a Boca Raton summer night set in, the large pile of wood within the circle of stones was lit. Soon the blaze was sending its warmth out several feet.

I was staring idly into the fire, the beer and liquor I had drunk starting to have the dulling effect I longed for. I was thinking about the next time I'd be with Nino and what to do about Parker when I was bumped purposefully in the shoulder. I turned to my right to find Parker standing next to me. He flashed his dazzling smile and all my worries seemed to melt away. And as always, that familiar fire began stirring in my loins. Why was I so susceptible to this man's charm? Was I driven purely by good looks and a big dick?

"A penny for your thoughts, handsome," he purred into my ear, and I felt the hair stand up on my arms and a tingle run through my entire body.

"I'm just thinking about the game tomorrow against the Barracudas. If we win, we will be up against the Panthers in a week for the title. The Stallions have not been this successful in so long—there's a lot riding on us."

"Don't worry, Andrew. I have a good feeling about tomorrow. We have a great team, with two great pitchers." He grinned. "We are going to knock them dead."

He put his arm around my shoulder and hugged me to him.

"Also, Parker, I can't get the fire out of my mind. Coach thinks it was set deliberately because he saw someone down by the building just before it caught fire. But why would anyone want to burn down the Stallions's headquarters? It just doesn't make sense. Unless they didn't want us to finish the season. Would someone go to those lengths to keep us from playing?"

I looked into his face for reassurance that my fears were unfounded. Was it my imagination, or was there a tensing of his features at my words and was his mouth a little too tight as it formed his smile of reassurance?

"Calm down, Andrew. Your wild imagination is getting the best of you. To be honest, I think the fire was simply an accident. That building is pretty old, and it may have just been a case of worn wiring. But, it's over and done with, and there's nothing we can do about it now. The field is still intact, all our uniforms and much of our equipment survived intact, and tomorrow's game will go on as planned. Don't worry any more about it. Just relax tonight and have a good time. Here, take a swig of this."

"What is it?"

"Just some special liquor I stole from my Daddy before I left for Florida. It's some of his best stuff. Much better than the swill they're passing around here. I've been saving it for an occasion like this."

I grabbed the bottle and took a long pull from it. It burned all the way down to my stomach. I wiped my mouth on my sleeve and handed it back.

"Thanks."

"Remember how we used to steal a bottle from my Daddy, sneak up to the hayloft, and stay up there for hours while you had your way with me?"

I laughed as he finished speaking. "As I remember it, Parker, you were the one who always had his way with me."

"Andrew, I know I made mistakes; hell, we both did. But things haven't been the same since we broke up. I haven't felt the same, and I sure as hell have missed you. I know we've drawn closer together since that day on the bus, and we've been hanging out more, and it just feels right. And, well, I'd like to give us another chance at a full-fledged relationship. I'm hoping you feel the same way."

At his words my heart pounded in my chest, while the rest of my body seemed to freeze in place. I had been expecting, anticipating, hoping to hear these words again. But a piece of me, a stubborn piece I was not completely proud of, wouldn't let me give up just yet.

"How can I believe you, Parker? Yes, things have been good between us, but so were they when we first met. And we both know how quickly things went downhill. When we met again at the recruitment in Miller Falls you had the chance to speak to me but you didn't. What has changed recently?"

"I know. I'm sorry. The signup for the tryouts was the first time I had seen you since we broke up, so it was hard for me, and having to see you with Nelson made it all the worse. I've come to realize the last few weeks how much I love you, how good you are for me, and how much I want to spend the rest of my life with you. I'm sorry for my actions in the past."

He sounded sincere, but I struggled to know if I really believed him. "Can I have some time to think about this, Parker?"

"Of course you can, Andrew."

I took another long pull from the bottle and was suddenly struck by the chill of the night. Parker saw me shiver, and opened his coat and wrapped it around me from behind, then hugged me tight. I instantly felt the warmth of his body, with all its familiar smells: his cologne, his sweat, and the unmistakable scent of male. I loved the feel of his strong arms, and I gently stroked the hair covering them. The feel of his hardness against my backside was comforting, assuring me that he was still physically attracted to me.

As I continued to drink the corn liquor, its effects seemed to increase tenfold. I thought I had learned to hold my liquor, but my legs and arms were beginning to feel very tired. Parker reached around me and began stroking my crotch. Despite the effects of the liquor, my cock was already half hard. Parker stroked it through the fabric of my jeans, quickly bringing it to its full hardness. I rubbed my ass back against his crotch, and he pressed his prick firmly into me. He reached higher and unbuttoned my shirt, then ran his hands through the thick hair of my chest before pinching my teats till they ached.

"Let's go to my truck."

I didn't need to be asked twice; I was swept up in his urgency as well as my own. We walked to his truck and he opened the passenger door. He sat on the edge of the seat, facing me, his legs spread wide, and pulled me in between them. He kissed me deeply and passionately, and I returned his kisses just as ardently. He pulled my shirt out of my waistband and pulled it open, exposing my chest. He bobbed his head and took my right nipple into his mouth, biting and sucking on it gently. I began moaning softly, and pushed his mouth down onto my teat. As he moved to the left teat his hands traveled all over my body, touching and squeezing my most secret, sensitive areas. Even as my relationship with Parker had gone bad, the sex had always been fantastic. He knew every inch of my body and was a strong and powerful lover. Images from our past sexual trysts flashed through my mind, heightening my arousal. His lips then sought mine again and his tongue was suddenly inside my mouth, exploring.

When he withdrew his tongue he licked down my stomach to my belt buckle. He loosened my belt and slowly undid the buttons on my jeans. All thoughts of previous issues with Parker had completely dropped from my mind. He pulled my pants down to my ankles and my briefs quickly followed. My cock throbbed in the cool night air. Parker pulled me to him again, his tongue once more sliding between my lips and exploring my mouth. My prick pressed against his, still covered in a layer of denim. He began rubbing his against mine, causing me to writhe in his grasp.

"Let's get you up on the seat."

Without further ado Parker slid off the set, grabbed me at the waist, turned me around, and lifted me to the spot he had just vacated. Beginning at my ankles, he licked up the entire length of my right leg, skipped over my crotch, and began working his way down my left. When he reached my left boot he unlaced it, slid it off along with my sock, and began sucking my toes. He took the right boot and sock off next and did the same. He worked his way back up to my crotch and pushed me flat onto my back. He laid my dick flat against my stomach and began working my ball sac. He licked both nuts, then took both of them into his mouth and rolled them around, savoring their flavor, then released them and began lapping at my bag once more. He let up from my balls and licked the shaft of my cock, up and down, ignoring the head each time. On his next swipe he engulfed the crown and simply held it in his mouth, breathing loudly through his nose. He held my cock head a moment longer, then swiftly engulfed my prick.

When he reached the root he sawed back to the top, then began rapid up-and-down movements. I gripped his shoulders to keep from sliding on the seat as Parker bobbed up and down on my stiffer. His mouth was warm and wet, and I knew it wouldn't be long before I came. I felt him slide a finger in next to my cock, withdraw it, and begin probing the crack of my ass with it. I lifted my ass off the seat far enough to grant him access. Once he had found the opening, he paused only a moment, then slid in deep. He struck the muscle deep inside me, which swelled from his ministrations; then he began thrusting in and out. Before too long I was on the edge of my release, and Parker knew it also (as he always did), for he plunged his finger in one last time, held it deep inside me, and froze on my dick, sucking for all he was worth.

"Here it comes," I cried as the first spurt shot from my stiffer.

Parker held me at the waist and took everything I had to offer. When I was spent he licked my cock clean and held it in his mouth till I was soft once more. He pulled me off the bench seat till my feet hit the ground, and then whirled me around and bent me back over it. A cool breeze blew gently across my ass. Parker spread my ass cheeks and I felt his tongue dart in between them. I moaned uncontrollably, and pressed my dick against the seat. Although Parker knew how much this turned me on, he had often been reluctant to perform this act on me while we were together. But there was no stopping him now as he swathed my crack, then paused to flick the tip of his tongue over the puckered opening.

After several minutes of eating my ass, Parker withdrew his face and I felt a cool unguent being liberally applied to my hole. This was followed by a fat finger sliding inside me to grease the interior as well. I braced myself across the seat as I felt the head of his cock press against my cornhole. He pushed firmly and, after the usual initial resistance, the fat head popped through the ring of flesh. He didn't hesitate but slid slowly, inexorably inside me. His prick was enormous, but it was the perfect fit I remembered, and he sank all the way in. Parker kissed the back of my neck, then grabbed me at the waist and began pounding my ass. His strokes were full and deep, and I held on to the edge of the seat as he plowed into me. As always, his stamina was impressive, and it was a good twenty minutes before he began to display the telltale signs of his approaching explosion. He sank into me a final time and sprawled heavily on my back as he filled me with his seed.

When he was done, he stayed inside me till he began to soften, then slowly pulled out of me. He turned me around and kissed me deeply once more. He then switched places with me on the bench seat, his pants still at his ankles, and pulled me into the warmth and comfort of his body. He retrieved the whiskey bottle from the floor of the truck and handed it to me. I took several long swallows, again feeling the liquid burn its way down my gullet to my stomach. I gave him the bottle and stepped back into his arms. I again felt the tiredness of before; my vision began to blur and I felt as if I was going to faint.

"Something's happening to me, Parker. I don't feel very good."

"Hold onto me, Andrew."

My voice sounded far away and slurred in my ears. I looked into Parker's eyes and only saw concern there. Or was there something more? I bent down to pull up my jeans, and saw the ground falling away beneath me, followed by complete darkness.

· · ·

The first time I awoke, shivering and naked, I faced a cold, gray dawn. I was lying at the bottom of a huge haystack. I quickly covered myself in as much of the hay as I could for warmth. I had no idea where I was or where my clothes were. I must have drifted off again, for when I opened my eyes a second time the sun was climbing in a bright blue sky. I was covered from head to toe in mud, and my head throbbed as if I had been kicked by a mule. I sat upright and rose slowly, on shaky limbs. It then struck me that I had missed today's game. The bus had left this morning.

I began shaking my arms and legs to work out the stiffness and get the blood fully flowing again. Because of my massive headache it was hard to remember the incidents from the night before. I looked around in a daze but did not see my clothes anywhere nearby. And there was nothing around that would hide any part of my nakedness. Not knowing what else to do, I sat covered in hay, my mind a jumble of thoughts. What had happened to Parker? And Kent? And the rest of the team? Why was no one looking for me? How had I wound up in a mound of hay?

As I was trying to decide what to do, I heard a vehicle slowly approaching. I peered out from underneath my hiding place and saw a truck. I could see the driver was male, but other than that I couldn't make out any other features. Not caring at this point who saw me in all my naked glory, I sprang up from the pile of hay and waved my arms to flag the driver down. The truck drove up next to the haystack and stopped. I gave a great sigh of relief when I saw Mr. Stanley step out of the truck. He stared at me with an alarmed expression on his face, then reached back into the truck and pulled a blanket from behind the seat. He came to me and wrapped the blanket around me.

"What the hell happened to you, Andrew?"

"I'm not sure, Mr. Stanley. We had a little get-together here last night, and I woke up still here this morning."

He stared at me with an odd expression on his face, then helped me to stand and led me back to his truck. Once he had deposited me on the passenger's side, he went around and got behind the wheel. He started up the truck, turned around, and headed out of the field, quickly approaching the main road. We drove past the town and headed back into the country once more. I didn't ask where we were headed, and at this point I didn't care. After a few more miles we turned onto a dirt road that was flanked by tall, shade-giving maples. After another mile or so, we approached a good-sized farmhouse. Adjacent to it were a small barn and a shed. Everything was in good condition, all fresh paint and newly mowed lawn. Mr. Stanley pulled around in the circular driveway and parked next to a screened-in front porch. White wicker furniture lined the porch itself, and all the railings were topped with flower boxes, each one filled with many colorful varieties I could not name.

"I don't need to tell you that you missed the playoff game yesterday, Andrew."

I turned to him in surprise.

"Yesterday? What day is today?"

"Today is Saturday, Andrew. Coach and Mr. Hughes were quite upset at your no-show, and concerned as well. They were of the mind that you had tired of baseball and had taken off with Nino Sabatini."

"Why would they think I skipped town with Nino?"

"On our way home after the game, several of the boys, including Parker, confessed to the party the other night, and said that you were there and that you drank quite a bit. Parker also said you left with Nino shortly after midnight. I've been looking for you in town all morning and figured I might as well check the party spot for any telltale signs of you. I'm glad to find you safe. Another good thing is that the Stallions won and will be in the final game next week."

While I was thrilled to hear of our win, I could not believe I had lost an entire day. What in the hell had happened the night of the party? Before I knew it, I began babbling to Mr. Stanley all about what had happened at the bonfire. I then proceeded to tell him of my relationship with Parker, both past and present, the preexisting rivalry between us as pitchers, my relationship

with Nelson, and the tumultuous fight that had ended everything.

Mr. Stanley listened quietly till I was done, then whistled in
amazement.

"Oh, to be young again. That's quite a tale, Andrew. And one
of the most convoluted ones I've heard in a long time. Well, this
is my house and you're welcome to stay the night. I can give you
a ride back to the boarding house tomorrow."

"I'm glad you came along when you did, Mr. Stanley."

"Please, for the time being, call me Richard."

We got out of the truck and I followed him up the porch
steps and onto the porch. He pulled open another screen door
and we entered a cool, dim kitchen. It was immaculate, and
smelled of pine.

"We need to get you in a hot bath before you catch your
death of cold, and get those bruises taken care of as well."

I stood there as if frozen in place till Mr. Stanley gently
pushed me out of the kitchen and up a wide staircase made of
dark wood. We turned left at the head of the stairs and entered
a good-sized bathroom. I hadn't had the presence of mind to
check myself for scrapes and cuts; the pounding in my head
and my chilled body had been my main concern. When we
entered the bathroom I let the blanket drop to the floor, suddenly bone-weary and too tired to even stand up. I would have
fallen had Mr. Stanley not reached out and grabbed my arm to
steady me.

He lowered the toilet lid and set me gently down upon it. He
then dropped to one knee and turned on the water in the tub.
He fussed with the hot and cold knobs for a bit, then leaned
back, seemingly satisfied. Soon steam filled the bathroom.
When the tub was three-quarters of the way full he turned the
water off, helped me to stand up, and told me to test the water
temperature. I dipped my hand in to find the water was almost

scalding hot, but I wanted in immediately. I placed one foot in the tub, swung my other in as well, steadying myself with Mr. Stanley's strong arms, then sank down beneath the water. I sat there motionless, the water rising to the level of my chest. I didn't have the strength to even wash my dirty, aching body.

A sudden movement out of the corner of my eye startled me; it was Mr. Stanley. Silently he grabbed a washcloth from a shelf above the toilet and dipped it in the water. He began washing me tenderly, starting with my face. The washcloth felt good on my skin, the dirt falling away as he scrubbed. He washed my face, then my neck and torso before dipping beneath the water's surface to cleanse my legs. Without warning his hand was in my crotch, rubbing vigorously. I was hard immediately, and without an invitation he gave my stiffer a few fast strokes with the washcloth before he tersely ordered me to flip over. I did as ordered and he washed my back and my ass, delving between the cheeks to scrub my hole, causing me to moan softly despite my aches.

When he was done, I stepped out onto the bath mat; he grabbed a large white towel and beginning drying me off. My cock was still at attention. He looked up at me and our eyes locked. I held my breath as he pushed me back once more onto the toilet; I spread my legs to give him full access to what he wanted. He wrapped his meaty fist around it and squeezed it several times.

"It looks like this needs my attention as well."

He gently stroked it, causing my balls to roll inside their pouch. I moaned softly and pushed back against the toilet seat lid. Clear fluid was beginning to leak from the slit in the head; he lapped it up gently, then swirled his tongue over the crown and down the thick shaft to my ball sac. He grabbed my bag in his right hand and pulled it to him, forcing the balls to knot at his mouth. He sucked the right one into his mouth and then the left before releasing them again. He then leaned into me and kissed me firmly on the mouth. I could taste my juices on his lips. He licked down my throat to my nipples. Both were swollen and pointing straight at him.

He sucked and bit each one, then licked his way down to my cock once more, engulfing the fat head and then sinking down its entire length. His mouth was warm, wet, and wonderful. He sucked me softly, then began vigorously sawing up and down, dragging his tongue across the knob on each upward stroke. I placed a hand on the top of his head, more to steady myself than to guide him. The bathroom was silent except for the sounds of his sucking and my soft moans and cries. I was getting close to coming, and he seemed to have sensed it, for he redoubled his efforts on my stiffer. After a few more bobs I cried out as my explosion overtook me. Gobs of cum erupted from my prick. He never hesitated, swallowing each drop with gusto. When I was done he released my dick with a wet popping noise and looked in my eyes.

I said, "Now it's your turn, Richard."

He stood up and I could see his prick outlined against the material of his pants. I undid the buttons and pulled his pants down over his thighs. His cock was fully hard, and his balls swayed slightly in their sac of skin. I grabbed his member in my right hand and held it tightly. It was hot and heavy to the touch; the by-now-familiar head the size of a plum. I spread his ass cheeks and probed his crack with an index finger. It was as hairy as the rest of him and filled with sweat. I opened wide and swallowed as much of his pole as I could in the first gulp. The smell of his crotch was strong. I slid back up from the midpoint and softly sucked the fat cock head. Richard moaned loudly and placed his hand on the top of my head. I grabbed his dick in my left hand and turned it sideways as if it were an ear of corn. Several thick blue veins pulsed along its shaft. I licked up and down the length of it, then turned it toward me once more. The rather large piss hole was leaking its early come, and I lapped up the salty juice eagerly.

When I looked up at him, his eyes were closed. He had removed his shirt, and his hairy stomach was rising and falling with his breathing. I grabbed his hefty ball sac in my left hand and swallowed his dick once again. When the enormous head hit the back of my throat, I stopped, willing my throat to relax, and the rest of it slid home. I lost track of time as my world revolved around this piece of meat in my mouth.

I released his nut sac to allow the large orbs to slap against my chin. The smell of his crotch was continuing to have an intoxicating effect on me. Suddenly, he began pumping his hips, driving his dick in and out of my mouth. I saw his balls roll up tight to the base of his massive cock, and knew his release was approaching. On my next stroke he cried out loudly and tightened his grip on my head as the first thick blob hit the back of my throat. More and more of the thick, ropy stuff spewed forth. When he was spent I released his prick and licked it clean. I stood up and he wrapped me in his arms and together we left the bathroom and went down the hall and into his bedroom. He lay me down on the bed and reclined beside me. Within minutes I was fast asleep.

• • •

When I awoke it was just growing dark outside. It took me a moment to remember where I was. Mr. Stanley was no longer beside me. I got out of bed, naked, and went downstairs to see where he was. When I reached the first floor I heard voices coming from one of the front rooms off the kitchen. Following the voices, I walked full on into a card game. There were four players at the round table: Coach, Mr. Stanley, Mr. Hughes, and another man I had never seen before. I guessed him to be about the same age as Coach. All four were drinking beer and smoking cigars. All were wearing only their underwear, except for Coach, who was completely naked. I realized this in the same instant that I remembered I was also naked. And surely they were furious at me for missing the game and would not want to see me. My immediate reaction was to go back upstairs, but my dick was trying to convince me it would be much more fun to remain. Before I could make a decision, Coach spotted me.

"Oh, Andrew! Don't run off," he said, rising from the table and coming to me. "I'm so glad you are OK. Allow me to introduce you to my companion, Albert."

"Greetings, Andrew," Albert said, extending his hand. "I've heard so much about you. And you have a lovely cock."

"Thanks, Albert."

"Now, Andrew," Coach began, "Mr. Stanley has filled us in on your whereabouts yesterday. My goodness, that's quite a tale. On behalf of the team, let me tell you I'm so glad you are OK. We waited for you yesterday morning, and searched the entire grounds. When you didn't show up, Parker said you must have lost track of time or had enough of baseball life. Then on the bus ride home the other players confessed to the party, and Parker said you left it with Nino Sabatini."

I looked at Coach for a minute before replying. Neither he nor Mr. Stanley had commented on the fact that I was supposedly at the party with Nino. I hadn't seen him in several days, so I sincerely doubted he was at the party. Or had I been that drunk? Something was not adding up here.

"I guess in all honesty I simply had too much to drink and wandered off from the group and passed out. When I woke up this morning I was sleeping in a stack of hay. I can usually hold my liquor, so I'm not sure what happened. My sincerest apologies for missing the game yesterday. Baseball is my life, and I would do nothing to jeopardize that, not for any man. You aren't going to kick me off the team, are you?"

"Well, you did break the rules about drinking before a game," Coach answered sternly, "but then, so did the rest of the team. But you alone missed the second most important game of the season. You are lucky that you are such a valuable member of the team and that you have done an outstanding job this season. I also know the rest of your teammates respect and care for you very much. Maybe I'm getting soft in my old age, or maybe it's just because I like you, but I voted to keep you on the team, and the managers agreed. It's good news for everyone, because we beat the Barracudas yesterday, so we face the Panthers next Saturday in the final matchup."

"Yes, Mr. Stanley already informed me we beat the Barracudas. Congratulations, Coach, that's great news! Rest assured, I'll be there!" All four men laughed at my remark.

"Well, I don't mean to interrupt. I'll let you get back to your card game."

"No worries, Andrew," said Coach. "Mr. Stanley has us over every Saturday night for a game of strip poker and then some. And since you're already naked, would you like to be the 'and then some?'"

Not knowing exactly what he meant, but not really caring, I readily agreed. I trailed Coach to the poker table.

All four men stood up and slid their chairs back from the table. Mr. Hughes, Mr. Stanley, and Albert removed their underwear and stepped to within a foot of the table, each man at an opposite point. I looked at Albert's cock first, as he was the unknown entity. His was as fully hard as the rest, but not as long. However, what he lacked in length he made up for in girth. It was good-sized, and would certainly stretch wide any asshole it entered.

"For your part in this, Andrew," Coach instructed me, "all that you need to do is climb up on the table and position yourself on your hands and knees. We'll do the rest."

I climbed up on the table and placed myself as Coach had directed. The table seemed a little loose, and I was startled when Coach gripped its edge and spun the entire top of it. When he stopped the top from spinning, I was facing Albert. I suddenly felt hands running lightly over my ass cheeks and, looking over my shoulder, saw Mr. Stanley sliding a finger up and down my hairy crack, then probing my shit hole. My own dick was as stiff as a board, but I was determined to keep my hands off it till the last man. Mr. Stanley paused and licked up and down my crack, running his tongue over my opening. He withdrew suddenly and spun me to the right. The same process was repeated with Coach. When he had lapped at my hole I was spun to Mr. Hughes, and then to Albert.

When I was whirled back to Mr. Stanley, he steadied the tabletop and I felt a cool, familiar substance being applied to my hole and all along the crack of my ass. This was followed by one of his fingers slipping inside me. When it was withdrawn I felt the head of his dick pressing against me for a moment; then it was in me all the way, with his balls slapping against me. This was all about Mr. Stanley, and a show for the rest of the guys standing around the table. He gripped me firmly at the hips as he hammered my ass. His lunges were full and deep, and the only sounds in the room were his thighs slapping against my ass cheeks and our collective moans. When he increased his thrusts even more I knew he was about to blow.

"Here it comes, Andrew!"

As I felt his cum flooding my hole, I used the muscles in my ass to milk him dry. Mr. Stanley collapsed on top of me and lay there till Coach hollered at him for holding up the game. He reluctantly pulled out of me, and spun me to Mr. Hughes. His approach was slow and gentle, his strokes long and deep. He was in no hurry, and I loved the feel of his cock inside me. Soon the rest of the men were jeering him, accusing him of hogging the goods. He didn't reply but simply kept up his steady pace. With no warning I felt my asshole being filled with his sweet stuff. When he was done he withdrew, kissed me softly on both ass cheeks, stepped back from the table, and spun me to Albert.

At this point there was no need to even use the glove grease; I had enough spooge inside me to allow him to enter me easily. After his first thrust I saw him grab something from the chair next to him and then I felt a strip of cool leather encircling my waist. I looked down to see that he had tied a belt there for an extra grip. As with the two previous men, Albert was no novice at pleasuring a man. His fat prick stretched me wide open. After sinking to the bottom, he paused a moment to allow me to feel his full girth, then pistoned in and out of me like a machine, his strokes full and deep, hitting the swollen muscle in my asshole each time. Waves of pleasure rippled through my body. I pushed back against him each time, forcing his cock in deep. His fingers dug into the flesh at my hips.

When he had shot inside of me, he quickly withdrew and spun me to Coach, who entered me as easily as Albert had done, sinking in to the hilt. He held his cock inside me, grinding the head against the well-stimulated muscle found there, then pulled out and began rapid in-and-out lunges. He gripped me by the hips and after only a few hammerings he spewed inside of me and lay across my back, drawing in deep lungfuls of air. When he pulled out of me he wiped the head of his dick on my ass cheeks and climbed off the table. He dried his face with his T-shirt and took a long pull on his beer.

"Now that was a wild ride indeed, gentlemen."

The four of them smiled their appreciation as I collapsed on top of the table. I was covered in sweat, my knees were shaking, and my asshole was plumb worn out. I could feel cum sliding down the back of my legs. Despite all this, I wanted more. Coach raised a bottle of beer to my lips and I drank half its contents in one gulp. When he pulled it away, I wiped my hand across my lips.

"Shall we go another round?" I smiled.

I could tell by the smiles and the expressions on their faces that they were thinking the same thing. But suddenly there was a furious pounding on the kitchen door. The four men exchanged anxious looks, and I was certain that whoever was calling at this hour was not expected. I climbed off the table while the four of them quickly dressed. Coach and Mr. Stanley exchanged worried looks.

Mr. Stanley went to answer a second, louder pounding, while Coach told me it would be best if I went back upstairs and stayed there till someone called me to come down. I left the dining room as if I were heading upstairs as he had asked, but instead I lingered in the hall leading to the stairs, tucked in the shadows. My mouth fell open when the door opened to reveal Giovanni, Lorenzo, Antonio, and Nino, plus three other men I had never seen before. The strangers were dressed in suits similar to the Sabatinis', so I guessed that they were somehow connected to the family business. And none of them seemed pleased to see all the company Mr. Stanley had.

CHAPTER NINE

Giovanni entered unbidden, followed by his sons and the three strangers. They filled the large kitchen, forcing Mr. Stanley to retreat to the poker table.

"Good evening, Mr. Stanley. Mr. Connors, Mr. Hughes." He ignored Albert completely. "We're sorry to bother you on this fine, fine evening, but I would like to have a word with you."

Although Giovanni's words were spoken in a friendly tone, there was an underlying threat to the whole situation. "The other one needs to get lost, and quick," Lorenzo barked.

A look was exchanged between Coach and Albert, and the man squeezed past Giovanni and through the doorway. When he had gone, the older man closed the door loudly behind him, then turned to face the three managers once more.

"Is there anyone else in the house?"

"No," Mr. Stanley immediately replied.

I don't know how he gave it away, whether it was his quick response or a look on his face that I couldn't see from where I stood, but I could tell by the way Giovanni scrutinized Mr. Stanley that he did not believe his response. He turned to his sons.

"Boys, check the house to make sure it's clean before we conduct our business here. If you find anyone, bring them to me."

The reality of my predicament hit me full force, and I turned to flee back upstairs. I had just made it to the top step when Nino appeared at the bottom of the landing and saw me. He quickly recovered from his surprise, and placed a finger on his lips, motioning me to keep silent. As if I needed to be told.

"I'll check the second floor," he said to one of his brothers who remained out of my line of sight. He motioned with his hand for me to continue my retreat as he began making his way up the stairs. I made it to Mr. Stanley's bedroom right as Nino reached the top of the stairs. I grabbed the clothing that Mr. Stanley had thoughtfully laid out for me. While I quickly dressed I could hear him making a pretense of checking the rest of the upstairs rooms. I sat on the bed and waited for him. Finally he came back to the bedroom and closed the door gently behind him. He sat down next to me on the bed. He had a sad look on his face, which was replaced with a smile as he took me into his arms and kissed me. He gave me several quick kisses, then pushed me to arm's length. A look of deep concern took over his features.

"What are you doing at Mr. Stanley's house?"

I could tell he was genuinely concerned about me, and slightly angry.

"What's the big deal, Nino? Mr. Stanley invited me over for a game of poker with some of his friends. A better question is, what is your family doing here? For the second time they are harassing Coach and the other two Stallions' managers. Over what? What is the connection, Nino? And have you been in town for the past several days?"

Nino didn't respond immediately, and I was suddenly quite sure that he was not going to tell me the truth about the situation unfolding in the kitchen and dining room below us. I began to get a bad feeling about the whole situation, a feeling that had been gnawing at me since the incident in the locker room. Nino startled me when he took my hands in his. Was his concern based on his fear for me? Would his family hurt me? Why did I so badly need this man in my life, dangerous or not?

"No, Andrew, I haven't been in town for the past few days. I've been away on business for my father. And please don't ask me any more questions about my family. I've told you all I can for the moment. It's best you don't know the rest of the story yet."

If Nino wasn't in town, he couldn't have been at the party and lured me away. So Parker had lied about that. But why?

"Nino, if it affects you, then it affects me. For the second time I'm asking, please tell me what is going on. I don't want my suspicions about your family to include you as well. Are the Sabatinis gangsters?"

I could tell by the hurt in his eyes that I had hit upon the truth. I felt like I had been punched in the stomach. He sensed my reaction.

"Andrew, please let me explain."

"Nino, did you get lost up there?"

It was Giovanni, and he sounded like he was at the bottom of the stairs.

"No, Pop, just being thorough. I'm coming down."

"Andrew, I have to go or you will be discovered. I still would like to explain what is going on here, but it will need to wait. I'll come and see you in a few days if I can, or sooner. Now, I need you to hide under the bed in case one of my brothers decides to double-check my work."

He kissed me good-bye and waited while I slid under the bed. Then he left the room, closing the door behind him. The house was preternaturally quiet, then from downstairs I heard several voices raised in anger, what sounded like blows being exchanged, and furniture being thrown about. This went on for several minutes, then silence reigned once more, only to be broken by the slamming of the kitchen door and the sounds of engines revving to life. I waited till everything was quiet, then waited another stretch of time before sliding out from under the bed and creeping downstairs.

Coach, Mr. Hughes, and Mr. Stanley were sitting at the table, or what was left of the table. It looked like something large and heavy had landed on top of it, and by the looks of them I was guessing it was one of their bodies. Three of the four chairs were smashed beyond use. And it looked like the fight had spilled over into the living room. Several lamps had been smashed, and the evening breeze was coming in through a window that had been relieved of its glass. Coach had a bloodied lip and the knuckles of his right hand were also torn and bleeding. Mr. Stanley was holding a raw steak to his eye. Mr. Hughes had a large purple lump on his right cheek.

"What the hell happened here?"

"Nothing for you to worry about, Andrew," Coach replied, apparently speaking for the group. "Mr. Sabatini and his sons are trying to push the three of us around, and we're pushing back, and they don't like that. No one goes against the wishes of the Sabatini family."

The room was silent in its destruction. Coach abruptly stood up.

"Well, I'll see you tomorrow, Richard. You too, Jonathan. Goodbye, Andrew."

Mr. Hughes said goodbye as well. Mr. Stanley and I followed them to the door, and I pursued Coach all the way to his truck, leaving Mr. Stanley standing mute in the doorway. As Mr. Hughes drove away, I stepped in front of Coach's truck door, blocking his entry.

"You've got to tell me what's going on. I'm involved with Nino Sabatini, so if there is something I need to know about him or his family, please tell me."

I saw anger rise quickly in Coach's eyes.

"You stay away from that good-for-nothing bum, Andrew. He's bad news, just like the rest of his family, and he will bring you nothing but trouble. You deserve better than Nino. You and Parker have a bright future in baseball; stick with him and dump that no-good Nino. Now, please go back inside and I will see you tomorrow."

With that he moved me out of his way, got into his truck, and drove off. I followed Mr. Stanley back inside but did not bother speaking to him since I was positive he would tell me nothing. I went upstairs and took a nice long, hot shower. When I came back downstairs Mr. Stanley was standing in the kitchen, waiting for me. Some of the vestiges of this evening's earlier destruction had been cleared away. He held his arms out to me and I stepped into them and he hugged me deeply.

"Please realize, Andrew, that we care very much about you. We are not telling you what's going on here for your own good. And it's probably best that I take you home tonight."

"Okay, Richard."

We left the house, climbed into his truck, and drove in silence down the winding roads till we were turning into Mrs. Jenkins's driveway.

"Thanks again for coming to my rescue this afternoon," I told him. "I don't know what I would have done without you. But I have to ask a final time: Won't you please tell me what's going on with you, Coach, Mr. Hughes, and the Sabatini family? I'm not just being nosy; I sincerely would like to help the three of you."

He stared at me as if he wanted desperately to tell me the truth, but fear was holding him back.

"If I thought you could help, Andrew, believe me, I would enlist your aid. Now I have no right to ask this of you, but I must echo Coach's sentiments again: Please stay away from Nino Sabatini. He will bring you nothing but trouble."

"I know, Richard. But what man won't?"

I kissed him on the cheek and hopped out of the truck. He waited till I'd made it safely inside before driving away. The house was quiet when I entered. I went upstairs, hoping to find my room empty and avoid an uncomfortable discussion with Kent. Thankfully, it was. I quickly undressed and crawled beneath the covers. I pushed away all thoughts, seeking solace in a good night's sleep.

· · ·

I slept straight through the night, waking to find Kent sitting on the edge of his bed, his concern evident on his handsome features.

"Where the heck have you been? No one has seen you since the night of the party. We all figured some local hunk showed up at the party, swept you off your feet with his charm and big dick, and you were now a farmer's wife. Parker finally told us you left with Nino."

"Very funny, Kent. Have you seen the farmers in this area?"

I quickly gave Kent a shortened version of yesterday's events, withholding from him the incident at Mr. Stanley's house with the Sabatinis. However, I did give him every juicy detail of the game I had played with Albert and the three managers. When I was done, he let out a long, low whistle.

"Man, you'd best stay away from that corn liquor. But it sounds like the fun you had last night sort of made up for it."

Just then there was a knock on the door and Parker entered. He came to the bed; I stood up and he embraced me.

"Andrew, I'm so glad you're OK. I was so worried about you. I've seen you drink before, and you can always hold your alcohol. But you were soused that night and determined to leave with that Sabatini fellow. I tried to stop you, but you were adamant."

I steeled myself after hearing what I knew to be a lie. Parker was up to something, and I needed to find out what it was. Till then it was crucial to not arouse his suspicions.

"Thanks for trying, Parker. I'm not sure what I was thinking. I couldn't have gone very far with Nino, because I woke up at the party site. Unless he dropped me back off there later. It's funny, though, that no one saw me. Oh well, I'm still alive and the Stallions are in the final game!"

Parker waited while Kent and I got dressed; then the three of us headed downstairs for breakfast. The usually quiet affair was boisterous that morning due to the glee over the big win, plenty of ribbing of me for my embarrassing drunken antics, and relief that I was back safe and sound. No one held any animosity toward me for missing the game, especially since they'd won. When breakfast was over, we headed to the field for practice. After going through the litany of exercises, we played several practice games, then stopped early. We hit the showers and then I went to my room.

I read my latest pulp novel by the window, sipping a cold bottle of soda I had taken from the kitchen and watching the world float by outside. It was a beautiful summer afternoon, the sky a pale blue interspersed with a few clouds. The scent of fresh-cut grass wafted past the thin curtains with the breeze. In this tranquil state I went over the events of the past two days for the umpteenth time. What had really happened the night at the bonfire? Why was Parker lying about Nino? When was Nino going to tell me the truth about his family? Would Nino be coming to see me?

I chastised myself. What was I doing with this potential bad boy? I had still been trying to sort out my feelings for Parker when Nino had entered the picture, and now he was proving to be a bigger complication than Parker. From a bad-tempered sot to a gangster's son—I sure could pick them. I had never been a believer in love at first sight, but ever since our first brief meeting, I had found myself longing for Nino during his frequent absences. His dashing good looks and rakish air and—truth be told—the element of danger were immensely appealing. He was like no one I had ever known or would ever know in Miller Falls.

My train of thought was abruptly cut off by the familiar roar of an engine and quick shifting of gears; the flashy red car pulled into the driveway and stopped in front of the house as a small cloud of dust rose and then settled. Nino was sitting behind the steering wheel, and my heart swelled at the sight of him. He opened the driver's door and stepped out. He was dressed in yet another suit of the latest fashion, this one a light gray, with a jaunty white kerchief in his breast pocket and bright white spats adorning his shoes. He literally ran up the walk to the front door in evident excitement to see me.

I heard his loud knocking, followed by several seconds of silence, and then more knocking, this time even louder. A few moments later I heard Mrs. Jenkins speaking, but I couldn't quite make out what she was saying. A short exchange took place, and then I heard footsteps on the stairs, followed by pounding on the door to my room. I counted to ten, so as not to appear too eager to see him, then slowly walked to the door and opened it.

Nino stood there, as dashing and as handsome as when I had last seen him at Mr. Stanley's house. As always, his white teeth flashed in a mischievous grin as he stepped into my room. I closed the door quickly behind him.

"Boy, that's some watchdog you have downstairs. I didn't think she was going to let me in. Usually I'm lucky enough to miss her."

When I realized he was talking about Mrs. Jenkins I couldn't help but laugh, even though I was still miffed at Nino for what had happened at Mr. Stanley's. Not waiting for a response, he grabbed me by the waist and pulled me roughly to him. He kissed me long and deep, then his tongue slid into my mouth, though my own tongue did not rise quickly to meet it. I could feel his stiffer swell beneath the fabric of his pants, and he pressed it insistently against my thigh. The smell of his aftershave combined with his raw animalness filled the air. When he realized that I was not returning his affection as ardently, he stepped back from me.

"What's wrong, Andrew?"

"It's your family, Nino, and what happened at Mr. Stanley's last night."

He was silent for a moment, but the anxious look on his face made me even more worried than I had been.

"Andrew, I do want to tell you everything, and I will, in good time. I am trying very hard right now to make a break from my family, as I've never felt I belonged with them and I want a different life than the one they have laid out for me."

He paused a moment, then began pacing the room.

"There are some things I have to take care of before I can talk to you about this. But I promise, I will tell you everything. Please trust me a little while longer."

I could not doubt the sincerity in his voice, and it was at that moment that my choice was made for me. I wanted to be with Nino, not Parker. I was only clinging to Parker because it had been so comfortable to be with him again. I stepped closer to Nino and he took me into his arms once more. I began rubbing his cock vigorously, and he began humping against my hand in his lust. He pushed me backward onto the bed and lay full-length atop me. Moments passed and I began to think he was asleep because all I could detect was the slow rise and fall of his chest. He suddenly rose up and looked me in the eyes. There was an intense emotion reflected there that scared but at the same time delighted me. My thoughts swirled.

I began undoing the buttons on his shirt, revealing the dark forest of hair beneath. I reached in and began stroking his nipples. He moaned softly in response and ran his finger lightly up and down my right cheek. Suddenly, he pushed my hand away, rolled off me, and stood beside the bed.

"Let's save this for the picnic."

"What picnic, and where?"

"I have everything we need in the car. There is a good-sized lake several miles outside town. It's very private, so no one will bother us. I want to make it up to you for all the time I've been gone."

"Is that where you take all your lovers?" I grinned.

He smiled back but did not reply. Once we were in the car, I idly watched the scenery roll by as Nino expertly worked the gears. A moment later I felt Nino's hand on mine. After almost an hour of driving, we started to climb into some low hills. Lazy white clouds spotted the sky, casting shadows on the ground, and a lone hawk make slow circles against them. We turned off the main road onto a dirt lane lined by tall spruce trees. After descending a gentle incline, we saw before us a deep-blue lake, dazzling in its reflective beauty. Nino pulled the car under a copse of pines and we got out. The warm summer afternoon was intoxicating. Nino opened the trunk and removed a checkered blanket. He carried it to the grassy bank of the lake and spread it beneath a tall pine.

"Have a seat, Andrew, while I unload the rest of the things from the trunk. It will only take a minute."

He returned with a large wicker picnic basket and a small ice chest made of wood. He set them down on the blanket and began removing items from the basket. There were china plates, silver utensils, sandwiches wrapped in wax paper, cold fried chicken, a jar of pickles, hard-boiled eggs, a foot-long length of salami, a wedge of cheese, and an apple pie. From the chest he pulled a large bottle of champagne and several dark bottles of beer. Finally he drew out a small, flat-bottomed crystal vase with a single red rose in it. This he placed in the center of the blanket.

"I'm impressed by your culinary efforts, Nino. This is quite a spread."

He stared at me sheepishly a moment before replying.

"I had some help from my mama. And this is her china and silverware from the house in town. She was adamant that I make a good impression on you. She lives in our main house in New York City but is in town for a quick visit. I told her about you and she is very excited for me. She has been secretly hoping that I would get out from under my papa's thumb and the family business. She told me this morning, when I picked up the basket and ice chest, that she had a good feeling about us. I do too," he finished, softly.

I smiled as I listened to Nino continue to expound upon the virtues of his mother, while he began uncovering and unwrapping the dishes she had prepared. He grabbed the salami and looked up at me with a twinkle in his eyes.

"I want to see you naked," he said, almost breathlessly.

I stood up, pulled my shirt over my head, and undid my pants. I reached down, undid the laces of my shoes, and kicked them off. I shrugged my pants and my briefs down to my ankles and stepped out of them.

"Leave your socks on, Andrew, and get on all fours."

When I was on my hands and knees on the blanket, he slowly unwrapped the salami and lay beside me. He grabbed it in both hands and lifted it to his mouth, slowly engulfing several inches of its length. I was instantly hard as I watched him. He let the salami pop from his mouth and began rubbing it around and over my lips. I opened my mouth and he slid it inside a good five inches, then began pushing it in and out of my mouth. It was cold on my tongue.

"Would you like to pretend this is me and have it in your ass?" he whispered.

"Yes, Nino," was my immediate response.

He crawled around behind me and told me to stay on my hands and knees. I watched over my shoulder as he produced a tin of grease from the basket and applied it liberally to my sweet spot, inserting two of his fingers to lubricate me inside as well. I then felt the cold head of the salami push against me. I winced in shock and pleasure.

"Sorry, how about warming that up a little bit more?" He crawled around till he faced me, again holding the salami out to me. "Open your mouth," he whispered.

I opened my mouth and he slowly slid the salami inside. I held it in my mouth, sucking on it, feeling its coldness seep into my mouth. After I had held it for a few minutes, Nino withdrew it and returned to my asshole. Once again I felt the thick end against my opening, but this time it was warm. As Nino pushed against me I pushed back, wanting this gargantuan slab of actual meat inside me. After much maneuvering the end popped through. Without stopping Nino slid half the salami's length into me till it was deep in my guts. The feeling was incredible. He pushed it in and out slowly, then paused a moment. I turned around to see him shedding his own clothing. He warmed the other end with his mouth for a good five minutes, and then knelt behind me, butt to butt, and greased up his own hole. I knew what was coming, and the thought was crazy. Nino placed the other end of the salami against his asshole.

"Push back against me, Andrew."

I did. I felt some pressure, then suddenly Nino's ass was pressed against mine, and I heard a low "Oh my gosh" escape from his lips. He remained still a moment, then rocked back against me, pulling the salami out of me and back into him. We began rocking back and forth, driving the salami deep each time. I could hear Nino's grunts when it was his turn to receive the stick.

While the real meat dick slid into me again, I spit into my hand, coated my stiffer, and began stroking myself. After several minutes of being penetrated and working my cock I shot my load onto the blanket. When I was done I pushed back against Nino with all my might, driving the salami deep inside him. He cried out long and low, and turning my head I saw his hand moving swiftly on his prick. When he had dumped his seed as well, Nino reached around behind him and pulled the piece of meat from his ass, and then mine. It exited with a loud suction, and my ass seemed to thank me for the relief as it eagerly retook its former shape.

"That was loads of fun, Andrew."

Without waiting for a response he pulled a bottle of cold beer from the ice chest, popped the top on his belt buckle, and handed it to me. When we had quenched our thirst, we began devouring the feast that Nino had brought. When we had eaten everything in sight, except for the salami we had pleasured ourselves with, we lay side by side in the cool grass and dozed for a bit. I awoke to find Nino staring at me intently, a smile playing about his lips.

He tenderly pulled me close, then flipped me on my back. He got on his hands and knees and positioned himself above me, facing my feet. His swollen member was poised above my mouth; his balls rested on the bridge of my nose. I gripped him at the hips and pulled his ass down and back toward me, placing the crack directly in my face. I parted his cheeks, exposing his hair-filled split, at the center of which was his spot. I wet my thumb and pressed it firmly against Nino's hole. He squirmed above me, pushing his ass back into my thumb. His cries were soon muffled as he filled his mouth with my stiffer. After several minutes of working his hole with my tongue, I opened my mouth and slowly engulfed his dick. He began slowly thrusting his stiffer in and out of my mouth, while I did the same to his mouth. After several minutes he began thrusting a little harder, and his moans increased. He suddenly withdrew my cock from his mouth.

"I'm going to shoot, Andrew."

He slid his dick out of my mouth till just the fat head was encircled by my lips, then let loose with a barrage of spooge. As I felt the stuff slide down my throat, I swallowed as quickly as I could. Nino took my prick back into his mouth right before my own torrent began shooting into it. When we were both spent he rolled off me and we lay on our backs, our stomachs rising and falling heavily from our exertions.

"Are you sure you want to know about the Sabatini family?" he asked out of the blue. "Once you do, there's no turning back."

"If we are to have any type of long-term relationship, Nino, we have to discuss it."

He held my hand, and I could see tears forming in his eyes.

"We've never talked about anything long-term, Andrew. Is that what you want?"

"I do, Nino."

He kissed me long and hard then raised up on one elbow.

"It's true that my family operates outside the law. To what extent, I honestly don't know. My mother has tried to keep me out of my father's clutches for years now. She sees something different in me than she sees in my brothers. She sent me to boarding school and then to college, but Pop insisted I come to work for the family. There was no denying him, nor my grandfathers on both sides, as well as my uncles—the family overrode my mother's wishes. She has appeared to accept this on the outside, but inwardly I know she is still fighting it. So, when I finished college I went to live in our main house in New York City, the intent being for me to learn the ropes, so to speak."

"How many houses does your family have, Nino?"

"I'm not sure, Andrew. There are probably at least a dozen spread along the East Coast, as well as some on the West. I've only been in a few of them. The house we had dinner in the other night and the one in New York City are the ones I frequent the most."

"So what is your family's business, Nino?"

"Simply put, it's making money. On anything they can: gambling, produce, whiskey. You name it, and my family is making money off it somehow, and not legally. But, as I am the newest one in the fold, I'm still not privy to all the details."

"What's Giovanni's beef with Coach, Mr. Stanley, and Mr. Hughes?"

"I'm not sure, Andrew. Pop has remained closed-lipped about that one. I do know it concerns a very large debt, and that the three of them are standing up to him, which makes him very angry. He's used to getting what he wants, no questions asked."

I leaned into him and was covering his forehead with kisses when a shadow fell across us. I looked up to see Nino's father standing above us, holding a gun.

CHAPTER TEN

Nino saw his father at the same time. He rolled away from me and stood up. His cock was still at full attention. Giovanni stared into Nino's eyes.

"Yes, boys, I prefer no questions be asked. Nino, get dressed and get back to your car. I need to speak to your friend here, the star pitcher, alone for a bit."

Nino stood up, silently facing his father, not making any move to get dressed. An age-old fight for dominance between father and son seemed about to play itself out in front of me. Giovanni had made eye contact with me, whether to try to intimidate me or not, I could not be sure. But now he turned his gaze back to Nino, clearly amazed that his son was not following his direct orders. Without warning he slapped Nino across the face with his open hand, knocking the slighter man to the ground. When I sprang to defend him, I found myself facing the gun.

"Now, do I have everyone's attention? Nino, get dressed, and get in your car. If I need to ask you again, it's very likely someone will get hurt."

The implied threat of bodily harm, undoubtedly to be carried out on me this time, propelled Nino swiftly to his feet. He purposefully placed himself between me and Giovanni as he began to dress, all the while keeping an eye on his father and the gun. When he was fully clothed, he turned around to face me.

"It'll be OK, Andrew."

He kissed me on the cheek, then turned to face his father once more.

"Papa, please don't hurt Andrew. He's a great guy, and I'm very much in love with him. If something does happen to him, you will need to deal with me."

I was surprised to hear words of love spill from Nino's mouth, and realized it was the first time they had been spoken aloud. By the look on Giovanni's face, he was surprised as well. And not pleased. But I thought I also saw a grudging respect.

"Go to your car, Nino. I have no intention of hurting him, unless he forces me to. He and I are just going to have a little chat."

Nino turned to look at me once more, a smile of encouragement on his face, then moved past his father and climbed the hill, soon disappearing over its crest, his shoulders held high. Not once did he look back.

I was reaching down to pick up my pants when Giovanni placed a hand on my arm.

"No need to get dressed just yet, Andrew. When I was visiting Mr. Connors the other day and we were first introduced, I could see you were quite a handsome young man, one with many talents that are not always obvious to the casual observer. I had business to attend to that day, so I couldn't give you my full attention. But then I learned through one of my business associates that you had caught the fancy of young Nino who, to date, has been reticent in this area. So now I will take the necessary time to fully appreciate my youngest son's tastes. Stand up straight and let me get a good look at you."

"How did you find us out here?"

"I make it a habit to know where my boys are at all times. Especially Nino."

Afraid of what he might do to me or Nino, I did as I had been asked. Giovanni took one step backward to afford him a better view. As he inspected me, so to speak, I took another long look at him. I could definitely see where Nino got his ravishing good looks. Take away the gray hair, 20 pounds and, say, twenty years, and I could be looking at Nino. Giovanni was an older version, but still a very handsome man.

He stepped closer to me and ran his free hand up and down my arms, squeezing the muscles in each and murmuring words of appreciation. He then did the same to my chest and stomach, running his fingers through the hairs on each and pinching both nipples. My legs were next, and Giovanni bent down and squeezed and worked the muscles in my calves and thighs. I was completely hard by this time. When he straightened back up, he saw this and slapped my stiffer playfully with his hand. He stared at it for a moment before grabbing it. He squeezed it several times, then released it and hefted my ball sac. He squeezed both nuts repeatedly, then released them.

"Very impressive, young man. I'm going to trust you to behave yourself and put my gun away. Now, turn around."

I did as instructed, my initial fear turning to feelings of horniness as Giovanni felt my back and then my ass, gripping my cheeks to gauge their firmness.

"Bend over."

When I complied he spread my ass cheeks, exposing my brown hole. I jumped when he pressed his thumb against it, and then I felt a wet finger probing where the thumb had been. He pushed gently against it till he gained access, then slid his finger in to the knuckle. He paused, then slid it in and out twice more before withdrawing it.

"Nice and tight, just the way I like them. Now stand up and turn around."

I stood straight once more and turned to face him. I felt like a horse that had just been examined to be hired out to stud. Giovanni took a step backward.

"Did I pass, Mr. Sabatini?" He didn't miss the note of irritation in my voice, and either that or my question itself brought hearty laughter from him.

"You are a young male in fine physical condition, and you

should have no problem keeping my Nino's desires satisfied. I didn't have a problem with Nino's choice of companion in the past, or what he did with him. However, even though you are only number two, you are another matter altogether. He's been talking crazy about leaving the family business and making a life with you. Not to me, of course, but I have my spies."

He paused for a moment, a wistful expression appearing on his face as he stared over my head at the lake. It almost seemed as if he was reflecting on something that had happened in his past, perhaps even when he was Nino's age. I cleared my throat discreetly to bring him back to the present, and he shook his head as if he had been in a dream.

"Now it's time for the next part of my inspection, Andrew. Get down on your knees," he ordered huskily.

I did as I was told, more curious now than afraid of what was coming next. Giovanni stepped closer to me so that his crotch was directly in my face.

"I make it my business to sample all my sons' male companions, and I make no exception with you. It only happens once, and they know and approve, and appreciate it. My apologies to you and Nino that it's taken me so long to get around to you, but I've had many other important business matters to attend to."

He undid his belt and unbuttoned his pants, then slid them down over his thighs along with his white briefs. His thighs were thick and covered in black hair. Giovanni took off his shoes and socks, then removed his coat, folded it, and laid it gently on the grass beside him. His shirt was next, revealing his chest and stomach. Both were covered in thick black hair, but unlike his thighs, these hairs were interspersed with silver. It was as if he had a permanent fur coat. His nipples were large, light brown, and puffy. And as for the saying "Apples don't fall far from the tree," in this case it was doubly true. His cock was enormous, club-like, and jutted out from his body with a slight upward curve. The head of it was the size of a small plum. A dense patch of the same silver-black hair grew at the thick base, with no real border between it and the hair of his stomach. His balls matched his dick, inside their gigantic flesh basket, the right one hanging lower than the left. I was certain that in his youth and, for that matter, his entire adult life, he had brought pleasure to a fair amount of men.

"Show me what you do for Nino, Andrew. And don't fret over the size, just take what you can."

I shuffled on my knees till the smells of his crotch filled my nose. I gazed up at the stiffer before me, and felt for a moment as if I were in a posture of worship. As I wrapped my hand around his prick, I wondered how many other men had heard those same words: "Just take what you can." My fingers barely met around its girth. As I stroked the thick shaft, his balls swayed in their flesh sac. After a few tentative strokes, I trailed my tongue up and down his stiffer, then swirled it over the fat knob. I let it slip inside my mouth, where I sucked softly on it. Keeping the large head in my mouth, I relaxed my throat and slowly but surely swallowed half his cock. I paused to adjust my breathing and attempted to take the rest, but only managed a few inches, leaving enough to wrap my left hand around.

With my right hand I kneaded his balls as I slid back up his dick. I again sucked the crown briefly, then started sawing up and down on his horse cock. With my left hand I jerked the part of his pole that I couldn't fit in my mouth. Giovanni placed his hands on my shoulders to steady himself and began thrusting his hips to match my bobbing head. The hairs on his chest and stomach were soon damp with sweat, which ran down to soak his crotch. Saliva was leaking from the corners of my mouth and mingling with the sweat. The combined smells were filling my nose on each downward lunge, driving me to increase my efforts on his stiffer. Before long, Giovanni's knees began to tremble. When his balls tightened in their sac, I knew he was close to spilling his seed. Sure enough, his next statement confirmed this.

"I'm gonna blow, lad!"

He groaned loudly and thrust his prick a final time into my mouth as a thick wad of his spunk hit the back of my throat and slid down my gullet. Again and again he groaned, each deposit getting smaller but still coming. There seemed to be no end to his flow. Finally he was done, and I eased up off his dick and licked it clean. I was amazed at the potency of a man his age.

"That was very nice, Andrew. I now understand why my Nino is so enamored of you. Now, let's see what else you can do."

He suddenly pulled me up and to him, and kissed me hard on the mouth. I returned his kiss with the same ferocity. When I released his lips I proceeded to plant kisses on his neck, then worked my way down to his tits. I pulled each point of flesh into my mouth and sucked and bit them, quite hard in fact, bringing deep sighs and moans from Giovanni. As I alternated between them, my efforts elicited an "Oh my God" from the older man. Without warning he grabbed my arms and wrestled me to the blanket, at which point he promptly fell on top of me.

His weight felt good as he began kissing me again and grinding his cock against mine. I raised my legs in the air, then wrapped them around his waist. He looked into my eyes and smiled, as it was apparent what I needed.

"Do you have any grease with you?"

"There is some on the blanket here somewhere."

Securing the tin, I handed it to him, then lay back down and lifted my legs again. Giovanni knelt between them and applied the grease liberally to my asshole, even sticking several fingers deep inside me. He tossed the tin on the blanket and positioned the head of his dick against my hole.

"As you can probably guess, Andrew, this is going to hurt at first."

"That's OK, Giovanni, I want you inside me."

Without further conversation he began pushing, and for several moments I didn't think my asshole was going to yield. But Giovanni was patient and insistent, and finally the large head popped through, eliciting a long, drawn-out gasp from me. He paused for a moment, then slowly pushed his entire length inside. I gripped his arms and gritted my teeth as his huge member went deeper and deeper. When I was sure I couldn't take any more, I felt his crotch hair brushing my ass cheeks.

"Are you OK, Andrew?"

"Yes."

"I'll take it slow and easy."

And, true to his word, Giovanni began slow in-and-out plunges with his cock, kissing me and biting my nipples all the while. I wrapped my arms around his hairy back and locked my heels in the small of his back. After what seemed an eternity, but in reality was probably a good twenty minutes, Giovanni quickened his pace considerably, and I knew he was getting ready to cum. After a half-dozen more lunges he cried out, and I felt his jism flooding my asshole. When he was done shooting he pulled out gently, then wrapped his arms around me and playfully stuck the tip of his tongue in my ear. He held me briefly, then rose and began dressing. Once he was fully dressed, he reached out a hand and pulled me to my feet.

"Now, Andrew, I've known the pleasures of a man, as have all of my sons. More times in my years than I can probably count, or care to. Each of us has a special male companion to whom we turn for certain needs; Nino has had you, and as I said, you are only the second one. But it cannot be, and has never been for any of us, a full-time, permanent, life arrangement. Part of Nino's destiny is to take a wife, raise children, and continue running the family business. I had to do it, and my father before me, his father, and so on. This is the duty of

Nino's brothers as well. The family must continue to the next generation, and the one after that. It pains me greatly to say this, it truly does, but since your affair is such a threat to this arrangement, as of this moment you and Nino must stop seeing each other. And you should know he is officially engaged to be married in the fall."

I reeled as if I had been struck. Nino was engaged! Why had he never said anything to me about this? Surely it had been to spare my feelings. Or had it? Would Nino have ever told me, or might he have just gone through with the secret wedding and kept me on the side? Of course he would have; that is what the male members of his family did. But he had made the fatal mistake of falling in love with me. That was not part of the game these men played. When I collected myself and stood up, Giovanni kissed me a final time on the mouth.

"Farewell, Andrew. Best of luck to you and the team."

With that he turned, climbed the hill, and disappeared from sight. A few minutes passed before Nino came walking down the hill. I was positive some exchange had passed between him and his father. He stopped a few feet from me and stared at me in silence. I opened my mouth to explain to him what had just happened, but he stepped to me and placed a finger to my lips.

"There's no need to tell me anything, Andrew. This is not the first time this scene has played out for me, and for my brothers it's ten times as many for each. I was hoping to keep our relationship a secret from my father, but he has eyes and ears everywhere." He paused, a tear appearing in the corner of his right eye, which he wiped away.

"And papa really likes you, whereas he never cared for my first companion."

I took Nino into my arms and hugged him fiercely, then brought him to arm's length. He was simply the handsomest man I'd ever laid eyes on, and I loved him dearly. I decided then and there not to bring up the subject of his engagement. Given the fact that I had been seeing Parker, and the nature of my special relationship with Nelson, it would be nothing but hypocritical. Plus, my stubborn pride wanted Nino to be the one to broach the subject. For now I would just ride out this storm to whatever conclusion.

"What can we do about this, Nino? Are you strong enough to stand up to your father and your brothers? Has anyone ever stood up to them and lived to talk about it? Will anyone else in your family even lend a hand? Perhaps your mom? Is there anywhere we can go that he won't find us? How about one of your many houses?"

The questions came tumbling out of me, and I could tell by the look on Nino's face that they were all questions he had already asked himself. He didn't answer for a moment, but stood there in silence.

"Mama has said several times that she wants a better life for me, but I don't see her going against papa to the extent we need. I honestly don't know what to do. Let's get you back to the boarding house and we can discuss it further."

• • •

We didn't speak on the way back, each of us wrapped in his own thoughts. Nino drove fast and recklessly, once forcing another car onto the grass roadside, but neither of us cared. The wind blew in our faces and for the time being we were together, consequences and the Sabatini family be damned. When he pulled up in front of the boarding house, we sat in silence for a moment, then he leaned over and kissed me deeply on the lips, not caring who saw us.

We got out and made our way to the boarding house, then my room. When we entered we found Kent there, and I asked him if he would leave us alone for a few hours. He must have sensed something in our attitude or appearance, for he left the room without an argument. Nino and I undressed and crawled underneath the covers. We wrapped our arms around each other and soon fell fast asleep.

Kent did not return till the next morning. Nino and I both got dressed and followed Kent down to breakfast. The rest of the team was very cordial to Nino; I wasn't sure if it was out of respect for me or fear of what his father could and would do in a fit of anger. Mrs. Jenkins didn't even notice the extra body. When we had stuffed ourselves with pancakes, ham, eggs, and toast, Nino and I went out onto the front porch and sat in the swing. I was the first to break the silence.

"Nelson is arriving today for his visit; he will be here for the final game. Rather than have him pay for a room in the hotel, Kent has agreed that he can stay in our room. We haven't told Mrs. Jenkins yet, but I doubt she'd notice another young man hanging around the boarding house. She certainly didn't notice you this morning."

"Okay. I have to go to Tampa today to check on a delivery for papa. I will also go see my mama to see if together we can formulate a plan of action. This means I will be gone for a few days. I'll come straight here once I return. And I look forward to meeting Nelson."

He kissed me on the cheek, then got into his car and drove out of the driveway and down the road, disappearing in a cloud of dust.

I was so distracted during that day's shortened practice that twice Coach asked me what was wrong, but I wouldn't talk about it. My mind was filled with thoughts of Nino, Giovanni, the Sabatini family, Parker, and, of course, the impending arrival of Nelson. When practice was over and I had showered out behind the house—the cold shower only adding to my sour mood—I walked to the bus station in town. I sat on one of the benches outside and idly watched two buses pull in and unload their passengers.

The riders swarmed off the bus, milling around till they found their waiting loved ones. The sight of so many happy people began to lift my mood, and I became more eager for Nelson to arrive than I had since receiving his letter. I was apprehensive as well, for in all my recent letters I had written glowingly of Nino and our blossoming relationship, but of course I had not mentioned what had been happening with Parker. He would be furious when he found out I had been seeing Parker again.

Maybe I wouldn't tell him, I told myself consolingly. I had chosen to be with Nino, so there was really no need to tell Nelson about Parker. The only trouble with that plan was that everyone on the team knew that Parker and I were in a relationship. Although we hadn't publicly announced it, it was pretty hard to miss in the close quarters the team kept. And while they also knew of Nino, they weren't ones to pass judgment. I didn't want to risk someone slipping in front of Nelson and mentioning Parker. Plus, it wouldn't feel right keeping it from him.

My thoughts were interrupted by the announcement that Nelson's bus had arrived. I smiled when I saw his face pressed to one of the windows; when he saw me, a grin spread from ear to ear. I fidgeted as the interminable line of travel-weary passengers exited, grabbed their scarred luggage, and trudged off down the street. Finally, Nelson was standing in front of me, holding a battered valise in his left hand. I looked him up and down and, as always, the sheer size of him was overwhelming. He dropped the valise and opened his arms. I stepped into them and he hugged me fiercely. He ground his crotch into mine, and I could feel the head of his cock through the fabric of his pants. Instantly, my own prick was aroused and begging for attention. Before releasing me Nelson blew gently in my right ear, causing my nipples to harden.

"Greetings, old friend," Nelson's voice boomed, carrying well above the noise of the crowd. "It's so good to see you."

We left the station and headed back to the boarding house. Mrs. Jenkins was on the front porch, hanging clothes on the line. After introducing Nelson to her, we entered the cool house and quickly climbed the stairs to my room. We met Kent in the hall; he was headed down to the pond with the rest of the team. We passed on his invitation to join them, then entered my room and locked the door behind us. Nelson was immediately on his knees in front of me, undoing the button on my pants. He slid his hand underneath my briefs and grabbed my dick, which immediately sprang to life. He pulled my pants and briefs down my thighs, causing my cock to burst free and slap hard against my stomach. Apparently enamored of the sound, Nelson grabbed my stiffer by its thick base and slapped my belly several more times with it. He then ran his thumb over the head and through the swollen slit, which was already leaking juice, then released me. He bent down and undid the laces on my shoes, then pulled them off, followed by my socks. Still on his knees, he reached up and pulled my pants and briefs the rest of the way down, and I kicked them off my feet. I pulled my T-shirt off and stood naked before him.

He looked me up and down, spit into his hand, moistened the entire length of my cock, and began stroking me roughly. My hips bucked each time his hand moved over the sensitive crown. My juice was flowing freely; a long strand was looping its way down to my foot. Nelson saw this, caught the strand on a finger, and gingerly steered it to his waiting tongue. After catching and swallowing the tiny morsel, he drove his tongue into my slit, lapping up the juice there before engulfing the fat head and slowly, deliciously, sliding down my shaft. He tried to make me laugh by puffing his cheeks out and bugging his eyes as if my manhood was too much to take. Amused but still flattered, I knew from past experience that he could easily swallow me, ball sac and all.

Nelson released my stiffer and began licking the insides of my thighs, his tongue tickling me and causing the skin there to turn to gooseflesh. He then nuzzled my nut sac with his nose before licking its soft skin. He pulled one of my balls into his mouth, rolling it around with his tongue and sucking on it gently. He released it to do the same to its twin, then let that ball plop from his mouth and trailed his tongue up and down my shaft. When he reached the tender head on his next upward swipe, he engulfed it and slowly sank down its length once more. His mouth was warm and wet, and felt incredible wrapped around my dick. Nelson stayed there, sucking softly, his breath exhaling gently through his nose and into my bush. He slid up once more till just the large knob was still inside, then began eagerly bobbing up and down on my cock. As was his forte, he swallowed my ball sac on each downward lunge, and the feeling was incredible. I looked down to see my stiffer disappearing and reappearing from his mouth as his nose poked into my belly. Before long I felt the familiar stirrings and knew my explosion was fast approaching.

Nelson sensed it as well, for on his next upward spiral he let my dick plop from his mouth and closed his eyes and stuck out his tongue. This was one of our favorite scenarios, and I was not about to disappoint him. I grabbed my pole, which was still slick from his mouth, and began stroking it furiously. After only a few passes, I cried out as the first white blob shot forth and landed squarely on Nelson's tongue. More and more of the thick white stuff followed. He waited till I was spent, then ate it all, licking his lips after doing so.

"That's the best meal I've had since I left Miller Falls."

We both laughed as Nelson stood up and pushed me back against the bed and then down on it. After covering my face and throat with kisses, Nelson stood up and quickly stripped out of his clothing. I relished the sight of his naked body, with all the hair, and all the curves and muscles that were as familiar to me as my own body. He crawled back on the bed and straddled my chest, his large member only inches from my face.

I ran my hands over his chest, covered in its soft, blond fur, then placed my hands on his muscular thighs, each also covered in light blond hairs. He scooted up farther on my chest till his balls were resting in the hollow of my throat. His smell became more intense, a combination of sweat, cock, and his overwhelming maleness. I reached behind him and gripped his ass cheeks. I wet my index finger and slid it along the crack of his ass to right where it met his lower back. Nelson cried out and shuddered in pure ecstasy as I rubbed the spot vigorously with my finger. This always drove him absolutely nuts.

Nelson rose up farther on his knees and positioned himself so that his nut sac was directly over my mouth. He looked down at me and smiled, then laid his balls right on my lips. I opened my mouth and let one drop in, sucked on it heartily, then did the same to the other one, before bathing the entire sac of flesh with my tongue. I grabbed his ass cheeks once more and spread them wide, then placed my finger against his spot. He moaned softly and slid up till his hole was staring me in the face. Not needing a second invitation, I spread him wide and slathered my tongue all along his crack, including his sweet spot. I then paused and stuck the tip of my tongue in him as far as I could, and Nelson let out a rather long, loud moan.

"Lick that hole."

I continued to work his tender spot as he began to pump his stiffer. Sweat was seeping down his ass cheeks right into his crack, and I was licking it up as it came.

"Here it comes, Andrew!"

Nelson pulled up and back from me just as he released his first blast. It landed on my cheek. He continued to coat both cheeks and my lips till he was empty, then sprawled beside me and licked my face clean. He then kissed me deeply, wrapped me in his arms, and we both drifted off. When we woke, Kent was still not back from swimming. Once we were dressed I showed Nelson the rest of the house, and then we went outside to see the grounds. We viewed the barn, the outside showers, and the outbuildings that now only housed rusted and broken farm machinery.

I was trying to come to grips with how or when I would tell him about Parker. He was going to be furious, I realized, not just because I went back to Parker, but because I kept it from him for so long. We came to the pond, where a few of the players were still swimming and lounging on the bank. Luckily, Parker wasn't one of them. I introduced Nelson around; then we moved on to what was left of the locker room.

Next we walked around the baseball field, which was in the best condition of anything at the Stallions' headquarters. When Nelson had seen all there was to see, we returned to the pond, which we now had to ourselves, and sat down on its grassy bank. I was silent for a long time, trying to screw up my courage.

Nelson knew me well. "What do you have to tell me, Andrew, that can be so bad? Please just say it and get it over with."

I just blurted it out. "I've been seeing Parker for some time now, in addition to Nino. I have chosen Nino and will be breaking it off with Parker, but I haven't told him yet."

I expected an immediate outburst, some type of recrimination, or even a solid punch in the chest, but nothing came. Nelson sat in shocked silence.

"Please say something, Nelson."

"I can't believe that after everything you went through with him you started dating him again. He was a mean, violent drunk. And unless you believe in miracles, I'm sure he hasn't changed one bit."

"I did think he had changed, Nelson. But some things are not adding up where he is concerned, and that is why I decided to make a break from him. And he never hit me—you know that."

He spun angrily toward me. "Well, I'm sure he would have gotten around to it."

He stood up and headed back to the house without another word. I stayed seated on the grass, stunned and hurt. But hadn't I known what his reaction would be? At least everything was out in the open now. But I hadn't gotten the chance to share my suspicions of Parker with Nelson. I stayed at the pond for a good while, missing dinner and not caring. I wanted to give Nelson time to digest the news and get over his anger toward me. When it began to grow dark, I headed back to my room. When I opened the door, I found Kent there with Nelson. They were laughing uncontrollably, and each was drinking a bottle of beer. Several empty bottles were on the table between the beds.

"Hey, Andrew. Nelson and I have been getting acquainted. Why don't you join us for a beer?"

Nelson acknowledged my presence with a nod of his head, but that was it for the next several hours. I sat on the bed while Kent and Nelson talked about everything under the sun: the Stallions and strategies for winning the final game, life in Miller Falls, and both of their aspirations for the future. Feeling like an outsider, I sat and got quietly drunk, giving one-word answers to the few questions that were asked of me.

As the beer continued to flow, I began to see a real spark between Nelson and Kent. I got up to piss, and when I came back into the room it was just in time to see Kent impulsively lean into Nelson and kiss him full on the mouth. Nelson eagerly returned the kiss and began pawing at the buttons on Kent's pants. Kent stood up and let Nelson pull his pants and briefs down to his ankles. Kent was fully erect and ready for action. Nelson went down to his knees and cupped Kent's huge sac of balls, then gave his thick shaft a few strokes before slowly taking the entire length deep down his throat. He paused, then slid back to the fat head and let it plop from his mouth.

"Join us, Andrew," Kent said softly.

I did as he asked and stood to Nelson's right. While holding onto Kent's prick, Nelson undid my pants and pushed them and my briefs down to my knees. I was as hard as a rock. He took the large crown into his mouth and sucked on it for all he was worth before returning to Kent's. He then alternated between the two of us, bobbing up and down on Kent's pole, then switching to mine. The only sounds in the room were Nelson's hard sucking and our collective moans and sighs.

I placed my hand on Nelson's shoulders to steady myself, and Kent followed suit, quickly grasping my hand as his explosion hit full force. Nelson slid up to his cock head and held it in his mouth as Kent released his flood. He swallowed audibly, then licked his dick clean, smacking his lips when he was done. He now turned his attention to me, sliding his hand up my legs till his finger expertly found my shit hole. He quickly withdrew his finger, wet it, and then returned to explore once more. He inserted its full length inside me, and after only a few quick pokes my seed was gushing down his throat to join Kent's. Just then there was a knock at the door and the voice of Mrs. Jenkins asking if one of us was willing to walk into town for some ice cream. Kent and I quickly pulled our pants up and Kent opened the door.

"I'll go for you, Mrs. Jenkins."

"Thanks, Kent."

She handed him some bills and went back downstairs.

"Would you guys like to walk into town with me? It's a nice night for it."

Nelson readily agreed, but I politely declined.

"I'm going to stay here and finish my magazine."

Nelson thanked me with a look, then he and Kent left. I never heard them come in that night, but when I woke in the morning they were both in Kent's bed, naked limbs entwined. I nudged them awake and we dressed and took our place in the large dining room for breakfast, where I introduced Nelson to the rest of the team. Parker froze when he saw Nelson, and the two glared at each other across the table. I was sure everyone could feel the tension in the room. However, being a true friend to me, Nelson took the first step to break the ice.

"Good morning, Parker. Congratulations on a great pitching year." Insincere or not, the greeting seemed to make Parker relax a little.

"Thanks, Nelson. I'm glad you can be here for the final game." And that was the extent of the exchange.

After breakfast we all headed to the field for practice, and Nelson tagged along. At the field I introduced him to Coach, Mr. Hughes, and Mr. Stanley, and Nelson took a seat on the bench next to Mr. Hughes. He watched us practice the entire day, joined us for supper, and then disappeared with Kent right after. The next day of his trip was the same as the first. Nelson was cordial to me but became inseparable from Kent, which made things awkward since he was sharing my and Kent's room.

To add to my anxiety, I had not heard from Nino. I had no idea if he was still in Tampa or New York City. And I had no way of getting in touch with him or his family. I could not go to the big mansion and simply knock on the door and ask, "Is Nino here? No? Well, do you know how I can get in touch with him?"

I'm sure that would get me nowhere, and the fact that I was looking for Nino would make its way back to Giovanni. All else considered, the man scared the hell out of me, and for good reason. What could be keeping Nino? Had he hatched a plan with the aid of his mother to get him out of his father's clutches?

I was sitting in my observation chair by the bedroom window after dinner, these thoughts churning in my head, when the door opened and someone entered. I was too disinterested to turn and see if it was Kent or Nelson.

"Andrew, can I speak to you for a moment?"

Recognizing Nelson's voice, I turned to face him.

"Certainly."

"I need to tell you that I am not happy that you started seeing Parker again. I need to be honest with you about that. I have seen a new happiness about you in the short time I've been here, but whether that's due to Parker or Nino, only you know. As you have told me you are breaking it off with Parker, Nino seems to be the obvious answer. I will do my best to hold my tongue and be civil to Parker, even though my first impulse is to punch him in the face every time I see him. But it will not be easy. Also, I am starting to have strong feelings for Kent. It's amazing that I never noticed him back home."

"I'm very glad for you, Nelson. Kent is a great guy."

Still reluctant to share my concerns about Parker, even with Nelson, till I knew more, I got up and went to him, wrapping my arms around him and hugging him tight. I could feel his stiffer immediately press against my crotch. As always, he felt good and strong in my arms, and he smelled great. We pulled apart and quickly undressed, our need for each other driving us. He kissed me, then pushed me on my back on the bed, and climbed onto it. He grabbed the tin of grease from the table between the beds, opened it, and spread the substance on my hole and inside me as well. He threw the tin back on the table, placed the head of his cock against my cornhole, popped through aggressively, and sank inside me to his balls. He immediately pulled out and began pounding my ass, his strokes hard and deep. I worked my asshole around his dick, squeezing it with my muscles on each of his upward and downward lunges.

"I'm almost there, Andrew."

He drove deeply into me a final time and held it there as his spunk flooded my asshole. When he was spent he withdrew, then flopped on top of me. I wrapped my arms around him and kissed his forehead. Suddenly, the door flew open and crashed against the wall. Nino was standing in the doorway, and the look on his face was not pleasant. Nor was the gun in his hand, which was pointed at Nelson and me.

CHAPTER ELEVEN

Nino entered the room and kicked the door closed behind him.

"Who the hell are you?" Nelson demanded.

Nino ignored him as his gaze remained locked on me.

"I've been knocking on the door for five minutes. Beat it, so I can have a moment with Andrew."

"I'm not going anywhere, mister!"

Nelson stood up as if to challenge Nino, who, in the perfect image of a young gangster, swung the muzzle of the gun toward him.

"You must be Nelson. Get the hell out of here. Now!"

Nelson looked at me, and I nodded my head yes.

"It's Nino," I said softly.

He then stood up and quickly dressed. When he was fully clothed he left the room as ordered, staring Nino down as he passed him. Nino was extremely agitated.

"What's wrong, Nino? When I didn't hear from you I was worried that something had happened to you. Obviously it has, or you wouldn't come into my room waving a gun."

He seemed surprised by the weapon in his own hand and set it down quickly. "I've broken ranks with my father, and he's about to call out his goons on me. When I heard noises in here and didn't get a response to my knocking, I panicked."

He stared at me coldly. "Does Nelson know about Parker?"

I almost gasped at this question.

"How did you know about Parker?"

As the question left my mouth, I knew I had just tipped my hand. And I could tell by the look on Nino's face that he realized it as well.

"I've been hanging around here long enough for word to get around. And it was obvious the other day when I interrupted the two of you. I also know he's an ex-lover. But we can talk about that later. Right now, I need you in a bad way."

Also willing to postpone this sticky discussion, I stretched back on the bed, my nakedness revealed to him, and his eyes drank me in. He began to undress, and when he was naked he walked to the bed, his cock hard and straining toward me.

"Slide up," Nino grunted.

He propped two pillows behind my back to help me maintain a sitting position. Once he had me where he wanted me, he knelt on the edge of the bed and swung his right leg over me. Both his knees were now pressed tightly to my hips. He then shuffled up my torso till his stiffer was literally staring me in the face.

"Open your mouth."

I did as ordered, the smell of his crotch flooding my nostrils as he placed his fat cock head on my tongue. I savored his flavor as well as the silky softness of the knob. But Nino was insistent to be inside me and pushed his cock in farther, causing me to tilt my head to allow his fat dick to slide down my throat. His meaty ball sac was resting against my chin, its scraggly hairs tickling it. His thick bush was mashed against my nose, and I inhaled deeply once more of his smells. He didn't move for several minutes but simply knelt there, his prick down my throat. I breathed gently through my nose as I sucked softly on his member, and Nino sighed contentedly. Without warning he slid back out to the fat head. He then slid his pole back in and began thrusting slowly, his balls slapping against my chin. I grabbed the sac and kneaded the twin globes roughly, while with my other hand I reached up and pinched Nino's nipples. They were fairly hidden in the forest of hair that covered his chest. As I brought each one to hardness, Nino moaned loudly and increased his lunges. I released his ball sac and trailed my finger beneath it and up the crack of his ass. I probed the hair-filled channel, then withdrew the digit, wet it, and rubbed the top of Nino's crack, where it met his back. As with Nelson, this spot also drove Nino crazy, and before I even had a chance to get my finger inside him, he was spewing into my mouth. I swallowed it all and squeezed his balls a final time as he withdrew his dick. He rolled off me and onto his back next to me. His chest and stomach were shiny with sweat. We lay there in silence, staring at the ceiling. He was the first to break it.

"Now, when were you going to tell me about Parker? How many other lovers do you have on the side that I don't know about, Andrew?"

I fought desperately to quell my rising anger as I told Nino of my previous relationship with Parker, including the ending, and how he and I had once again become attracted to one another but that I had again broken it off. Of course this was not the whole truth, but most assuredly it was my intent. But news of Nino's engagement had stung, which I realized, ashamedly, made me take a small amount of pleasure in keeping this bit of the puzzle from him. As I was speaking, Nino jumped off the bed and was pacing the room.

"Do you still love Parker? If so, you need to be with him, not me. I don't want to share your love with anyone else!"

Despite my best efforts, my own anger quickly boiled over.

"Like I have to share your love with your fiancée?"

Nino recoiled as if he had been struck. He turned away from me and stared at the wall. When he turned back to me, his anger had increased tenfold.

"How the hell did you find out about Mabel? Have you been spying on me, Andrew Duggan?"

So, he was not even going to try to deny it. I said coldly, "No, your father told me at the lake. When he was testing me out to be sure I was 'worthy' of his youngest son." I fairly spat the last words at him.

"He had no right to. It was up to me to tell you."

"And when was that going to happen, Nino? Years into the marriage when I ran into you and your wife at a baseball game? In the market? On the street? I'm not the only one who's been keeping secrets and should have been upfront right from the beginning!"

I was now also on my feet, pacing the room in tandem with Nino.

"I overlooked the fact that your family operates on the wrong side of the law because I had fallen in love with you, and you with me. Or so I thought. Parker may be a lot of things, but a gangster he isn't. But if you are afraid to choose your own life, and insist on getting married to Mabel, then that new life will not include me."

"What are you saying, Andrew?"

"We're through, Nino. Go back to your fiancée and your criminal way of life. I don't want anything more to do with you."

I turned to the window, afraid to see Nino's reaction to the words I had just uttered. But there was no response to my tirade. He quietly dressed and left my room, closing the door behind him. I watched as he got in his car and drove slowly away, tears streaming down my cheeks. I felt as if I had been kicked in the balls.

"Goodbye, Nino," I whispered.

• • •

Coach was giving us two days off before the game. Nelson was still staying in our room, and he and Kent were beginning to spend more and more time together. Nelson also did odd jobs around the boardinghouse for Mrs. Jenkins, ran errands for Coach, and helped out the team however he could.

He was well liked by everyone. He and Parker had even managed to avoid any confrontations.

My sadness over the breakup with Nino had evolved into anger, and I was now mad at him and the whole world. Nelson did his best to make me feel better, as only he could, but he was being pulled more and more into his relationship with Kent. And he had not even met Nino till our showdown in the room, so what real advice could he give me? Parker knew that something was troubling me deeply, based on the fact that I had been avoiding him since my return from Mr. Stanley's house. Plus, he was keeping a safe distance from Nelson, and trying to be on his best behavior. And how could I tell him about Nino when I no longer trusted him? If Nino was out of my life for good, what did it matter? Or should I tell Parker in case Nino or his family sought retribution? Or did I even care to warn him? I didn't know what to do about any of it.

Even though Coach had given us time off, Mrs. Jenkins had not. Both of her housekeepers were out sick, so we were forced to make our beds, clean our rooms, and bring all our laundry downstairs. She also had us helping her with all the rest of the normal household chores—those she didn't already have Nelson's generous assistance with, that is.

An hour before lunch on the day before the final game, we escaped her watchful eye and gathered behind the barn, Nelson included. Joshua, our unofficial leader, had called the meeting.

"Guys, we need to slip out of here and go somewhere for the rest of the day or else Mrs. Jenkins is going to work us all afternoon."

The rest of the team agreed, and we all sat pondering the best place to go.

"Why don't we spend the day at the pond?" Parker interjected. "We can raid the kitchen and run to the grocer's for cold beers and anything else that strikes our fancy. I also have a bottle of whiskey in my room."

Everyone loved the idea, and Joshua laid out the plan. Parker, Kent, and I were to head to the grocery store in town for the beer and extras. Joshua, Dizzy, Mark, and Trevor were to steal any leftovers from the icebox while Ethan, Heath, Nelson, and Nicholas distracted Mrs. Jenkins, who kept a famously close watch over her kitchen. Excited by our cleverness at foiling Mrs. Jenkins's plan for us, and at the thought of an afternoon spent at the pond, Parker, Kent and I ran all the way into town, not stopping till we stood on the grocer's porch.

"Parker, why don't you run up the street to the icehouse and get us some ice for the beer?" I suggested. "Kent and I can get the beer and groceries."

"Will do."

As Kent and I entered the store we were greeted by Mr. Johansen, the store owner, busily sweeping the floor. He ran the store with his wife, Martha.

"Hello, Mr. Johansen," Kent and I chimed.

"What can I get for you today, boys?"

"We need a salami stick, a loaf of bread, a wedge of cheese, some pickles, and some bottles of beer and soda."

"Wonderful. Help yourself to the beer and soda, and I will be right back with the rest."

The interior of the store was cool and dim. The butcher area was in the back, and the smell of fresh meat and blood filled the air. An entire glass display case near the cash register seemed to hold every novelty sweet imaginable. In the far corner opposite the register stood two enormous ice chests, at hip level, that held cold beer and soda. A large freezer was next to the chests; it housed ice cream of all varieties. Kent and I gathered two dozen bottles of beer and half as many sodas, making several trips to place them all on the counter by the register. Mr. Johansen returned shortly with the rest of the goods. As he rang them up, I looked at the salami stick, remembering the picnic with Nino. A deep sadness pervaded me that I fought strongly to overcome.

"Can we have some peppermint candy sticks as well?"

"Sure thing."

Kent paid for our purchases, which Mr. Johansen placed in a cloth sack. We had just left the store and were waiting for Parker to rejoin us when there was a commotion in the street a few buildings away. A large circle of people had quickly formed around what was undoubtedly an altercation of some kind. We ran to the knot, and we could hear the sounds of a struggle coming from within the circle. But I couldn't see who was fighting because there were so many men encircling the combatants. Suddenly, the ring broke as one of the fighters was knocked through it.

The man fell on onto his stomach at my feet, almost knocking me down. A distant fear crept into me as a certain familiarity about him struck home. As he struggled to rise, his back still to me, a second man charged through the ring of men: It was Nino. He had a reddish-purple bruise on his right cheek, and blood was running from his nose and mouth. His suit was dirty, and the right sleeve was torn at the shoulder.

As the man on the ground struggled to regain his feet, I saw that it was Parker. He had fared worse than Nino. Both eyes were starting to blacken, and blood was running from his nose. A part of me wanted to cry out to them to stop, but another part of me, a bigger part, wanted to see Nino get the brunt of the beating. Parker charged Nino, who met him with a vicious right hook that again sent Parker reeling outside the circle of onlookers. The crowd was egging both men on, its bloodlust reaching a fever pitch. Parker was again trying to get up, but this time it was even more difficult. Out of the blue, someone yelled, "Police!" and the crowd began dispersing. Then Nino saw me. He started to speak, stopped, then simply stared at me as if he were seeing a ghost.

I leaned down to help Parker. "Just leave us alone, Nino. Just leave us alone."

I could see the hurt on his face. "Andrew, you don't understand," he began, but I cut him short.

"No, Nino, you're the one who doesn't understand. I want
you out of my life."

He started to reply but stopped himself, turned, and disappeared into the crowd.

I helped Parker to his feet just as two policemen arrived.
One officer stopped to talk to some of the remaining onlookers,
while the second one came over to us.

"Are you OK, mister? Do you know who the other guy
was?"

Parker looked at me, then the officer.

"I don't know who he was, officer. I've never seen him
before. I was headed to the icehouse when he began harassing
me about tomorrow's game."

The officer addressed Kent and me. "And what about you
two? Do either of you know who the assailant was?"

I was straight-faced and serious. "I was in the store getting
some groceries for a picnic we are having, so I didn't see the
fight start. Once we came outside I did get a good look at the
man, but I didn't recognize him."

Kent echoed my statement.

A peculiar look appeared on Parker's face, but he said nothing as he dusted himself off the best he could.

"Can you give me a description of the man?"

"Aw, let's just let it drop, officer," Parker offered. "I've been in
worse fights, and I doubt I'll be seeing him anytime soon."

"Okay, mister. But if you run into him again, don't hesitate
to come to the station." With that the officer turned and joined
his partner.

"Are you OK, really, Parker?"

"I'm fine, Andrew. It's hard to believe how some folks can
get so heated over a simple ball game."

I knew it had been over me, but at this time I was not going to contradict Parker's story. Without further discussion the three of us began to walk back to the boarding house. Parker stopped at the front steps and turned to me.

"You know, I don't think I'm up for a swim right now. I'm going to go to my room and lie down for a while. You guys go and have a good time with the rest of the team, though. Don't worry about me; it's nothing, really. A few scrapes and bruises. Andrew, you know firsthand I've had much worse."

Part of me wanted to stay with Parker and mend his wounds, but I realized that was an old and dying part. A bigger part was telling me that Parker was not on the up and up. I had a strange premonition that there had been more to the fight than me. What game was Parker playing?

"Okay, Parker. If you're sure you'll be fine by yourself. We'll check on you when we get back."

Parker went inside, and we met the rest of the team behind the barn as planned. The boys had done well in the kitchen, securing an apple pie, cold fried chicken, a watermelon, and a jar of pickled eggs. They had also grabbed several towels. Suddenly, we heard Mrs. Jenkins in the house, hollering several of our names. Knowing she would not restrict her search to the house, we ran pell-mell to the pond.

· · ·

It was another beautiful afternoon, with the temperature well into the nineties. The sky was pale blue and cloudless. We headed down the slight incline that led to the pond. The blue of its water was juxtaposed against the green of its grassy banks.

Dizzy spread out the blanket and we quickly set upon our horde of food. We ate, drank beer, and chattered like magpies. Everyone was excited and ready for the next day's game. When the food was gone, some of us dozed on the luscious green grass, while others swam or took a walk around the pond. When I woke from my nap everyone had regrouped. Joshua stood up and addressed us.

"Last one to the buoy is a rotten egg."

Gleefully we hopped up and stripped off our clothes. Lighting out for the water, we fanned out behind Joshua, cocks and balls flopping as we ran. When I neared the water's edge I assumed a diving position and hit the water with outstretched arms, in the midst of the team. I went deep, feeling the chill of the water, then quickly stroked to the surface alongside my teammates. We all began swimming toward the buoy as fast as we were able. It was a good half mile to the platform, and I was breathing heavily when I saw it looming near. It was accessible by two ladders that were nailed to the floor of the platform. Their ends disappeared beneath the water's surface.

As I reached the ladder and climbed to the platform, I found only Joshua already there, lying on his back on one of the foam mats, placed there to protect swimmers from splinters. Joshua rested on his elbows, his big dick lying to the left. I lay down to catch my breath as the rest of the team reached the buoy and climbed aboard. We lay in silence, letting the sun dry our bodies. I was almost asleep when someone began rubbing my stomach. I opened my eyes to find it was Joshua, and he was stiff as a board.

He looked into my eyes, and I stared back at him. As he leaned over to kiss me, I raised my legs in the air. He accepted the invitation, crawled between my legs, then bent down and began licking my asshole. He stuck his tongue in as far as possible several times before replacing it with his middle finger. He spit on his finger and slid it deep inside me. The rest of the team watched us.

Joshua withdrew his finger and spit several times into his hand. He filled my crack with his saliva, then spit several more times. The second batch he spread over the shaft of his thick cock. He grabbed my ankles and placed them on his shoulders, then shifted closer to me and placed the head of his cock against my wet hole. He pushed once and was inside me, sinking all the way in till he struck the special muscle buried deep within me. I moaned softly as Joshua bent forward and kissed me. As he began pounding my ass with slow, but full and deep, strokes, I eased my feet from his shoulders and locked my ankles in the small of his back.

"Christ, your ass is tight!"

In response I rose up and bit his right nipple, eliciting a long moan of pleasure from him. After several minutes I wrapped my arms around Joshua, pulling him down on top of me. I began thrusting upward to meet each of his downward lunges, all the while whispering enticements in his ear to drill my ass harder. The only sounds on the platform were his thighs slapping against my ass cheeks. Joshua drove deep one final time, then gripped my earlobe in his teeth. I felt his cum flooding my cornhole. When he was spent, he kissed me a final time before withdrawing. He dove into the pond to rinse off while the rest of the team continued to stare at me with lust-filled eyes.

"Well, who's next?" I asked demurely.

Dizzy raised his hand. "I'll take a crack at you."

"Let's have at it, Dizzy."

As Joshua climbed back onto the platform, Dizzy knelt between my legs, spread spittle on his prick, and entered me quickly. He wasn't as big as Joshua in the dick department, but he was fat, and he knew how to use it. Each of his thrusts were full and deep, causing me to arch my back and forcing long drawn-out moans from deep within me. After a good ten minutes he filled me with his spooge, and Trevor was up next.

As the afternoon stretched on each of my teammates, and Nelson, went two rounds with me. They were simply insatiable, as was I. Nelson was the last for both rounds, and when he had released inside me for the second time, he rolled off me, his chest rising and falling rapidly. The team lay sprawled around me on the platform, some dozing, while others simply lay there with satisfied smiles on their faces. In my need to forget Nino I was ready for a third round, but we all decided it was probably best to head back to the house since it was nearing dinnertime. We dove into the pond to rinse off, then swam back to shore as a group.

At the back door of the boardinghouse we were greeted by Mrs. Jenkins, who was very angry with us for not helping her that afternoon and for stealing precious food from her kitchen. She declared that there would be no dinner served in her house that night. Shame-faced, but satiated, we climbed the stairs to our rooms. I had just sat down on my bed, with Kent and Nelson on Kent's bed, when there was a knock on the door. I said, "Come in," and Parker entered.

"How was the pond?"

"It was a beautiful day for a swim, and the water was very refreshing. Are you feeling better? What did you do while we were gone?"

"I spent most of the afternoon hiding under my bed from Mrs. Jenkins. She was not happy to find no one here to help her. I think she finally coerced Coach into doing some heavy lifting for her in the barn. It was quite comical. Do you want to play some cards?"

"Not really, Parker. It's been a long day and I'm beat. I'm going to do some reading and get to bed early. I'll see you tomorrow at breakfast."

"Okay. Goodnight."

After he left, Nelson and Kent excused themselves to go for a walk. I sat in my chair by the window, which had become a sanctuary for me, and stared out the window till the sun went down. My thoughts were focused solely on Nino and the life we could have had.

I was in bed before Nelson and Kent returned. I tossed and turned for most of the night, unable to stop thinking about the game, Nino, Parker, and their fight in town. A small voice inside my head was trying to tell me something about that incident. I knew I was missing something. But my mind seemed to just circle around it in the swirl of thoughts about my breakup with Nino and the pressure of winning tomorrow's game. It was hard to ignore the fact that in the ten years the Stallions had been a team in the Bush League, they had never even made it to a final game. I finally managed to doze off but woke before sunrise. I went and sat in the chair by the window once more, careful to not wake Kent and Nelson as I watched the sun come up and another beautiful summer day unfold.

"Good morning, Andrew."

Nelson was standing by my side; I had not even heard him get out of bed.

"Good morning."

After a few minutes Kent joined us, and we dressed and went downstairs to breakfast. I greeted Parker, but that was the extent of our conversation. Everyone was remarkably stoic before the big game. I ate hurriedly, eager to reach the field. I was the first to arrive and was going through my warm-up exercises when a sudden thought struck me: What happened *after* today's game? If we won, would I sign a longer contract with the Stallions? And what if we lost? I shut my mind to those paths and focused only on my warm-up pitches.

Within minutes Coach, Mr. Hughes, and Mr. Stanley arrived, and shortly thereafter the rest of the team began straggling in. When everyone was present, Mr. Stanley blew his whistle for attention. We quieted immediately.

"Men, the Panthers will be arriving in a matter of minutes. I just want to take a moment to congratulate all of you on a stellar season. The Stallions have never had such a spectacular showing. Whatever today's outcome, be proud of this team and of each of your individual contributions. Also, I have it on good authority that there may be one or two major league scouts in the stands today, so show them what you've got. Now, have a good game today, and do your best."

When he finished speaking, the entire team cheered. And just then two silver buses pulled into the driveway and headed toward the playing field. When the first one came to a stop, the players exited the bus, introductions were made, and best wishes were shared all around. The second bus was full of Panther fans. Soon the biggest ball game of my life was underway.

We drew first blood, with two earned runs in the bottom of the first. The Panthers' pitching held us scoreless for the next four innings, however, while their batters worked Parker to too many full counts and walks, then drove in three in the fifth on a missed curveball that sailed right over the heart of the plate.

In the top of the sixth, Coach relieved Parker with me. They got some solid hits against me and eked out two more runs, but thanks to our resurgent offense, at the end of the eighth inning we found ourselves leading 8 to 5. It was a pretty safe lead going into the ninth, but we'd have to hold them and hope their bats didn't heat up any more. As the Stallions headed out to take their places on the field, Parker pulled me aside.

"Andrew, Coach wants to see you in the locker room pronto. He said it would only take a minute. Something to do with Nino Sabatini."

At the mention of Nino's name, my heart sank in my chest. I knew Coach actively disliked Nino. Did Coach have news of him, either good or bad? Or had Giovanni paid Coach another threatening visit? And why was Coach in the locker room at such a crucial moment in the game? That couldn't be a good sign. Parker saw that I was in distress.

"You'd better hurry," he said.

I rushed into the locker room. It was eerily quiet.

"Coach? Parker said you wanted to see me. Coach?"

I saw a sudden movement out of the corner of my left eye, which was followed by a sharp pain behind my ear and then darkness. When I came to, I was sitting in the back of a speeding car. My arms were bound behind my back, and I was bound at the ankles as well. A filthy gag was in my mouth. Lorenzo Sabatini was sitting beside me, pointing a gun at my head, and Antonio was driving. A stranger was sitting in the front passenger's seat. The car careened around a corner, promptly depositing me on the floor. Lorenzo grabbed me by the shirt collar and unceremoniously yanked me back onto the seat.

"Slow down, Antonio, you idiot. You want to get us all killed?"

"Shut up, Lorenzo. Papa told me to get to the warehouse as soon as possible."

We kept going at breakneck speed, the dust from the road roiling within the car, causing us all to choke. Suddenly we turned off the main highway without slackening our pace. After what seemed like several hours—but was, in reality, probably only half of one—the air became thick with the smell of fish and salt. We were nearing the ocean, which meant we were heading for the warehouse district that Antonio had alluded to.

Soon the ocean smells were punctuated by the strident cries of seagulls. The car turned sharply again, and I saw the ocean to my left and what appeared to be rows of warehouses. Several wharves stretched out to the water on our left. Antonio stopped abruptly, this time depositing both Lorenzo and me on the back floor.

"You goddamned fool, Antonio. This is the last time you ever drive with me in the car!"

Antonio's response was lost to me as Lorenzo this time pulled me up by my hands, forcing a cry out of me as the ropes chafed my flesh.

"Fortunately for you, Lorenzo, this is the warehouse that Papa told me to come to: Number 9."

But which wharf or section of the coast we were near I had no idea, and my hopes sank. Even if someone made the connection that the Sabatini family had kidnapped me—which, at this time, seemed highly doubtful—how the hell would they know where to start looking for me?

Antonio and the stranger got out of the car. The stranger opened the back passenger's door, Lorenzo pushed me out of the car, and I landed face first on the ground.

"Remember what Papa said, Lorenzo! No rough stuff. At least, not yet."

With that ominous statement ringing in my ears, Lorenzo came around from his side of the car, pulled me to my feet, and half-yanked, half-walked me to a door in the side of the building. Antonio ordered the stranger, whom he called Marco, to keep watch outside. The door had no window, and when Antonio opened it we faced a Stygian blackness and a smell reminiscent of an outhouse in a fish market on a hot August day.

Antonio stepped inside and Lorenzo shoved me roughly behind him. As my eyes adjusted to the gloom, I surveyed the interior. I heard Antonio fumbling to our right, followed by an audible click, resulting in several low rows of lights coming to life overhead. Even their excessive number barely kept the darkness at bay. I quickly saw that the darkness was masking a hoard of broken boat parts, empty metal barrels, fishing hooks and miscellaneous fishing gear, and various sundry goods.

I was denied a more detailed examination as Lorenzo pushed me through the maze to a corner of the warehouse where we faced yet another door. This one looked like it was barely being held up by its hinges. Although Antonio opened it gently, I still expected it to fall on us. We went through the doorway single file into what appeared to be a small bedroom. The furnishings consisted of a bed, two chairs, and a small table with a dirty lamp that gave off a sickly glow. Another floor lamp stood in the corner but was dark. There was one window directly above the bed, so filthy that it allowed no light into the room and—I quickly noted—barely big enough for a small child to fit through.

Antonio turned around to face me and I saw a surprised look on his face. A blinding pain behind my right ear resulted in total unconsciousness for the second time that day.

CHAPTER TWELVE

A loud thumping sound coaxed me slowly from the dark place I had been dwelling in. As my eyes adjusted once again to the gloom of the tiny room, the smell of rotten fish assaulted me. The feeble light from the lamp revealed that I was lying spread-eagled on the bed, atop a blanket that had seen better days. On the table next to the bed were several glasses and two ashtrays overflowing with cigarette butts. I was naked, and each of my wrists and ankles was tied to one of the four metal bed frame posts. A disgusting rag was tied into my mouth. My cock was standing as rigid as a flagpole. My clothes were folded neatly and in a pile on the table. The mysterious thumping sound suddenly ceased.

I tested the ropes and found them secure, dashing my hopes of quickly freeing myself and getting the hell out of there. While I was going over other possible escape scenarios in my mind, the door opened, casting a bright light into the room. A figure stepped into this light and approached the bed. When it was right next to me I recognized Marco.

He didn't speak, only checked my arms and legs to ensure they were still secure. He then glanced at my prick, throwing a look over his shoulder at the open door. He turned and shut the door, came back to the bed, bent over my crotch, and took the head of my dick quickly into his mouth. He sucked the fat knob lustily, while he caressed my balls with his left hand. He looked up at me, smiled, then swallowed my stiffer to the root, forcing it deep down his throat. He continued kneading my balls with his left hand, while with his right he began stroking my prick as he noisily slurped on it. He was very talented, and it was apparent he wanted me to cum as quickly as possible, most likely for fear of being discovered. I was not in any position to deny him. The feel of his mouth on my pole soon wrung a forceful explosion from me. He was startled when the first spurt hit the back of his throat, but he quickly recovered and swallowed all my jism. When I was spent he swirled his tongue over the still-swollen crown, then stood up and left the room without looking back.

I dozed off, and when I woke I couldn't determine what hour of the day it was, or even if it was the same day. Suddenly, the door opened again and two figures entered the room. As they drew closer I could see it was Antonio and Lorenzo. Antonio was carrying a tray. He set it on the small table. Lorenzo pulled a metal chain beneath the lampshade standing on the floor by the bed, flooding the small room with light. He then sat in the chair nearest to the bed.

"Andrew, I'm going to remove the gag so you can eat. Don't bother hollering, because there's no one within miles of here that is going to help you. I'm leaving your hands tied, for obvious reasons."

He removed the piece of cloth and took a bowl of what smelled like minestrone soup from the tray.

"If you're going to kill me, Antonio, then why bother feeding me?"

"Papa said to take care of you till he got here. He's taking care of a business matter. I figured you were hungry. If you're not, I can take this away."

At the smell of the soup, I suddenly realized that I was hungry, and a small measure of my hostility subsided.

"I will eat it."

Antonio sat on the edge of the bed and fed me the soup. It was delicious. When it was gone, he held a glass of water to my mouth and I drank half of it. He then set the glass on the table and left with the tray. As soon as he was gone, Lorenzo came to the side of the bed.

"You sure are pretty, Andrew. Let's see if you're as good as Nino says you are."

I wasn't sure since our breakup if Nino had trashed me to his brothers or not, or if Lorenzo was just trying to goad me. But by the sounds of it, I was to pleasure yet another member of the Sabatini family. I figured what the hell, the first two were pretty good. Not that I had any say, considering that all my limbs were bound. Lorenzo began to undress, and I was amazed at how similar his body was to Nino's. His chest and stomach were covered in the same black hair as Nino's, but there was more of it. Lots more. It was a veritable forest. His nipples were dark and hard and almost obscured by the hair. Lorenzo laid his shirt and undershirt on the chair, then unbuttoned his trousers and slid them down to his knees, revealing white briefs. The underwear clearly outlined his massive cock and balls.

Lorenzo made sure he had my full attention before sliding his briefs down to join his pants and then pulling both down and stepping out of them. His dick, though still soft, was long and thick, the head nicely shaped. His balls were large. The hair of his torso continued uninterrupted past his crotch and down his legs. My eyes followed his hands down as he removed his socks. When he stood next to the bed in all his naked glory, he was quite an impressive sight. His body was so similar to Nino's, just with a few extra pounds and muscles in the right places—a level of maturity Nino had not yet reached. Lorenzo stroked himself to full hardness, then knelt on the edge of the bed. His impressive prick was bigger than Nino's by several inches, though not as big as the old man's.

"Give me any trouble, Andrew, and you will regret it."

"I'll behave myself, Lorenzo."

He crawled onto the bed and swung his left leg over me to straddle my chest. He tucked his knees tightly to me and rose up so his stiffer was inches from my mouth. Up close it resembled a small club protruding from his crotch.

"Open wide."

I opened my mouth and stuck out my tongue, and he placed just the head on it, then slid the fat plum inside my mouth. I sucked it greedily, rolling my tongue around the silky knob and running it through the tiny piss slit. Lorenzo jerked forward and moaned loudly each time I probed the tender opening. He withdrew his dick, shuffled up farther on the bed, and rested the shaft of his cock on my nose. I licked up and down the thick piece of flesh, then slid down as far as the ropes would allow to suck his balls. They were heavy in their sac of flesh, and their scent drove me crazy. I took each one into my mouth, rolled it around, then spat it out. I stretched further, striving to reach his shit hole with my tongue, but the ropes wouldn't allow it. Lorenzo moved back down my chest and quickly shoved the entire length of his prick down my throat. Due to the position I was lying in, I had to turn my head sideways so he wouldn't choke me.

Just then the door opened again, and out of the corner of my eye I saw Antonio approach the bed. He smiled when he saw the activity, and pulled the chair to the side as if watching a spectator sport. Lorenzo acknowledged his presence with a smile, then placed his hands behind my head and began thrusting his cock in and out of my mouth. His ball sac slapped repeatedly against my chin. I lost track of time as this serious piece of meat filled my mouth and throat. Suddenly, Lorenzo's thrusts increased to a fever pitch.

"I'm gonna cum right in your mouth, Andrew!"

He ceased his thrusting and held my head still; the first gob hit the back of my throat and slid slowly down. More of his cum followed, and I swallowed the heavy flow as fast as I could. When he was spent he climbed off the bed, the hair on his body glistening with sweat.

"That was spectacular, Andrew. Nino sure was a lucky man. And I can't wait to try that sweet ass of yours. Hey, Antonio, this guy is good at sucking cock. Give him a try."

A wide smile appeared on Antonio's face as he stood up and began to undress. He quickly revealed that he too had inherited the hirsuteness of the males in his family. But whereas Lorenzo and Nino were well-muscled and carried no extra fat, this son of Giovanni was packing a few extra pounds around the waist and in the ass, giving him a cuddly appearance that Lorenzo and Nino did not have.

His prick was stiff as a board, and ready for action. I could see his early juice leaking from the tiny slit in the head. And while it appeared Antonio had been cheated in the length department, though only in comparison to his father and brothers, it was by far the fattest of the four, with the size of the head rivaling Giovanni's. His balls were enormous as well, and both hung very low in their flesh sac. Antonio climbed on the bed and moved till he was kneeling on the pillow next to my head. He turned to Lorenzo.

"Can I untie his hands so he can do what I like?"

"Fine, Antonio. But remember, Andrew, no funny stuff, or I'll put a bullet in you."

"I get it, Lorenzo."

To punctuate his statement he took Antonio's seat in the chair, a pistol clenched in his hand. Meanwhile, Antonio had untied my hands and was thrusting his fat dick in my face.

"I want you to stroke it while you take only the head in your mouth."

"Got it, Antonio. I respect a man who knows what he likes."

With my hands free I was able to turn on my side to better service Antonio. The young gangster extended his arms behind his head, grabbed the bed railing and slid down till he was sitting on one of the pillows. His prick was sticking straight out and facing me, his ball sac supine on the pillow. I spit several times into my hand before wrapping it around the fat shaft. I began jerking him slowly while I licked and sucked the plum-sized head. Several times I had to spit on his thick shaft so my hand did not chafe him. I also wet the middle finger of my free hand and began exploring Antonio's hairy ass crack. After much probing he spread his legs wide enough to grant me greater access, and I found his hot hole. I pushed against the ring of flesh and my finger slid in as far as the angle would allow. Antonio moaned softly and began pumping his hips against the digit.

Out of the corner of my eye, I saw Lorenzo smoking a cigarette while he watched the action on the bed. With his free hand he was stroking himself. Antonio's stamina proved to be less than that of his father and brothers, and before I knew it he was moaning and thrashing on the bed. His balls had snugged up tight inside their sac, and on my next lick of his cock head he did not announce his eruption but simply pulled his stiffer away from me and blasted his load all over my face. He then scooped it up with two fingers and fed it to me, making several swipes till my face was clean.

"I guess I get sloppy thirds," Lorenzo said. "Leave his hands free."

He stubbed his cigarette out in the ashtray on the table and went to the door, opened it and disappeared. He returned momentarily with Marco, handed the gun to him and ordered him to sit in the chair and keep me covered. He then crawled onto the bed once more. He grabbed me by the ankles and flipped me on my back again. Without saying a word he undid each of the ropes that bound my ankles, then pushed my feet up and over my shoulders.

"Hold these for me will you, Antonio?"

Antonio laughed and did as his brother had instructed. Lorenzo knelt above my hole and gently ran his tongue up and down my ass crack, flicking his tongue over my opening and inserting the tip as deep as it would go. After several more swaths he sat back on his haunches.

"Marco, toss me that tin on the table."

Marco tossed the requested item to Lorenzo, then sat down again. Lorenzo smeared it across my sweet spot, and along the shaft of his dick. The fact that they had a tin of mitt grease gave me pause, but I guessed anyone had access to it, and especially the Sabatinis, considering how often they'd been lurking around our games. I felt Lorenzo's fat cock head pushing against my hole before popping through and burying itself deep within me. He pulled out quickly, then sank back in, pumping with long, deep, slow strokes.

He then reached up and snatched my ankles from his brother's grasp, placing them over his shoulders. Antonio swung around till his ass was right above my face, and I was more than happy to oblige his wordless command. He spread his ass cheeks, exposing his brown hole. I inhaled deeply of his heavy, musky scent, then licked the area between his nut sac and his puckered opening. Antonio groaned his appreciation and grunted when I hit his spot dead on.

"Lick that hole!"

I ran my tongue over the puckering opening as Antonio began bucking up and down on my face, grinding his asshole against my tongue and lips. While one brother writhed on my face, the other was filling my ass with his substantial cock. Marco held the gun on me, enraptured with the lusty proceedings. Lorenzo's thrusts continued deep and powerful, hitting bottom each time before pulling out to plunge inside once more. He leaned over and began biting and sucking my nipples, then spasmed as I felt his spunk flooding my ass. He pulled out quickly to allow Antonio to suddenly lift off my face, swing around, and lay his seed on my face for the second time. Once more he fed it to me, then flopped on the pillow beside me. Lorenzo got off the bed and lit another cigarette. Antonio did the same.

Just then the door opened and Giovanni entered. And he did not appear very happy. He tossed his coat on the empty chair next to Marco and walked around the sides and end of the bed several times without speaking, his hands clenching and unclenching at his sides. Lorenzo and Antonio watched him warily, seemingly waiting for an outburst. Giovanni stopped at the foot of the bed and stared at me with a mixture of sadness and thinly disguised malice. It was obvious something had taken place that was going to seal my fate. Suddenly, the gangster smiled.

"Is he all broke in for me, boys?" Giovanni said with a laugh in his voice.

His sons stared at him in open wonder, as did I. After several seconds had passed with no response, Giovanni whirled on his sons.

"Well?"

This time a slightly sinister note had crept into his voice, one that I'm sure his boys had heard before.

"You bet, Papa," replied Antonio. "And he is still fresh and ready to go again, even after pleasing us twice."

Surprisingly, I saw a grudging respect in Giovanni's eyes. He turned back to me.

"The good ones always are, aren't they," he said, almost beneath his breath, to no one in particular. "The good ones always are."

Giovanni moved to the side of the bed and began undressing, slowly, almost tantalizingly, his eyes never leaving mine. He knew I craved him and was not afraid of his monster prick. Lorenzo and Antonio were staring at it as well, whether in reverence or jealousy I could not be sure. Without being asked,

Lorenzo tossed his father the tin of grease. Giovanni scooped out a generous portion of the grease and slathered his pole with it, then crawled onto the bed and coated my hole and the area around it.

The bed sagged beneath his weight. Without warning, he grabbed me by the hips and expertly and with little real exertion flipped me on my hands and knees. I tried to relax as I felt his bulbous crown push against the outer ring of my sweet spot. I knew I could accommodate his girth because I had the day of the picnic. When the large head popped inside me, I grunted loudly and arched my back as his thick cock slid deep inside me. I felt the head bump against my secret muscle as Giovanni rested his weight across my ass.

"You like that piece of meat inside you, don't you, son?"

"I do, Mr. Sabatini."

The old gangster held his dick inside me, and I felt his crotch hair tickling my ass. He tweaked both my nipples between his thumbs and forefingers, then gripped me firmly at the hips, slid back out about halfway, and plunged in to the hilt again. He began long, lazy thrusts inside me, making me feel every inch of his prick.

Although he had twenty years and 20 pounds on his two sons standing beside the bed watching us, hard dicks in their hands, Giovanni certainly surpassed them in style and technique. I loved the feel of his belly as it banged against my ass, and the smell of the sweat that was running off him in rivulets and drenching me. After much grunting and gasping, the old man sank into me a final time and let out a loud, long moan as he spewed his juice deep inside me. Surprisingly, he stayed hard inside me till I thought he was going to have another go. When he finally did pull out of me, my asshole slowly returned to its normal size. He grabbed his white T-shirt and wiped the sweat from his forehead.

"That, my boys, is how you take care of a man. A good one anyway. Thanks again for the ride, Andrew."

He punctuated this statement with a sharp slap on my left ass cheek as he climbed off the bed. When he finished dressing, he looked at his watch and frowned. Was he expecting someone?

"Keep an eye on him, boys. I'm going to check on things and be back in a few minutes. Marco, you come with me."

"We'll keep an eye on him for you, Papa," Antonio replied.

Lorenzo and Antonio also got dressed, then thankfully turned me on my back before once again tying my wrists and ankles to the bed frame. They skipped the gag this time. Lorenzo took a seat in the chair again and lit another smoke, while Antonio stood idly by him, seemingly deep in thought. I stared at the dirty ceiling, surprised to find myself wondering where Nino was. Shouldn't he be here with the rest of his nefarious family? Was that who Giovanni was expecting? Had he really made the break he had talked about?

As promised, Giovanni returned, alone. And this time he was more than agitated; he was furious, his face an unhealthy shade of red. He didn't speak to his sons, but simply stood at the foot of the bed and stared at me as if he were about to deliver a sermon or a sentence. Even though he was not a tall man, he was still a very imposing figure.

"Andrew, do you know where Nino is?" he blurted. He seemed to immediately regret his question.

"I haven't seen Nino in several days, Mr. Sabatini. Isn't that what you wanted?"

He stared at me, his face turning an even darker color. So Nino was missing. That explained Giovanni's wrath: He had lost control of his youngest son!

"I haven't seen him either, Andrew. I sent him to handle some business for me in Tampa, but he never showed up at the customer's place, and I haven't seen him since. Nor has anyone in the family, or anyone who works for me. The last I heard of him, he was in a street fight in Boca Raton. Just like a common hoodlum."

He paused for effect, then continued his tirade.

"Well, Nino's whereabouts had no impact on today's game, and will have no impact on your fate."

"I have no idea what you're talking about, Giovanni. But I can guess it means no good for anyone involved."

He held up his hand to silence me.

"Please, allow me to continue. It truly saddens me to have had to resort to these means to ensure compliance from Mr. Connors, Mr. Hughes, and Mr. Stanley. My business partners and I have been trying to acquire the Stallions since the beginning of the season. You are probably not aware of this, but betting on sporting events continues to thrive as a favorite pastime in this great country, so several years ago my associates and I started investing heavily in various athletic events. These sound business investments have garnered us large financial rewards, all up and down both coasts. Now, I'm sure you know that Mr. Connors is a part owner of the Stallions, along with Mr. Stanley and Mr. Hughes."

If he was waiting for a reply, I did not give him one.

"I see. Well, something that you are probably not aware of is the fact that Mr. Connors likes to bet money on baseball—on any sporting event for that matter, but baseball is his preference. Suffice it to say that, unfortunately, Mr. Connors is a lousy gambler and has racked up considerable debt, which he is finding difficult to pay off. I'm sure you've noticed the ratty uniforms, the broken-down bus, the dilapidated headquarters. And it seems several players left at the end of last season because their paychecks began to be—shall we say—spotty, and eventually for some, totally absent. This was the impetus for the recruiting sojourn that brought you to Florida.

"These events are all connected by the fact that Mr. Connors has been using the team's money to pay off his gambling debt, and keeping it—until recently—a secret from Mr. Hughes and Mr. Stanley. And when that money ran out, having heard I was in the business of lending funds, he began requesting loans from me to keep his creditors at bay. Sadly, Mr. Connors quickly got behind in his payments to me. As a way to free him of this terrible debt, I proposed that he transfer his interest in the Stallions to me. My plan for next season was to have a team that wanted to win at any cost, and make some money in the bargain before heading to the majors. But Mr. Connors steadfastly denied my request, subsequently placing many people in jeopardy, including you.

"See, instead of giving up, he searched for five new players, including two new pitchers, hoping that if the Stallions were on top this season, he could make money by betting on the games and thus pay me back. But here comes the second twist: Knowing that the Stallions have always been losers, I had already bet large sums of money *against* them."

He paused to catch his breath. I noticed a line of spittle running from the corner of his mouth.

He continued, "And what happened then, Andrew?"

I spoke with a certain amount of stubborn pride. "With the new recruits the Stallions became a formidable team and began racking up win after win, resulting in you losing a considerable amount of money. Did I hit the nail on the head, Mr. Sabatini?"

"Yes, you did, son. My losses have indeed been heavy, as have those of my colleagues who, as you may well imagine, are not happy. So I was left to wonder what to do about this problem, specifically what to do about these two new amazing pitchers who would potentially lead the Stallions right to the playoffs and the final game. Should I get rid of them both? Just one of them? Or do I coerce one or both of them to throw the last game, thus collecting on all my debts and amassing a small fortune? Well that was the plan, till my foolhardy son fell in love with one of them."

His last statement hit me like a blow to the face.

"So I turned to the second pitcher. The one not in love, or should I say only pretending to be in love? The one who wants to make it to the majors, no matter what price he has to pay: murder, arson, betrayal, or revenge. The one who hates the small town he came from and would do anything to leave. Who hates the other pitcher enough to turn against him, even though at one time they were lovers."

He paused again, as if to let the words sink in. A sick dread was forming in me as I realized the full implications of what Giovanni had just said. I was speechless. Everything was beginning to fall into place around Parker's behavior: the newfound solicitousness, his professed love for me, his possible role in my blackout the night of the bonfire. It had all been part of a master plan to ensure the Stallions lost the final game of the season, if they indeed made it that far. Seeing that I wasn't going to respond, the gangster continued his diatribe.

"Okay, Andrew, it's time for the final piece of the puzzle to fall into place. There's someone outside who is anxious to see you."

Giovanni went to the door and opened it. Someone was standing on the other side of it, but the bright light and Giovanni's body impeded my view. I could hear Giovanni talking to the unknown person in low tones, followed by soft laughter; then Giovanni stepped aside and the person came into sight. Even though I was expecting it to be Parker, I was still shocked and enraged when my suspicions were confirmed. I pulled against my ropes violently, the need to do bodily harm to this vicious man consuming me completely. Parker simply smiled wickedly at my efforts as he and Giovanni stood at the foot of the bed.

Giovanni slung his arm around Parker's shoulder, pulled him to him, and kissed him fully on the mouth. So Parker had become Giovanni's male companion. As the two men continued to kiss, Parker began stroking the front of Giovanni's trousers, and it was plain to see by the swelling there that the older gangster was responding. The sexual appetites of this family were amazing. Giovanni gave Parker a final kiss before my ex-lover sank to his knees in front of him. He slowly unbuttoned Giovanni's pants and slid them and his briefs down to his knees. Parker rose up on his knees, lightly gripped the large cock head, then expertly guided the large piece of flesh as Giovanni slid the whole thing down his throat. I could actually see Parker's throat stretched by the huge prick. But I knew that even the talented Parker could not take the entire gigantic dick. Giovanni placed his hand on the back of Parker's head and began pumping in and out of his mouth. With his left hand Parker hefted the gangster's bag of balls. Giovanni muttered "Sweet Jesus" as he used Parker's mouth; saliva was running freely from both corners. The only sounds in the room were Parker's noisy sucking and Giovanni's bear-like grunts.

"I'm gonna blow right in your mouth" was Giovanni's next outcry, and he moaned long and loud as he flooded Parker's gullet with his spunk. Parker's throat muscles worked furiously to swallow the heavy load. Giovanni stepped back from Parker as he withdrew his cock, allowing Parker to suck on the large crown before the length of flesh began to soften. Lorenzo and Antonio watched slack-jawed, their eyes filled with lust.

"Now take care of my boys."

Lorenzo and Antonio dropped their pants and briefs in front of Parker, who was still on his knees. He immediately began giving their cocks the same treatment as their father's had received, taking turns swallowing their impressive pricks. Both brothers were moaning softly, and Lorenzo had slung his arm around Antonio's shoulders. Parker quickly brought both men to noisy, powerful explosions. When he had drained them dry, they stuffed their dicks back in their pants and stood waiting to see what their father was going to do next. They didn't have long to wait. Giovanni began speaking to me once more, with Parker standing by his side.

"Yes, my young friend. Parker has been in on this since several weeks after arriving in Boca Raton. I first met him by accident at the recruitment in Miller Falls. I recognized right away how ambitious he was, and he recognized a kindred spirit in me. Once you both had made the team and began racking up wins, I began to get nervous. And I don't like to be nervous. I began to feel Parker out, so to speak. We joined forces and began to formulate our plan. I was still hoping to recruit you to the cause as well, but when we first met in the locker room I knew that you would not go along with it. And that day I visited you and Nino at the picnic I was sure of it."

"Did Nino play a part in your deception?"

Giovanni didn't respond for the longest time, and I was beginning to think he wasn't going to, when he finally did.

"Unfortunately, no. My youngest son has proved to be a disappointment to me and our family. He never had the stomach for our line of work, and once his mother insisted he go to college, it was all over from there. Initially all he knew was that Mr. Connors owed me money. But since taking up with you he somehow became wise to my larger plan."

He paused a moment, then turned to Parker. "Anything you'd care to add?"

"I'd be happy to, Giovanni," he sneered. "Yes, Andrew, you were a fool in love, just as you were when I first met you. It was so easy to get back into your good graces. You love my cock so much you can't see straight. It began as soon as we arrived in Boca Raton. And you weren't simply drunk at the bonfire, of course; I drugged you on purpose so you would miss the game, casting doubt on your commitment to the team and on your own ability. You never even noticed I wasn't drinking the whiskey. I also set the fire in the locker room. My intent was for the whole facility to burn down, permanently crippling the team and forcing the sale of the Stallions. But the fire was discovered too soon. Finally, that fight in the street with your boyfriend, Nino, whom you reprimanded: The truth is, he had discovered my little game with his father and was coming to the boarding-house to warn you. But you made it pretty clear that day that your loyalty lay with me, so he turned his back on you. And so today, after getting you out of the way so I could pitch the final inning, I deliberately allowed four runs in the top of the ninth, then intentionally struck out with two outs and bases loaded in the bottom of the ninth, cementing the Stallions' heartbreaking loss. By doing so, I am guaranteed a pitching spot on one of Giovanni's major league teams when the new season starts."

His smugness was unbearable. I felt a searing new hatred toward Parker, but also for myself. Why had I been such a fool? Why had I not learned a lesson from my first go-round with him? I could not contain myself.

"Well, Parker, you finally got what you wanted." My voice was thick with emotion, and I was trembling. "You know, you may have taken a shortcut to pitching in the majors, but I intend to get there the right way, and maintain my pride in the bargain."

The look in Parker's eyes told me that my words had the sting of truth, but he quickly disguised it with bluster.

"You were always a small thinker, Andrew," he fairly snarled at me. "We both know who the better pitcher is and always will be. You were simply fortunate to strike the fancy of Mr. Stanley with your big cock, eager mouth, and willing ass. You have no real talent and everyone on the team knows it. I should have given you a larger dose that night at the party; that would have ended it right then and there. Regardless, you will never make it to the majors or play on any other team for that matter." He turned Giovanni. "Let's be done with this."

Giovanni grabbed his coat from the chair and removed a gun from a holster inside.

"Andrew, I warned you to stay away from Nino, yet you chose to ignore that warning and started him down a path he can never return from. It saddens me to say this, but now both of you will need to pay the ultimate price. And you will be first."

He raised the gun and pointed it at me, when, suddenly, shots rang out from outside the room.

CHAPTER THIRTEEN

Giovanni lowered his gun, grabbed his coat once more, and produced a second gun. This one he handed to Parker.

"Parker and Antonio, follow me. Lorenzo, you keep an eye on Andrew till we see what's going on outside. I'll knock three times before I come in. If anyone else tries to, shoot them."

Giovanni opened the door slowly, peered around its edge, then moved quickly through it, followed close on his heels by Parker and Antonio, the latter shutting it softly behind him. After an agonizing eternity, more gunshots sounded outside the room, but farther away than the first volley. Suddenly, the door flew open and Nino and Nelson came bursting into the room. Lorenzo, momentarily startled by the unexpected entry, raised his gun, but Nino was already firing his. A small round hole appeared in the center of Lorenzo's forehead, and he crumpled to the floor without a sound. Nino moved quickly to the bed and undid the ropes that bound me. Nelson positioned himself by the door, a gun in his right hand.

"What's happening, Nino?"

"Why, I'm here to rescue you, of course, my love."

Although he tried to keep his voice light and gallant, I knew he was scared to death of the action he was taking.

"Papa, Antonio, and one of my cousins, Marco, are outside the warehouse looking for whoever fired those shots. Parker is with them." When he said "Parker," it sounded like a curse word.

"If Papa catches us, we are done for. I've gone against his wishes, and he cannot allow me to live and still retain his place in the family."

"What will you do if he finds us, Nino? Or if another member of your family does?"

"I'm prepared to do whatever it takes to protect you, Andrew." He looked at the body of Lorenzo on the floor as if it were evidence of his words, then pulled me to him and kissed me firmly on the mouth.

"Get dressed; we need to get out of here before we are discovered."

I retrieved my clothes from the table and quickly dressed while both men kept an eye on the door. When I was ready, Nino handed me a pistol.

"Do you know how to use this?"

"Of course, I grew up on a farm. Guns were part of our life."

As we approached the door Nelson dropped his guard and lowered his gun, hugging and kissing me, his relief at seeing me safe evident all over his face.

I hugged him back fiercely. "How did you get here, Nelson?"

"When you disappeared during the game and I didn't see Coach in the dugout, I went to look for you in the locker room. After a frantic, fruitless search, I ran into Nino."

Nino picked up the explanation from there as Nelson resumed his position at the door, listening for footsteps.

"I never went to Tampa. I went to see my mother instead to finalize a plan to get out from underneath my father's control. While there, I ran into a man who works for my father. He and I had a secret liaison a few years ago, and he has never stopped loving me. He knew there was a plot to throw the game, but that was the extent of it. He said he would contact me when he had more details. When I came back to Boca Raton, I saw Parker coming out of our house with my father. It was obvious the two were involved in something, and my instincts told me it was to throw the final game. I was coming to warn you when I ran into Parker. My anger got the better of me and I confronted him.

You know the rest. After the final game had started, my ex-lover showed up in Boca Raton, having learned more details of the plan: Parker was to throw the game in the last inning, after you had been kidnapped and taken to the wharf. And the plan was to take me as well, so I stayed out of sight. When I got to the game you were gone, but I ran into Nelson. He immediately agreed to help me. Now we need to get the hell out of here."

Nelson stepped back and Nino, holding his finger to his lips, slowly opened the door. He poked his head out, then motioned for Nelson and me to follow him. Guns raised, we weaved our way through the mass of junk in the warehouse to the outside door, which was wide open. Nino stepped to the door frame and surveyed the area, then gave us a nod to follow him. As we left the warehouse I saw an unfamiliar man lying to the right of the door near a pile of broken boxes. A pool of blood surrounded his head and stained the front of his crisp white dress shirt. A few feet past the man was the car that had delivered us here. Next to it were two vehicles that I didn't recognize: One had to be Giovanni's and the other Nino's, who had obviously not driven his red sports car to avoid being spotted or tailed.

"You guys go get in the car while I cover you," Nino whispered. "I'm not sure how many men are lurking around here, so stay low as you go."

I ducked and followed Nelson to the nearer of the two cars. He slipped into the front seat and I took the back. Then Nino darted to the front of the car and slid in behind the steering wheel. As he started the engine, Nelson turned to me.

"I was so afraid we'd get here too late, Andrew," he said softly.

"Your timing was perfect. A few moments later and I would most certainly have been dead."

As Nino put the car in gear, Marco came around the far end of the warehouse. He immediately saw us and began firing. The first shot shattered the windshield, spraying glass all the way into the backseat. The next few shots plunked into the engine itself. The three of us leaned out the windows and began returning fire until the man jerked and fell to the ground. At the same time Nino winced and grabbed his right arm. He had been hit. Immediately blood began seeping from the wound.

"Nelson, you're going to have to shift the car while I steer. My right arm is quickly becoming numb and will soon be useless." The car began to move, jerking along till the warehouse was behind us and we felt a bit safer.

I leaned over the seat, alarmed at the sight of so much blood.

"We need to bind that arm, Nino, to stanch the flow of blood."

"It looks worse than it really is, Andrew. The bullet passed clean through."

"I don't care. Stop for a second."

I reached beneath my shirt to my undershirt and tore a strip off the hem, then wound it around Nino's arm above the wound and tied it tight. He winced a little but gave me a smile of encouragement. When my ministrations were complete, I sat back in the seat while Nino maneuvered the car with his left hand and Nelson worked the shifter. It was slow going, but we were making gradual headway down the pier. Suddenly, steam rose from the hood, accompanied by a loud thumping noise. One or more of Marco's bullets had done more damage than the engine could stand. Although we had put a little distance between ourselves and the warehouse where I'd been held captive, we were still deep within the warehouse district. The car gave a final violent shudder, and Nino coasted it to a stop.

"That's it for our transportation," Nino said "Maybe it's best that we part company here. I'm at a disadvantage with this bloody arm, and I'd prefer it if at least you two made it out of this alive."

"We're not leaving you, Nino. We're in this together, no matter what the outcome."

He leaned into me sideways to protect his injured arm, and kissed me deeply.

"Thanks, Andrew. I needed to hear that. Okay, let's find a place where we can fend them off till the cops get here. I gave them an anonymous tip that gunshots had been fired at this warehouse and that the Sabatinis were involved."

"Police! What? Was there no other way?"

"I wasn't sure that Nelson and I could fully pull this off on our own, Andrew. My father has a lot of family members working for him, and then his other cronies who make up the extended family. We would be fighting against a sizable force if he had time to get the word out."

We left the disabled car just as more gunshots rang out. Several wooden crates exploded around us, sending splinters flying everywhere. One wood shard penetrated my right cheek; when I placed my fingers on the spot they came away bloody. Nino grabbed my arm, pulling me out of a semi-daze, and the three of us ran toward a large fishing boat that was tied up at one of the docks. As we boarded more shots were fired, and pieces of the deck exploded around us, forcing us down behind the gunwale.

"You two stay here while I go into the cabin and see if I can get this thing started. Maybe this will be our way out of this mess," Nino said.

Nelson and I stayed put as Nino began crawling toward the cabin. Silence reigned over the wharf. Unable to sit still, I peered above the gunwale just in time to spot Giovanni and Antonio running toward the boat. Nelson and I rose up and fired off several rounds simultaneously and saw both gangsters stumble and fall on the wharf a few feet from the boat. Nelson turned to me.

"Do you think they're dead, or just wounded?"

"I can't tell from here, Nelson. But we need to make sure because if we do manage to get out of this mess, and they're not dead, they will track us down if it takes the rest of their lives."

"I'll go check, Andrew. Keep me covered."

Nelson left the ship in a crouched run, then darted behind some barrels a few feet from the two men. He watched them for several minutes, while I scanned the area behind him for other signs of pursuit. Suddenly Nelson ran to Giovanni and put a bullet in his forehead, moved to Antonio and did the same, then returned to crouch behind the barrels. At the same time I heard a noise behind me and to my left. I went around the ship's cabin and almost cried out when I saw Parker standing there, his back to me. At the same time, Nino emerged from the cabin and found himself facing Parker, who immediately got the drop on him.

"Good riddance, Nino!"

Nino also saw me, and his expression alerted Parker, who fired at Nino and then turned to me. I saw Nino topple off the boat and heard him hit the water as I fired, then watched Parker fall to the deck. I hurried to him and shot him two more times, to be sure, then reached down to make sure he was dead. Hearing a noise, I whirled again and almost put a bullet in Nelson as he came around the corner of the cabin.

"Easy, Andrew, it's me."

"Parker shot Nino as he came out of the cabin. He fell into the water. We've got to find him before the police or more of Giovanni's men arrive!"

Nelson and I scanned the water but saw no sign of Nino. Frantic, I dove in and began swimming among the moored boats, desperately searching. I didn't want to cry out in case more of the Sabatinis or their henchmen were still about. After searching the half-dozen boats, I swam past the boat we had been on to check the pilings beneath the wharf. Finally, exhausted, I climbed a ladder back to the dock, where Nelson helped me up. Tears were beginning to form in the corners of my eyes.

"I can't believe he's gone, Nelson."

"We don't know that for sure, Andrew. I've learned that Nino is a pretty resourceful guy. He may be just hiding, hoping his family will think he is dead."

Suddenly, sirens sounded in the distance. Help had finally arrived, but it was too late. Nelson grabbed my arm.

"We have to get out of here before the police get here, Andrew. If we don't, we will have to explain our presence here, plus several dead bodies. It's best that the law doesn't associate us with this gunfight. Let's get to Giovanni's car and get the hell out of here."

We ran. The sirens kept getting louder. When we reached the car, Nelson jumped behind the wheel, cranked the engine till it roared to life, and we drove off in the opposite direction from the sound of the sirens. We chanced upon a side road at the other end of the warehouse district that, after several minutes of twists and turns, deposited us on the main road; a sign read BOCA RATON. Nelson and I smiled at each other, and he drove on slowly to keep from attracting any attention. We passed several police cars, their sirens wailing, and one ambulance, which made me wince with sadness. Finally, I could see the boardinghouse in the distance.

"We need to ditch this car so no one connects us with Giovanni."

"Let's drive to the pond from the opposite direction and push it into the water. It's deep enough."

"Good plan."

When we were at the pond's edge we got out of the car and pushed till it rolled of its own accord into the water. It gained enough momentum to keep going when it hit the water, and soon all that we could see was the roof; soon that too was gone. We circled around the pond and came to the back of the boarding house. As we were just going up the back steps, Coach came around the corner of the house.

"My God, Andrew, I'm so glad to see you alive. I saw a car at the pond and was coming to check it out. Your face is bleeding, come inside and tell me what happened!"

He hugged me and ushered me into the house. The three of us made it to my room, where I collapsed onto the bed, overcome by the day's terrible events. Coach took a handkerchief from his pocket, wet it with spit, and attended to the cut on my cheek.

Nelson looked around the room and his face fell. "Coach," he asked, "has Kent already left for home?"

"He should be at the bus station now. If you hurry, you can catch him."

Nelson turned to me. Tears were in his eyes.

"I think it best that I go with Kent and stay away from Miller Falls for a while. I would think the same goes for you. I will be in touch some way as soon as I can."

I stood up and held out my arms. Nelson stepped between them and hugged me fiercely, then kissed me on the lips.

"I love you. Good luck!"

"Same goes for you, friend."

Nelson sped from the room and Coach lay down beside me.

"What is going on, Andrew? We were so worried about you. I don't know if you know this, but we lost the game. Parker was pitching very erratically in the last inning."

I filled Coach in on what Parker had done, and then all the events surrounding and following my kidnapping. When I came to the part where Nino had fallen off the ship, I began to cry. Coach held me in his arms while I wept, his body pressed to mine.

After he comforted me for a few minutes, he started thinking aloud. "We'll need to hide you for a few days and then get you out of town. It's probably best not to go back to your parent's house for a while either. Wait, I have an uncle on the West Coast who I'm sure will take you in. We'll go to my house and I'll call him from there. Once you're settled out there, I can put you in touch with some recruiters for the West Coast leagues. I'll also tell Mr. Hughes and Mr. Stanley that you are still alive and well. Okay? Now you pack your things while I pull my truck around out back."

I packed what few belongings I had and met Coach in his truck behind the boardinghouse. As we drove away I lay across the seat so no one would see me.

. . .

The sun had barely risen when Coach dropped me off at the bus station two days later. I had slept most of the time at his house, and worried about Nino the remainder. I thanked him for all his help, hugged him goodbye, and told him I would call him when I reached his uncle's house. He drove away and I sat on the bench, absorbed in my own thoughts.

I had said goodbye to Mr. Hughes and Mr. Stanley that morning at Coach's house. Coach had apologized profusely to everyone for what his betting had resulted in. But we had all agreed that what was done was done. We couldn't fix it now. The baseball season was officially over, with the Stallions losing to the Panthers. All the managers knew that Parker had purposefully thrown the game, although we had no official proof. And with me in hiding, there never would be any.

It had been two days since the incident at the wharf, and I had not heard from Nino. I was increasingly sure that he was dead. The story had been all over the papers. They didn't come out and say that several gangsters had been gunned down at the wharf, but they did intimate that the Sabatinis' business dealings were questionable at best. The story had made the front page, with Parker's involvement still undetermined. But thanks to the efforts of Coach, Mr. Stanley, and Mr. Hughes, no one knew I had been kidnapped. The story told to the rest of the team was that I had to return to Miller Falls for a death in the family. The paper had named the gangsters involved, but there had been no mention of Nino. Had his wounds prevented him from swimming to safety?

As my bus pulled up to the curb I took my place in line, my mind a million miles away. An image came to me unbidden, but I could not push it away: The treacherous and very much dead Parker, dead by my hand. It was fitting justice for the man who had been plotting against me since several weeks after arriving at spring training. His jealousy of my skill as a pitcher and his eagerness to make it to the major leagues no matter the price had led to many deaths, including his own and poor Nino's, and almost mine as well. The world was better off without the likes of Parker. When it came my turn to board the bus, I chose the seat at the back.

I tuned out the chatter of the other passengers and instead filled my head with memories of Nino: His strong arms covered in their black fleece, his piercing blue eyes beneath those bushy black eyebrows. His full lips, covering my body with kisses or wrapped around my cock as he brought my seed boiling up out of me. Oh, Nino. Why had I doubted him just because he was trying to protect me from the awful truth about his family?

The bus pulled away from the curb and headed down the short main street and out onto the dusty road that would lead to the main highway. I stared out the window, watching the farmland roll past, mile after endless mile. I soon dozed off, but awakened as the bus pulled into the next small town. A few passengers exited the bus, and a few more got on. I paid no attention to them as the bus pulled away from the station once more.

I had just turned back to the window when someone sat down beside me. As there were plenty of empty seats on the bus,

I turned to express my irritation at this intrusion and ask the passenger to please move to another seat. When I did, I found myself staring into a familiar pair of light blue eyes beneath bushy black eyebrows. My heart leapt in my chest: It was Nino. He put his arms around me, pulled me to him, and began kissing me passionately. I returned his fiery kisses, then held him at arm's length, still not believing it was really him. He was not wearing a shirt underneath his sport coat. He seemed to read my mind.

"Yes, Andrew, it's really me. You're not seeing a ghost."

"Nino, I saw you take that second bullet and topple off the fishing boat. I looked and looked for you but had to leave before the police arrived."

Nino slid his coat off, revealing a large white bandage on his left shoulder. A matching one appeared on his right arm, replacing my torn piece of shirt.

"I saw you jump into the water after me, but I didn't want to yell to you in case my father or more of his henchmen were around. It suddenly hit me that the world thinking I was dead was the best way out of this predicament we're in. So, I hid by the pilings beneath the wharf till the coast was clear. When I thought it was safe, I made my way along the shore as best I could for a mile or so, then came ashore. It was tough going with one arm, and many times I didn't think I was going to make it. But the thought of being with you kept me forging ahead. Once I left the water, I had no choice but to walk back to Boca Ration. With nowhere else to go, I hid in the burnt-out locker room, where Coach found me the first night. I made him promise not to tell you because I knew you would come straight to me. He told me of the plan you two had formed, bandaged me and nursed me back to health, then drove me to this little town last night. I've been sitting in this bus station all night, waiting for you to arrive. Although Papa, Lorenzo,

Antonio, and Marco are dead, the Sabatini family is large, and if they thought I was alive I'm positive other relatives, in legion with many unrelated family affiliates, would have taken up the search for me as soon as they regrouped. But now I am finally free, and the West Coast sounds like a perfect place for us to begin a new life together."

He pulled me to him once more and kissed me repeatedly, then slid against the wall of the bus.

"But right now, Andrew, all I want to do is hold you."

I slid across the seat and rested my head on his chest as he wrapped his arms around me.